the love factory

elaine proctor

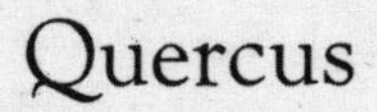

First published in Great Britain in 2018 by Quercus
This paperback edition published in 2018 by

Quercus Editions Ltd
Carmelite House
50 Victoria Embankment
London EC4Y 0DZ

An Hachette UK company

A CIP catalogue record for this book is available
from the British Library

PB ISBN 978 1 78429 684 1

10 9 8 7 6 5 4 3 2 1

Typeset by CC Book Production

Printed and bound in Great Britain by Clays Ltd, Elcograf S.p.A.

For Linda Proctor 1924 – 2017

I had my existence. I was there. Me in my place.
My place in me.
'Human Chain' Seamus Heaney

And for my children Lucia and Jacob
Who are my bloodwood

Chapter One

Anna sat up in her bed warmth and waited for her natural impatience to tip her towards the waiting day.

She slid from under the bedcovers so quietly that the *hargh-gggg-p-p-p-whooshnrrrr* of her husband's snoring continued without the slightest increase in pitch or rhythm. Then she ran lightly down the stairs with Liebe, her hunting dog, at her heels.

If she'd known what turmoil the day was to bring she might've slowed her pace, but unlike some in her family, Anna was not burdened with prescience.

She pulled open the kitchen door and sucked in a lungful of frosty air; she smelled the city in it and the liquid green of the underground stream at the bottom of her garden.

As she breathed in she whispered to herself, 'I am,' and, as if willing it would make it so, she said, 'at peace.'

There was fox scat on the stonework; the big male must

have passed by in the night. She heard the distant sound of the early train.

Liebe scratched at the gate at the far end of the garden, her pied orange and white body luminous in the dark day. 'Coming,' called Anna softly.

The dog and her owner both loved the unruly allotments that ran along the edge of the railway line behind the house, each small garden tended according to their owners' fancy; some grew flowers, others, like Anna, vegetables. Most started off every spring with a burst of enthusiasm and then let their beds fade to nothing by late summer. Only a few managed to keep something alive through the cold.

Just about all the families on Carlyle Road had a strip of earth to tend here. Anna liked to think it brought them closer together but, in truth, it was the two tornados that had twice torn the roofs off their houses that had made them allies. If past storm patterns continued, they were about due for another.

The grind of a sash window opening disturbed the darkness of the house next door. Anna saw a young man, pale-skinned and lanky, flip over the sill and onto the frozen grass. Liebe stiffened into pointer bird-hunting-alert.

The intruder turned back to the window . . . for one more kiss . . . *oh Lord* . . . from her neighbour, Farhad.

Anna watched the kiss pass from sweet-goodbye to fuck-me lust. She could have been inside their mouths, for the sudden heat they put out. She watched as Farhad fumbled with his lover's belt.

The encounter that followed, both their bodies half-in, half-out of the window, was over quickly. The lover pulled his trousers up, pecked Farhad on the nipple, and stumbled away over the grass. Farhad stood in the window bare-chested in the freezing dawn, watching him go.

And Anna stood to full attention in the perpetual spinach patch – impossible for Farhad to miss as he turned to close the window.

She longed to bend down and tend to her beds, to pretend that she'd not witnessed their coming together, but it was too late for that. She could see thought-ripples cross Farhad's face; *Ah shit*, he seemed to say. *Do you judge me? Will you tell my mother?*

Anna waved at him, an awkward flick of the hand – as if to say *Your secret is safe with me – although I can't say it didn't shake me up so early in the morning.*

He waved back.

Anna could see that Farhad would have preferred not to have to take his pleasure in so clandestine a way, and she turned away.

Released from watchfulness, Liebe ploughed joyfully into a flock of half-frozen pigeons huddled on the grass. They took to the air in a cloud and swept away over the rooftops of London's Kensal Rise.

Every morning the live creatures in Anna's life lined up to be fed in their established order; dog, cat, boy, man, snake. There used to be a girl in the line-up too but Anna's daughter was far away now, eating whatever they served up in her university canteen.

Anna filled a bowl with oatmeal and handed it over to her son, Luke.

'Ta,' he said and he glanced up at her.

Luke was a darter, inserting himself into the adult world just long enough to get the gist.

He ate six meals a day and snacks in between and still he was always hungry.

She poured a cup of freshly brewed coffee for her husband, Peter, released a small cloud of crickets into the aquarium-home of Luke's red-lipped herald – and wondered if her farmer ancestors feeding their flocks had felt *plentiful* in this way?

Peter took a long swig of coffee and scraped his chair back on the wooden kitchen floor. He pecked Anna on the forehead – she leant briefly into his kiss.

Anna could see that he was thinking about the day ahead as he gathered his phone and his keys. The tilt of his elegant head, pale-skinned and hollow-cheeked, precluded chatter. She lingered on his lightly freckled hands.

'Come on, Lukey,' said Anna. 'It's nearly half past.'

Luke got up and put his bowl into the sink. The sharp peaks of his shoulder blades through his T-shirt made Anna want to feed him beef stew and potatoes.

He and Peter left the house noisily.

'See you later,' shouted Anna from the kitchen and waited for the front door to bang shut before she and her small animal posse trickled into the lounge and settled into the armchair by the window.

The *little death* of her family's daily departure always filled Anna with an oddly flippant grief, yet grief it was. It meant she had to stop sheltering in the practical pleasures of being a farmer/mother/wife, and haul herself up the stairs to get on with the task of adding a thousand words to her exacting book. It was a difficult transition.

Anna closed her eyes and a fragile silence filled the long room, scattered with shoes the size of ocean liners and too many books.

Bar the arrival of her two children, she had always measured the passing of time not in births, marriages or deaths, but in the great books she'd read, and later, the lesser ones she'd written.

She recalled *Don Quixote*, say, which she first read aged sixteen, but also the volatile condition she found herself in as she turned its pages.

This was even more true of the books she'd written, especially if the labour had been hard, and the latest was the toughest yet. She dreaded nothing more than the dull silence of the days when her powers failed her.

Thankfully, in the quiet of this morning, her book people began to shuffle into view. She could stay this way for hours, suspended between worlds.

The doorbell rang – as shocking to her state as if Luke's pet viper had escaped its tank and sunk its teeth into her ankle. *It's the postman; quick hello and he'll be gone. Please, please, be the postman.*

Anna put her ear to the front door and called out, 'Hello?'

'*Sì*, Anna, it's me!'

'Nonna?' she asked in surprise.

'Are you going to let me in?'

Anna pulled open the door.

Her grandmother looked up at her, small, bent, and crackling with outrage 'In case you were wondering, I am still alive.'

The old lady stood on the doormat in a faded knockoff Louis Vuitton jacket and diamanté sunglasses, a suitcase at her feet. A suitcase?

'*Oh, che cosa, Nonna?*' said Anna. What have you done?

'I did nothing, *di nulla*, I swear,' said the old lady.

The last time Nonna had been sent to Anna's house it was because she poured a glass of water over an eighty-five-year-old fellow resident at the retirement home. When Anna chided her, she snapped, 'Dear God in heaven, Anna, the man told me the same story THREE times, and it was *agonia* the first time around . . .' and then she shrugged as if she was the wronged one.

'I'm here because I have the feeling,' the old lady said gravely.

'What kind of feeling?'

'You know the kind.'

Anna raised her hand. 'Don't say another word.'

She didn't want to hear about her grandmother's foretellings. The old lady opened her mouth to object.

'Zip it, Nonna!' said Anna.

And she did.

Anna took a breath. 'We'll give them a chance to cool off, then I'll take you back to the home.'

There would be no thousand words today.

Anna's grandmother came from a long line of worriers.

'Not worriers, Anna!' she'd exclaim. 'Seers!'

She smelt of anise, favoured hot curlers over a blow-dry and had her nails painted pearl-pink every ten days. Her mission, her very reason for being, was to ensure that her children and grandchildren *rose up*, and to achieve that, they had to dodge the bullets of life's misfortunes.

'To be a winner,' she said, and it sounded like *weener*, 'you have to catch the trouble before it catches you.'

'Yes, Nonna,' said Anna, aged just five.

'The ones who suspect nothing, they are the *what*?' she would ask.

And Anna would say loudly, 'THE LOSERS.'

'Exactly,' her grandmother would say and pat her head. 'Watch out for that, Anna . . .' and she pointed into the unknown future with her eyes blazing. 'Watch out!'

And Anna did watch out, her whole life long, until she could see trouble coming from a thousand miles away. Except the trouble that mattered, that is, like the day her mama was rushed into St Mary's intensive care, and never came out.

Chapter Two

There was trouble in the way Peter opened the garden gate that evening. And in the way he paused, as if to prepare himself, before completing the journey to the front door. But it was the totally unexpected nature of his trouble that took Anna by surprise. *What did he mean he'd lost his job?*

'Just that.'

'But what about us?' she asked before she could stop herself.

'For Chrissakes, Anna! I don't know.'

Peter had been waiting a long time for the university to give him tenure but he never doubted that they would. Instead, his head of department that morning had suggested he look for another job, 'Out of the capital, perhaps, for someone of your age? So sorry, Peter.'

Peter had told Anna the bad news as he stood in the kitchen with his coat still on.

Later, she remembered the look on his devastated face but

just then she was too blinded by this catastrophe to see him clearly.

She'd always taken her husband's long and secure employment as a given. It covered their basic life needs; food, and a roof over their heads, to say nothing of Nonna's retirement home, the children's university education, and some slim pickings put aside for retirement. But for Anna, most important of all was the freedom it gave her to write.

She was especially grateful for that when Sofia and Luke were babies and the longing to relieve her isolation and *make* something was strong. She put the children in her double stroller and went walking, drawn to the noise and clatter of London's street markets, each one further from home than the last. When she found the Queen's Market in Newham, it seemed to her like a new country; there wasn't a native Englishman in sight apart from the grumpy geezer selling bananas.

The route Anna took led them past a battered school building. On the wall outside was a poster for an immigrant advice centre.

One day she pushed her stroller over the broken door jamb and knocked on the door.

'What can you do?' asked the young woman manning the desk.

Anna shrugged. 'Not much.'

'Can you fill in forms?'

'Yes. I can do that.'

Anna volunteered for a few hours, three times a week. She filled in applications for amnesty, for disability support, assisted housing and schools, and in this way she came to hear the stories of the people who had washed up there. She met the children of women who had been trafficked and the ones who had arrived parentless, hanging onto the coat-tails of unscrupulous adults out to make a living from their plight.

Before Anna knew it, she'd been therc a year. The people who frequented the market assumed her to be local and nodded their heads in greeting.

It was many years later, when Anna's first two books were long finished, that the character of Boubakar began, uncertainly, to show up in her mind. She willingly followed the young Malian boy looking for his mother in London's immigrant outskirts, into a world of war and people trafficking and tragedy.

A little bit at a time, Anna began to write a book about how those who know the worst live amongst those who do not.

Peter seemed to accept the modest earnings Anna was able to contribute to the family economy, but whenever she tried to explain her work to him, it opened a rift between them. Like the evening not so long ago, in the perfect peace of their autumn garden when he'd asked, 'How'd it go today?'

'Oh, hard,' she'd said. 'Some days are hard.'

'Why do it then?'

Anna had looked at him as if to say, *Are you serious?*

The pot on the stove began to bubble and hiss. Beef stew was a favourite of Luke's. Anna had made it as part of her campaign to build up his bony shoulders.

Come dinnertime he devoured his helping and asked for more. As he ate he watched his silent father with uneasy attention.

'Did someone die?' he asked quietly.

His slightly flushed alarm stuck in Anna's gut.

'Don't be silly, *caro*,' she said, and ruffled his hair, 'Jump into bed and read a book. It's cold in here.'

He left reluctantly.

Anna and Peter stumbled through the clearing the table part of their evening in silence. It had taken her a long time to adjust to her husband's insistence that he be left alone when times were hard. 'Let me sort it out in peace,' he would say. 'Please.'

As she loaded the dishwasher Anna had to stop herself from hissing in anxious self-regard, *What's going to happen to my book people, Peter?*

The ringtone Anna reserved for her daughter rang out behind her. She and Sofia spoke often. Free wireless connection meant they were no longer exchanging news but rather chatting idly as they pottered. Anna used the time stealthily, to notice if Sofia looked tired, or whether she'd washed her hair.

Today, though, if she was honest, she clung to the conversation because she took comfort in her daughter's shining almond eyes.

'*Che cos'hai Mama?*' asked Sofia in Italian, which is what the children and Anna did whenever they wanted to get to the bottom of things.

'*Va tutto bene.* I'm fine, just tired.'

Later, when Anna crawled under the sheets, she found Peter already there.

'Sorry,' he said.

'No, please.'

'Yes, I'm sorry. I've made a bit of a mess of it all.'

She reached for him.

'I should've published more, learnt code, read environmental science, chemistry, politics . . . I'm a dinosaur, Anna.'

'Sshsh.'

They lay very close in the hope that it would bring comfort. She wrapped her arms around him and held on tight.

They lay like this until the house was still, then Anna reached for her husband in a different way. She stroked his lean limbs and dug her fingers into his hair. Slowly, gently, he turned to face her. He lifted himself over her and parted her legs until their bodies rocked together in familiar and consoling lust.

'Anna, you know cousin Giovanni was squashed under the tyres of his own tractor because he didn't heed his mother's warning!' said Nonna on the phone first thing in the morning

'Nonna, *per favore*,' said Anna, crouched at the side of the empty garden bed that had offered up a lavish crop of carrots in the autumn.

'But there's trouble coming, my child.'

'It's already here, Nonna,' snapped Anna. 'Peter lost his job.'

'*Oh, santo Dio*,' whispered the old lady. 'That was it.'

'Now tell me what to do, please,' said Anna.

'I don't know, *bella*, this I don't know,' said her grandmother.

'Right. That doesn't help me.'

'Just pay attention Anna! There is more to come.'

Anna turned the soil with a small garden fork. A vagrant carrot, shrivelled and almost black, emerged in her turning. She shook the soil off, frozen-fingered, and took a bite – it still held some of its taste. She snapped what was left in two and gave half to Liebe, then she went inside to take refuge with Boubakar and his people.

She found only silence when she opened her computer to work. She gave it a few minutes and then reached for her headphones.

Anna had written each of her books to a different playlist. Her father had helped her put the latest one together from his vast collection of African music. It was made up largely of a traditional Mande repertoire. He'd also thrown in some Puccini and Verdi for moments when she needed opera.

She put the headphones on her head, turned up the volume, and tapped her fingers to the music's quixotic beat.

From her earliest years, Anna's father had shared with her his love of music. A professor at the Royal College for thirty years, his knowledge was encyclopaedic, but it was how he reached for it after Anna's mother died that revealed to her its redemptive grace.

Many nights would see the three of them – Anna, her brother Stefano, and their father – listening to music on the sofa, or better still, playing together. Her *nonna* once said that after they lost their mother the three of them were like separate vines, too frail on their own, but capable when wound together.

She dialled the number of the small house in the Swiss village to which her father had retreated when he retired, but it rang unanswered. He was probably out walking his dogs.

Anna sat back in her chair and evoked him anyway. After all, he lived in her; he and his grit. Had he not packed her and Stefano's school lunches for years after their mother died, brushed their hair and cooked their dinners, when all he wanted to do was follow his beloved into the next world?

He had honoured them with his care. How then could she let Boubakar and his story go without a fight?

Anna turned away from the desk. If her imaginative world was made timid by the blow of Peter's news, perhaps the outer world would be more responsive?

She hit the redial button on her phone and called her friend and agent Lisbet Marais.

'How the fuck are you, Anna?' she said, 'And where's my manuscript?'

Lisbet was a South African with a mouth like a sewer. It was she who'd plucked Anna's first book out of the mountain of submissions years ago and become its cheerleader. She'd transformed a promising book into a pretty good one, even if the world mostly didn't notice.

Anna said, 'Peter's lost his job.'

In her strong South African accent Lisbet said, 'Fuck me . . . wait . . . what?'

'His head of department gave him the boot.'

'But academics never lose their jobs, they are carried out feet first.'

'Not this one.'

'Jesus, sorry, *bokkie*.'

She called Anna that whenever she was ruffled. The first time she did it Anna had asked, 'What's a bokkie?' and Lisbet had looked up and said, 'Little buck. You know, big eyes, soft muzzle, delicious in a stew.'

That was Lisbet, at once sentimental and effortlessly cruel.

Anna took a deep breath and asked Lisbet to bring forward the publishing date for her book by six months.

'What did you say?'

'I need to publish sooner, Lisbet, tomorrow actually.'

There was silence on the other end of the phone. They both knew how immovable publishing dates were. That's why Anna felt compelled to explain herself. 'It could save my life.'

'No, dear girl, it won't do that.'

'I can have it finished in a month if I really push.'

Lisbet let out a great booming laugh. 'Are you out of your mind?'

Quite possibly, thought Anna, and an image came to her of Peter, Luke, Sofia and Nonna, splitting apart and hurtling through space in an explosion of unmet need.

She jumped when she heard the hooter blasting outside in the street.

What day was it?

The hooter sounded again. Anna sat up. Bugger!

It was her friend Bouchra picking her up for Wednesday yoga. She made it into the passenger seat before she realised that she was still wearing her threadbare bedroom slippers.

Chapter Three

'Breathe in, right into the back of your chest,' said Stokely, their yoga teacher of eight years. 'Let your hips settle into the floor, release your neck.'

Stokely, so named by his Jamaican father after the militant leader of the Black Panther Party, was an inspired teacher. Wednesday yoga had become a cherished space in the lives of Anna and her two best friends, Bouchra and Nadia.

Stokely seemed to know instinctively when they needed shoring up and he did it with unusual skill.

'*Torschlusspanik*,' he said quietly to Anna as they stood poised to begin the sun salutations.

'What's that?'

'It means gate-shutting panic.'

'Yeah. That about sums it up.'

Torschlusspanik was exactly what Anna was feeling. She had long ago stopped wondering why German words held such attraction for Stokely. He didn't speak the language and had no cultural crossover with the country but the sounds of the words themselves, as well as their meaning, delighted him.

Anna always began yoga class knotted up like a tree branch and when it was over her muscles felt long and supple. She often had her best ideas upside down and thinking of nothing at all.

Not today though. Today, only her concern not to disrupt the class got her to the end.

'Oh, shit,' said Nadia as Anna shared her news. The three friends stood in the parking lot outside the yoga studio with the winter drizzle turning to sleet around their heads.

'Shit is right,' said Anna.

'So now what?' asked Bouchra.

Before Anna could answer, Nadia enveloped her in a hug, and murmured protectively, 'It's too soon for such questions, Bouchra.'

'Sorry . . .' muttered Bouchra. A dynamo Syrian, she hated uncertainty. 'But what's the plan, Anna?' she asked, unable to stop herself.

Anna leaned further into Nadia's embrace and closed her eyes.

Bouchra turned up at Anna's front door that afternoon with a lamb and eggplant curry in a large orange pot. Her visit was not unexpected.

Nadia wasn't far behind and she brought dhal.

The two women took occupation of Anna's kitchen table as if it were a war room.

'So?' asked Bouchra.

'I'm going to finish my book and hope it sells,' said Anna.

'What makes you think it will?' asked Nadia.

Anna took a breath. 'Nothing.'

'That's reassuring,' Bouchra muttered.

The friends had known one another for a long time. They'd met at the school gates and their children had grown up in each other's houses, eating Syrian, Aeolian and Indian food. Even when Bouchra's husband's business success took her to a wealthier neighbourhood, and her children to private boarding school, the women remained as close as sisters. Except, it must be said, on the question of money.

Bouchra's Syrian grandparents had fled upheaval in the Middle East and she'd been raised with the certainty that havoc and hardship were part of life's long road and that one needed to be ready for it.

Anna knew Bouchra's frustration with her lack of ambition in this regard had grown over the years. 'Tell me, Anna, do you not want to help the children buy a flat one day? It's the only way to get on the ladder.' Or, '*Habibty*, do you have to wear that out *again*? Stop by my place, I have something better.'

It was a measure of Bouchra's self-control that she didn't now say: *What did I tell you Anna!*

Nadia ladled rice and dhal into a bowl, added it to the food already in front of Anna and said, 'Eat.'

'Can't . . . sorry, not hungry.' Anna saw her two friends exchange a glance over her head.

'Anna?' said Nadia more gently now.

It took a moment for her to look up. 'I don't know how to do anything else.'

Anna felt herself flush with shame; *how then will I save us?* She asked herself.

'You can cook,' muttered Nadia.

'And you're a good mother,' said Bouchra.

Anna lifted her head and looked at them both. 'Maybe I should bottle that?'

In the silence that followed, Nadia reached for the bowl of dhal forgotten in front of Anna and began to slurp it up herself. Nadia was famous for her terrible table manners. Anna had always loved her for that imperfection.

'You could edit other people's manuscripts?' said Bouchra.

'Whoa there,' said Nadia with her mouth full. 'She can't spell, or tell the difference between *that* and *which*.'

'True,' said Anna.

'Maybe she's better in Italian,' offered Bouchra magnanimously.

''Fraid not,' said Anna.

A dull silence settled on them.

Ever the pragmatist, Nadia got up to fetch the phone message pad from the table in the corner and said, 'OK, so what are you going to cut from your monthlies?'

'The hairdresser,' said Anna.

'Lord have mercy,' murmured Bouchra under her breath. 'What about the grey?'

'Yoga?' said Anna.

'No,' said Nadia.

'Not yoga,' agreed Bouchra.

'How much does Nonna's retirement home cost?' asked Nadia.

Anna paused and then said quietly, 'Too much.'

'So, where will you put her when she moves in?' asked Nadia.

'In a tent in the garden?'

'That's not even funny, Anna.'

Anna felt her panic rise: what would happen to her thousand words a day if Nonna moved in? She knew better than to say that to her friends, today of all days, but she could feel the constriction of the world that it would bring - it was her deepest fear.

'They can't stand the sight of each other, Nadia,' she said instead.

'Who can't?'

'Nonna and Peter, you know that. How are they going to live in the same house?'

'Holy shit, you white people suck,' said Nadia and folded her arms across her chest.

'Well, she can't move in with me,' said Bouchra out of the blue, 'as much as I'd like to help.'

Anna looked at her. Bouchra's 'no-ask-zone' had shown itself more frequently the wealthier she'd become, until going to a movie, or out to lunch, became a test of who could calculate the precise three-way split of a bill, including the tip.

'Are you mad? I would never ask that of you,' said Anna.

'No, she wouldn't,' agreed Nadia, 'despite your five empty bedrooms, and, for the record, neither would I.'

Bouchra picked up Nadia's bowl, now empty, and the plate of untouched lamb stew in front of Anna, and crossed over to the sink. The silence rang with unspoken feeling.

The front door opened, 'Ah, sorry,' Peter said as he appeared in the kitchen doorway a few moments later. He looked as if he'd stumbled into a coven of witches. Anna wondered if he felt the bite of conflict in the air.

'Good grief, is that the time?' Nadia got to her feet.

As Bouchra passed him in the doorway she said, 'Sorry to hear your news, Peter.'

He nodded. 'Thanks.'

And they were gone.

Anna watched Peter put the cardboard box he was carrying down on the table; she could see it contained some of the photographs that had adorned his office. She wanted to say how sorry she was, but the line of his fine jaw seemed set against talk. *Her* talk, that is.

Chapter Four

'Will I have to leave university?' Sofia asked when Anna gave the children Peter's news.

'I could sell my saxophone,' said Luke.

'That won't be necessary,' said Anna.

She couldn't even dare to consider Sofia's question. The truth was that even if they lived frugally, she'd calculated their meagre savings would take them through only eight more months.

To help that go as far as possible Anna had cancelled some standing orders, the house insurance, which she knew to be unwise, and Liebe's pet coverage. Sadly, these savings affected almost nothing at all.

Anna swigged back half a glass of red in one gulp and said, 'We could save a lot of money if Nonna came to live with us.'

Sofia looked at her and said, 'Seriously?'

'Oh, dear God,' said Luke. He said that often, ironically, but today the words fell out of his mouth, fully felt.

'Why doesn't she go and live with Uncle Stefano on Salina?' asked Sofia, referring to the family's ancestral home on an island in the Tyrrhenian sea off the coast of Sicily. 'Then she can have as many bedrooms as she wants without evicting anyone.'

'Oh, *bella*, she feels too "with it" to give up on city life,' said Anna. 'As much as she loves to visit, it would drive her mad to live amongst the widows and the fishermen.'

'Will you give her my room?' asked Sofia.

'No, love.'

'Where will you put her then?'

'Not my room?' said Luke. His room, his cave, his place of retreat and reconfiguration. What sixteen-year-old could do without it?

'Your study's too small for anyone to live in,' said Sofia.

There was a moment of silence, during which Anna could sense the forming and reforming of the silent arguments in her children's heads.

'Give her Sofia's room,' Luke said. 'I mean, she doesn't even live here any more.'

'I do on the weekends.'

'Only sometimes.'

'I need somewhere that's mine, Luke.'

'What? To store your shoes?'

Anna closed her eyes.

'Tell her, Mama,' said Luke.

Anna raised her arms for quiet and when they were both looking at her she said, 'Nobody wants this, least of all Dad and me. Just let me think it through. OK?'

The manager of the retirement home greeted the news of Nonna's imminent departure with unseemly relief. Anna seized on it and offered him payment for a two-week notice period instead of the usual four. He accepted.

To help herself recover, Anna threw the frisbee for Liebe in the allotment garden. As she watched it spin, long and low, over the beds she thought; *There go my thousand fucking words.*

The truth was, Anna didn't know what else to do. Even the many hours she'd spent on the phone enquiring about menial editing jobs had come to naught.

She couldn't blame the employers. Oh, she was educated, two degrees and a shitload of living, but there were thousands of younger candidates pounding at their doors. None of them had been out of the job market for as long as she had and all of them were masters of the digital universe.

Anna took the frisbee from Liebe's mouth and threw it again. She could see Farhad making his way across his back garden towards her and wondered if his somewhat uncertain gait had to do with a lingering embarrassment over his clandestine morning visitor or whether her news had made the rounds of Carlyle Road.

Life had not always been kind to Farhad and his mother. He worked as an accountant to support them both and pay for his evening coding course at the University of Westminster.

He had permanent dark rings under his young eyes. *Thank goodness then for his secret liaison* was all Anna could think as he settled in nearby to turn the earth in his raised beds.

'Sorry to hear Peter's news,' he said.

So that was it.

'Yeah.'

'Any plans?'

'No.'

Silence.

'I'll think of something,' she said.

'*Inshallah*,' he muttered.

'With Him or without,' she replied.

Farhad's passion was for peonies. It was the hours he and Anna had shared in the allotment, each working on their respective beds, that had cemented their fondness for one another. Every summer he invited the allotment holders and their families to celebrate the full spectrum of his blooms, from white, through pink, all the way to almost black. His mother served tea, and small portions of densely sweet kulfi, and people sat about on picnic blankets while the trains passed to and fro.

'You won't tell my mother, will you?' he asked when Anna sat on the edge of the raised bed beside him.

'Tell her what?' Anna asked.

His silence was grateful. 'We got together in the shed all summer but it's too bloody cold now,' he said. 'Too cold and too grubby.'

'Where did you meet?' she asked.

'On the twenty-seven bus,' Farhad smiled, 'three mornings in a row.'

'What was it about him?'

Farhad looked at her, uncertain, and then he said, 'I knew he would share my *stuff*.'

'What stuff?'

'He calls them my "perversities".'

'How's that?'

Farhad smiled.

'Well?' she said, expectant.

'The first day I saw him he was as butch as can be. Suit and tie, the whole . . . you know.'

'And then?'

'The second day; black leather trousers.'

'Right.'

'And the third day he wore lipstick.'

'Oh.'

'What I mean is, I knew I wasn't going to have to be one thing with him.'

'As in?'

'Man, or woman.'

'OK,' said Anna.

'Did I just freak you out?'

Anna looked at him and she smiled. 'No, but I think I was born twenty years too soon.'

A dark curl drooped across her eyes. She paused to push it back and saw Farhad peer at it closely.

'Do I have slobber in my hair?' she asked. It wouldn't be the first time Liebe's foamy drool had ended up there.

'No,' Farhad cocked his head, 'but how come when you tie a scarf around your head it looks like destiny put it there?'

Anna knew the flattery was Farhad's way of shoring her up. 'Oh . . . I wish.'

It felt to Anna as if the only thing that had fallen on her in the last twenty years was vomit . . . baby, child, and drunken teenager.

And her books, her books had fallen on her too, thankfully, although they weren't much help in this crisis. Anna and Farhad paused at the doorway to the shed. She watched as he stashed his spade in the corner, and she said, 'Someone's had sex in here, for sure.'

Farhad said, 'Safe to assume that everyone's at it.'

'Oh, I wouldn't say that.'

He looked at her.

'Not often anyway.'

'Don't laugh,' he said, 'but along with the sex, we dream about matching dressing gowns on the back of the bedroom door and standing hand in hand in the queue at Tesco.'

'Now that's perverse,' she said.

Chapter Five

When Anna went to pick her grandmother up from the retirement home she found her sitting on her bed, fully dressed, with her small, crumpled hands in her lap.

'She got dressed last night and slept on top of the sheets,' said the carer.

'I didn't want to keep you waiting,' said Nonna.

Anna walked over to hug her.

Nonna muttered into her neck, 'I'll be good, Anna, no more arguments with Peter.'

'Shush, Nonna.'

'And no telling the future. I swear.'

Sofia had taken a few days to accept that she had to give up her room and the doing of it was more challenging still. Anna had had to call on Bouchra's bossy organisational skills to pull it off.

'Throw that away, Sofia,' she'd said as Sofia held up a lump of painted clay, the fruit of a toddler pottery class.

'But I made it.'

'I can see that.'

Bouchra then picked a short pink miniskirt out of a pile of used clothing intended for the small group of Syrian refugees given safe-haven in London. 'And what's this? No Syrian girl will wear this.'

'What, not even inside the house?' asked Anna.

'Nowhere!'

'Well, I heard that Syrian underwear is the raunchiest in the world, somebody has got to be wearing that,' said Anna.

'That's different,' said Bouchra.

'O-K . . .'

'Don't judge me, Auntie,' said Sofia. 'It was my Justin Bieber phase.' She took the skirt from Bouchra and put it on her head.

Bouchra smiled. 'Better.'

When Anna's books and manuscripts had been stashed in boxes in the shed at the bottom of the garden, and all Sofia's things installed in the office, mother and daughter surveyed the fruit of their labour.

Anna must have looked crestfallen at the cramped space that would house her child, because Sofia said, 'Aw, Mama, it doesn't matter. I'm not here that much.'

Anna moved Nonna into Sofia's room, box by box. She packed away her clothes, as per her instruction: '*Cara*, hang the outfits together, like that, see, blouse, skirt, jacket.'

'Really?'

'That way I don't have to look high and low when I want to dress.'

'Right.'

Then her nonna said, 'I will have soup for lunch.'

Soup? But what about Boubakar? Anna felt sure that today he would be there, if only she could get away.

Anna made the soup. Then she took refuge in the bathroom. She leaned against the cold tiled wall and hung her head. The peace was all too brief.

'Anna, is that you in there?'

Her nonna had a nose for despair.

Anna covered her ears in case the old lady chose that moment to say, 'Trouble comes in twos, my child, and there has only been one.'

And, of course, she did. She said exactly that.

Anna swallowed down the urge to shout, 'Way more than two, Nonna! And more coming down the pike.'

Instead, she waited for calm to return to her, and then she opened the bathroom door.

Her nonna lay on the bed, her pillows puffed just so in preparation for her afternoon nap.

Anna stood in her doorway. 'You going to be OK here, Nonna?' she asked quietly.

The old lady looked up at her and patted the space on the bed beside her.

Anna crawled onto the bed. It had been a long time since she had lain beside her grandmother. She rested on her back for a moment and asked herself, 'What, *deargodinheaven*, do I do now?'

The answer, oddly enough, lay on the pillow beside her.

Anna reached for Nonna's slim paperback and opened it. It was entitled *The Sheikh*. On the cover was a male model with a distinctly Palm Beach look, thick eyeliner stood in for his exotic origins. A half-naked blonde was on her knees at his feet reaching up for his protection.

'Nonna, is this yours?'

Colour crept across the old lady's cheeks. 'Ruby left it to me,' she said, somewhat sheepishly.

Ruby Costello had been Nonna's partner-in-crime at the care home until she'd passed away a few months previously. The two old ladies had shared a love for the Good Lord and very dry martinis; they would regularly partake of the latter and then pray together.

More than once Anna received a phone call from her nonna late at night:

'We are on our knees, Anna.'

'Are you?' she'd said and she could barely hear for Ruby's raucous laughter in the background.

'I mean really on our knees. Praying.'

'Yeees?'

'And we can't get up.'

They would both be laughing now. Then Anna would phone the night desk and the person on duty would have to go over and haul Nonna and Ruby to their feet and drive one or other of them home in a golf cart.

Ruby Costello, fabulous drunk, and bequeather of trashy erotic stories.

'Now shush, child, I need a nap,' said Nonna.

Anna's grandmother closed her eyes and folded her arms across her chest like Sleeping Beauty.

Anna opened the book and began to read. The Sheikh of the title had everything – money, power, a beautiful body, lust *and* decency. Would he save the heroine? Would he see her beauty and pluck her out of the sea of equally lovely others? Oh, most definitely, yes.

Preposterous! Yet here there would be no unhappy endings, no dark-winged grandmothers, no mothers dying too soon or husbands losing their jobs. And here was sex.

And camels, and the moon rising over the desert sand.

In spite of the crudeness of the language and the absurdity of events as they unfolded, Anna felt a warmth flush through her limbs. Her body couldn't care less about the quality of the words. It scorned her judgement and allowed itself to be stoked to lustful wakefulness.

That her nonna, the *trouble comes in twos* octogenarian, now snoring gently beside her, also took comfort from the union between the sheikh and his fair inamorata seemed to her, just then, to be entirely fitting.

Anna read on hungrily, aware only remotely of time passing. She read until she was finished. Then she sat up in bed and said to herself, 'My God.' She hugged the book to her bosom and whispered, 'I can do this.'

Chapter Six

Anna woke early. After feeding the dog, cat, boy, man, snake and now grandmother, she headed over to her local library and read her way through their small shelf of erotica, Anaïs Nin's classic *Delta of Venus* and a collection of Angela Carter's fairy tales.

The following day she left lunch in the fridge for Nonna so she could stay at Waterstones on Piccadilly until dinner time. She found a comfortable chair in the far corner of the sumptuous corporate cathedral and gave herself over to sexy tales of all descriptions. If any of the young people who worked there wondered if Anna might buy one of the tomes she was devouring, they were too polite to say so.

There were moments, in the course of that very long first day, when she would willingly have followed any one of the people browsing the shelves into the bathroom on the fifth floor and thrown herself at them just to get some relief from her lust. *Bugger the bathroom*, she found herself thinking, *what are the gaps between bookshelves for?*

It wasn't as if she hadn't read erotica when she was a young woman, but it seemed to her, now, that an overabundance of gorgeous tales had made their way into the world while she had been turned away. She would *love* to be able to write this. This was pleasure, languid, glorious, reading pleasure, tastier by far than *The Sheikh*, and rooted in great company; Henry Miller, Mary Gaitskill, Alice Munro . . .

Anna happened on an excerpt from *The Lover* by Marguerite Duras which pinned her to her chair and then sent her, finally, stumbling up the steps to the fifth-floor bathroom with the intention of relieving her lustful body herself.

But there was no relief to be had.

What settled on her, as she leaned against the partition wall of the loo, with her knickers around her knees, was the bruising awareness that her erotic life – her actual life and the modestly tender communion she shared with Peter – was a pale shadow of what they both wanted and needed.

Later, she would see that she had long known that, but never in her body, salty and sharp, the way she did now.

She had felt such fervour only once before. Her lover then, in her very first months of university, was Billy Jones, a visiting student from Ontario. Their eighteen-year-old bodies took to one another like missing parts of a bewildered whole. His hands were big, big enough to hold Anna in one hand as he lifted her up, and rough-skinned from working on his father's farm.

Once they'd kissed and she'd unbuttoned her white cotton shirt, she and Billy Jones didn't leave her dorm room for six straight days. They travelled into unchartered territory with their bodies, and it seemed, to her at least, that their hearts and minds had followed. Her craving for him looked a lot like love, and loving people hadn't always ended well for Anna. *You'll lose him too. You will lose him*, said the voice inside her head – the certainty of it drove her mad.

She could not allow that, so she kept Billy Jones prisoner with her bodily delights. She even watched him sleep to ensure that he didn't slip out in the night or, worse still, die right there and then.

When the proctor finally pounded on their door he found the two of them asleep on one another's bony chests, stricken and half-starved. They were both sent home – she knew it meant she would never see him again.

No one in her household said a word about it. She wanted Stef, at least, to make a joke about how most people got a drinking habit when they went to university but she had to go and get addicted to a brainy farmer from Ontario.

The truth was that it had shaken young Anna to her marrow to be faced with love and its shadow of loss.

Later that afternoon, an eager bookseller dug up Darcey Steinke's *Suicide Blonde* followed by what appeared to be hard-core fetish porn which made Anna's head hurt. Even in this Eden of stories, she had found her limit.

She put it back on the shelf and headed home early to

cook ragu alla Bolognese. She needed building up for the task ahead.

As Anna brushed her teeth before bed, the lingering sexiness of her day's reading came back to her. Peter paused on his way to bed and looked at her in the mirror.

'What?' she asked.

He read her face for a moment, then craned forward and kissed her on the lips.

How reliable he was when it came to detecting sensual possibilities in his wife's dark eyes.

She felt her husband reach for her hand and her heart sank. She made herself take it and tried to think of something funny to say.

In the twenty-two years of their union they had found ways to make light of their differences. She'd teased him for being a stitched-up Englishman and he played along.

'Your daughter just sang Puccini standing on a bucket in the kitchen. If you don't feel some joy you are from an unknown planet.'

'You do it for both of us, Anna, that's why I love you,' he'd said and he kissed her on the nose.

Now he kissed her hand. She let him do it. He kissed her skin all the way up her arm to the tip of her ears, and all the while she held her breath and hoped that he would realise that today was not the day for it. At least not for her.

He pulled himself up and reached over to kiss Anna on the mouth.

Her will failed her at that moment and her whole body screeched *run*.

Never before had she felt this way. Of course, there'd been times when she'd thought *Oh well, here we go again, do I have to?* And mostly she'd found joy and pleasure in it. Other times she'd been the eager party. In truth, she loved sex just as much as the next woman.

But this? This was beyond any such subtle negotiation.

Peter moved to the edge of the bed. 'I'll sleep in Sofia's room.'

'No, please.' She shook her head. 'Sorry. There's no need for that. I'll go to the study. You're already in bed. Please. Sorry. I'll go.'

Sorry, sorry, sorry.

She didn't go to the study, she went downstairs trailing Liebe and Lily-the-cat, and she sat at the kitchen table trying to understand what had just happened.

A tear escaped from her right eye. It was always the right; she wondered if she had a blocked tear duct on the left. Then she turned off the light and walked out of the front door into the pitch-black night.

The neighbouring streets were dark and empty. Liebe's breath made clouds in the cold. It always helped her to walk; each step quieted the rumbling alarm that seemed now to be her constant companion.

As she passed the small block of council flats on the corner she saw the Arab couple emerge at the top of their stairs and walk towards their front door. She had met them only a few times. They had arrived in Carlyle Road after the last tornado and had yet to apply to the allotment committee for their assignment of land, so she'd had less to do with them than most of her neighbours. Anna made a note to herself to remind Farhad to invite them to his peony fest in the spring.

The couple looked down then, and saw Anna and Liebe on the pavement. Anna lifted her hand and waved. A soft smile lit up the man's face. *'Baraka Allah fiki!'* he said.

It was thanks to Bouchra that Anna knew that he had said 'God bless you.' He said it gently as he turned into the flat. She felt the benevolence of the blessing fall on her cheeks, like warm summer rain.

Chapter Seven

Anna was late getting to the Romance Writing Workshop because Nonna insisted on two poached eggs for breakfast and the London overground was in a spasm – an incident on the tracks, said the tired-looking man in a blue uniform.

The room where the workshop was taking place was already over-hot and airless by ten o'clock in the morning. Anna made her way to the last empty chair. On the table in front of her was a gift bag containing two books. One of them was *The Sheikh*. The writer of that, and thirty-five other books, was to be the after-lunch speaker. If you want to crack the code, this is your woman, thought Anna, and she turned towards it all with an open heart.

Ten o'clock to lunchtime went by in something of a fog. Anna tried to extract *instruction* from the *you-have-a-great-story-to-tell-and-we-all-know-love* claptrap that spilled into the room from the publishing executives. The words formed a smoky halo around Anna's head. There was only one other person in the room who displayed any signs of bewilderment.

She was young and wore a ring in her nose. Anna watched her bent over her mobile phone, perhaps to relieve herself from having to pretend she understood.

To the question, 'Who is your favourite movie heroine?' she answered, 'The rabbit-murderer in *Fatal Attraction*.'

Anna wished she was sitting next to her.

At lunchtime she found herself in a small teashop managed by two Polish cooks and a skinny Asian student wearing a University of Durham T-shirt. By the time Anna was given her pot of Russian Black and her stodgy scone and cream there were no tables left. Then she noticed the girl with the ring in her nose sitting at the table by the window.

'Mind if I join you?' asked Anna.

The girl shook her head and returned to her phone. Anna sat at the table and poured her tea. She could hear the tic, tic, tic, of the girl's phone keyboard as she typed.

'It's weird in there,' said the girl, finally.

'Certainly is,' said Anna.

The girl smiled. Anna sipped her tea.

'I'm Anna,' she said.

'Cordelia.'

The two young women at the table next to theirs were deep in conversation. One was ginger haired, the other a brunette, English girls with fine skin and sharp chins. Their conversation had a peculiar intensity.

'Ben wants to get married in the church in Baxley but

Dartington is so much closer for the parents,' said the redhead.

Out of nowhere, her friend began to cry. Both Anna and Cordelia heard her low sobs but neither looked up. Their discretion bound them together.

The redhead handed her weeping friend a tissue, but she refused it. She reached for her hand. Anna saw her brush her lips over the brunette's skin. It was a lover's kiss.

'Be my maid of honour, Angelica.'

'Please, don't.'

'Be my maid.'

The brunette simply looked at her lover as tears poured silently down her cheeks.

The redhead signalled frantically to the waitress who sloped over with the bill. Finally, the two women got up, the brunette still sobbing quietly.

Anna, Cordelia and the waitress watched, agog, as the redhead took her lover into her arms and they stood, still as stone, breathing in one another's grief. Then she led her out by her hand.

When the door closed, Anna saw them split apart like separate planets and walk across the zebra crossing in the rain.

'Blimey,' said Anna under her breath, 'now that's a romance.'

'Shit, yeah,' said Cordelia.

Anna wished she'd gone home after lunch because the woman who wrote *The Sheikh* was as dull as ditchwater. Anna wanted to ask why she talked about writing in such a pedestrian manner and, in fact, now that Anna knew better, why she wrote the way she did. What about the rich tradition of erotic writing that had kept her in a swoon in Waterstones? Where was the influence of all of that?

But of course Anna didn't ask, what the hell did she know? She was a newborn babe.

The author of *The Sheikh* seemed now to be intent on weeding out the imposters in the room. As part of that mission she insisted that each of the participants invent an opening paragraph for a book, then read it out loud.

'Any volunteers?'

Sheila from Surrey, with a red scarf and dark brown hair, shot her hand into the air; 'Mary took off her nurse's uniform and stretched to relieve her aching back. It was only when she had taken off her bra too that she became aware of Dr McDougal sitting in the corner by his locker. She blushed pink and whispered, "Sorry. I didn't know you were here . . ." He silenced her with a gesture and said, "Please," his eyes dilated, his breathtaking eyes, "don't stop."'

'Brilliant. Love it! Who's next?'

Not me please, Anna prayed, but in vain. She read haltingly and with apologies to Billy Jones, 'I can't stop myself from kissing him . . .'

'Really? Present tense! And first person?' said the author. 'Never do that. Start again.'

But what about Alice Munro and Marguerite Dumas? Anna wanted to snap, they wrote sexy stories too, you know, and would you refuse them the pleasures of the present tense? But

Anna already knew the answer; if you were Marguerite Duras or Alice Munro you wouldn't be sitting in this room, so shut up and do as you're told. And she tried, conjugating as she went, 'I couldn't stop myself—'

'She,' said the author.

'What?'

'She, she, she.'

'She couldn't stop herself . . .' Anna continued so quietly that the author had to lean forward to hear her, '. . . from kissing him in the corridor of her University dorm—'

'I can't hear you.'

Anna glanced up.

'I mean, I can't hear a word you are saying,' said the author.

Anna knew she was done for, that the woman hated her and her pompous bloody sentence and that she was going to make her pay.

'Read it again,' she barked.

This time Anna returned to her tense of choice and by so doing inflamed the tension between them;

> 'I can't stop myself from kissing him in the corridor of my university dorm but I do have the good sense to wait until we are inside the room to unbutton my red cotton blouse. The next thing I know, I mean, really know, is that six days have passed and the proctor is pounding on my door. In the world of me and my boy from Ontario there was no time, there was only his skin, and my heartbeat, my smell and his touch. My

craving for him looked a lot like love, and loving people hasn't always ended well for me. *You'll lose him too. You will lose him*, said the voice inside my head - and the thought became a swarm of red ants, or bees, and it sounded like a storm on a tin roof.

Anna didn't dare look up. The silence in the room felt soup-thick and maybe even malevolent. Then the scribe of *The Sheikh* looked around and said, 'Anyone else?' and so consigned Anna to the dunces' corner with the LOSERS.

That's when Cordelia put a slip of paper on the desk in front of her that read, *I'm busting out. Coming?*

Anna found Cordelia perched on a garden wall eating a doughnut. She handed one to Anna.

'Thanks.'

They munched as they walked along the towpath that ran beside the river.

'That was good stuff, your paragraph,' said Cordelia.

'Argh, I don't know. It certainly wasn't romantic.'

'It was kind of sexy'

'Thanks.'

'You write literary fiction?'

Anna nodded. 'Not making much of a living at it though.'

'Yeah,' said Cordelia, 'I need to do this so I can finish my PhD without having to live under a bridge.'

'What's it on?'

'Kierkegaard.'

Anna laughed at this surprising young woman. 'Sorry, no offence.'

'None taken.'

'Why him?'

'You really want to know?'

'I do.'

'It's weird, but I just find his ideas about us flawed mortals irresistible.'

'Why's that?'

'Because they're so bleak,' and she chuckled

Anna looked up and their eyes met in the glancing way of strangers, and she said, 'I'd like him then. My husband says the only thing I trust myself to write about is misery.'

'My mum thinks it's all a waste of time,' Cordelia went on. 'The first of us to get to university and look what I do with it, *wallow*.'

She smiled. Anna finished her doughnut. 'What would Kierkegaard have made of today?'

'Best not to ask that.'

'I *am* asking.'

Cordelia laughed a great bark of sound and Anna knew she'd found a twin soul.

'I've bored most of my friends to death talking about him so I'm looking for a new victim. If you're willing, so am I,' said the young woman and then she glanced at her phone. 'Got to go now though.'

It turned out that Cordelia worked at a steak and chip restaurant in Leicester Square, which she said was like being slowly suffocated to death by a mountain of greasy French fries.

They hugged briefly outside the Tube station.

Cordelia scribbled her email address on a card and gave it to Anna. 'Hope to see you again.'

'Yeah, me too. Thanks for the doughnut.'

Chapter Eight

Peter busied himself with folding the newspaper at the breakfast table; he did it so long and so lavishly that Anna stopped loading the dishwasher to watch him. Luke, too, glanced up from his oatmeal.

When all the energy in the room had been colonised by the folding and turning and folding again, Peter looked up at Anna and asked, light as air, 'You planning to do some work today?'

Anna glanced at him then looked away. She wanted to tell him about the romance workshop and *The Sheikh* but the moment wasn't right. Luke was in the room and the paper-folding ritual had warned her away from opening her heart.

'I'm going to write,' she said quietly, 'like I always do.'

'I don't know,' said Peter, and he cleared his throat. 'You could be up there spinning silk for all the money it brings in.'

Anna could see the light blue vein on Peter's fine temple. She had the sinking feeling that the true cause of her husband's fury was not their financial predicament but her flight from their bed two nights ago.

'I'm hoping to change that,' said Anna.

Luke got up and put his cereal bowl in the sink. He paused there, anxious. The three of them seemed, all of a sudden, to be poised on the tip of a pin.

Anna forced the alarm from her face and gathered up her husband's dirty breakfast plates.

'How long until you can submit the manuscript?' he asked.

'It's not clear yet.'

'You said that before Christmas.'

'Don't be an idiot, Dad,' said Luke quietly.

Anna dropped the plates into the dishwasher. 'Lukey, don't forget your saxophone.'

She saw him observing his father, watchful, and the Italian was out of her mouth before she could stop it. '*Papa e solo stanco*.' He's just tired.

'*Quindi tu dici*,' said the boy. So you say.

As with Sofia, Italian was Anna's default language when things felt like they were slipping from her grasp. When they were first married she'd given Peter lessons but after a few weeks he'd declared himself unteachable.

How many times had she said the same thing about her husband? *He's just tired*.

He was afraid now, to be sure, and helpless, and for that she felt only compassion. But it was also true that there was a fault line in him that produced a belligerent self-absorption. It robbed him of his capacity for kindness and blinded him to things he should see.

'Time to toughen him up,' he'd declare each Sunday morning of Luke's childhood, and he carted the boy off to play in the junior league of the local football club. Luke would run up and down the field in a blur of misery while his father screamed, 'Kick it! Argh! Run for it, Luke!' from the side of the field.

When Luke turned eleven he sat down on the step in the hall and said, 'I'm not going, Dad.'

'What did you say?'

'I'm not going to football today.'

'Oh yes you are, my boy.'

'No,' Luke said quietly, 'I'm not.'

And that was that.

Not long after, Luke joined the cross-country running team at his school and spent his Sundays happily loping across the green spaces of Richmond Park and Hampstead Heath. Peter never went to watch him race.

It wasn't maliciousness, she knew, her husband was raised in a home chronically short on love. It meant that he couldn't imagine what his son needed, nor get the measure of his role as his teacher and guide.

'Come on, Dad, let's go,' Luke said and he turned and headed into the hallway, willing his father to follow.

But Peter did not move. Instead, he looked at Anna and asked, 'Do you even know what the word count is?'

'About seventeen thousand,' said Anna.

'I thought there'd be more.'

'Dad!' shouted Luke, from the front door.

Anna whispered, 'Not now, Peter.'

He got up out of his chair and strode up to her, hidden as she was from Luke's view. He leant the whole rigid length of himself against her body. She felt the ridges of the kitchen counter in her back.

He spoke very quietly, in her ear, 'I thought there'd be more,' he said, 'Anna.'

And then he was gone. She wanted to call out after him *Me too! I thought so too.* But she said nothing.

The word count on her manuscript was sixty-seven-thousand four hundred and twenty-two.

Anna didn't tell Peter that because she knew it didn't matter anymore.

She would have to let Boubakar go - and with him all of the world as he knew it. It may not have to be forever, but for now she would have to give up what he had allowed her to imagine about *difference.* She would lose the chance to make something of what she'd learned in the years she'd worked at the advice centre and would have to turn her back on the extraordinary people she had come to know there; displaced people, itinerant, hungry, distrustful, and so very vulnerable. She would have to let it all go if she was going to stand a chance of saving her family.

'But why can't you do both, *cara,*' said her grandmother

when she saw Anna's grief. 'Money work in the morning and this boy's story in the afternoon?'

But Anna knew she couldn't play host to both the sheikh and Boubakar. If they went toe-to-toe, the actor in the eye-liner wouldn't stand a chance in hell.

And neither would she.

Anna sat in the gloom of her winter kitchen. She sat until she was able to pull her computer to her, close the file named *BOUBAKAR* and drag it to the archive folder on the left of her screen.

Chapter Nine

After dinner Anna sat at her computer to write a story that would not be too sad, not too sweet, that would be sexy in just the right way – a story that might give someone a little pleasure. It did not begin well.

> Simon came to us by the number 17 bus. He brought with him a backpack full of dirty clothes and a lifetime of disappointment . . .

Anna considered the line. *Jesus, cheer up, will you!* said the voice inside her. She tried again:

> Simon came to us on the overground from Crouch Hill. He had a cheeky grin.

Her heart began to thud as she recognised that *The Sheikh*

would never begin with those words. She could see that she didn't have the nous to emulate the erotic story greats, but did it have to be this banal?

> Simon came to her on the *Victory*. The forty-two-foot yacht cut a line through the still water of the bay, straight to her belly. She waved to him, her long hair whipped wild by the wind, her white cotton shorts bright against her tanned, lean legs. One look at her and his eyes darkened black and limpid with lust.

Anna stopped again, *ah no*, *The Sheikh* was not that either, it was more sly and self-aware. Or was it just that she missed Boubakar?

She heard an unfamiliar ping and a text message popped onto her screen. It was Cordelia.

How is it going, Anna?

She sat upright and answered eagerly, Horribly! You?

It seemed somewhat magical to her that she and her new friend were having a written real-time conversation when they knew one another so slightly.

Well, I just wrote my first story.

Congratulations! Did you use the present tense?

I did.

Send it to me if you want a second reader.

Yes please. I'm doing it now before you can change your mind. You want to meet for a drink?

Love to.

Anna couldn't know then what would become of this first modest collaboration, but she felt her spirits rise. She turned back to Simon and his forty-two-foot yacht, and she wrote:

> Simon came to her on the *Victory*. She didn't know it was him, of course, but the whole of her insides flipped over at the sight of the man flying up the rigging to attend to a knot in the mainsail. The power and grace in the deckhand's wide, rippling back kept her riveted as the yacht slid into its berth.
>
> The deckhand? Then why did he remain onboard when the other crew disembarked?
>
> And it came to her that he was the owner of the beautiful vessel. He was also waving madly at someone on the jetty. At who? At her! And now he was off the boat and walking straight towards her and as he got closer she could see his eyes darken, black and limpid with lust . . .

No, no, no! Anna wanted to shout, why could she not write a credible first encounter?

Cordelia's email with the attached story popped into her mailbox just then. Anna clicked on it, grateful for the distraction from her own struggle.

She scanned the opening paragraph, stopped, and went back to the beginning to read it more carefully.

Cordelia had written a wild-ride erotic story, peppered with Mancunian slang and extreme, transgressive sex.

When she got to the end Anna sat for a time while the

shock of it passed. The scribe of this rampaging sexy story revealed a whole new aspect of the bright-spark academic Anna knew Cordelia to be. The result was a volatile mess, but it was also packed to the gills with exuberant boldness.

'Sheesh, Cordelia,' said Anna when they met for a drink to discuss it. 'Your story should've come with a disclaimer.'

'What?' she said, and colour bloomed across her cheeks.

She looked, Anna thought for a moment, like the red queen in *Alice in Wonderland* with her ginger hair cut in a sharp bob, and her glowing cheeks.

'I mean, I love it, but do you think they're going to even consider publishing it?' she asked.

'Well, they do have an imprint called Red Hot Passion.'

'I think they mean old people passion.'

'Are you saying old people don't partake of a bit of rough?'

'I think a lot of their readers won't know what half these things are; I mean, I don't even know what "fisting" is.'

Cordelia sat back in her chair. 'Where've you been, Anna?'

'In the wilderness of middle age, apparently.'

'Where, I'm told, fetishes abound,' said Cordelia with a twinkle.

'Wish I'd known that too.'

They were silent for a moment and it struck Anna that even talking about *this* felt comfortable with Cordelia; it was as if she'd known her all her life.

'How do you know this stuff?' she asked at last.

'What?'

'About sex, fetishist sex in particular.'

'Well, I read,' said Cordelia. 'Right now, Martha Nussbaum's essay on objectification is lighting my fire.'

'Martha Nussbaum?'

'Moral philosopher and an intellectual light for me and my chums.'

'How?' said Anna.

'For starters, she suggests that there are times when being treated like a sex object – no, she actually calls it "a mysterious, thinglike presence" – can be liberating.'

'OK . . .'

'And that sometimes it allows us to reach out to another person, purely sexually. And to trust them, you know, with our dignity. That's the idea anyway.'

'Martha Nussbaum,' said Anna quietly and she wondered, again, what else she'd missed. She didn't tell Cordelia that she sometimes sounded like a book rather than a person, because she could see that the ideas gave the young woman a mooring in a choppy sea, and goodness knows everyone needs that.

'I also have the odd skirmish with men I don't know, by way of research,' said Cordelia and she blushed again.

'What, like you hook up with complete strangers?'

'Yeah.' She shifted in her seat.

'And you do fisting and the like?'

'Not yet. I haven't done that, that . . . myself.'

'OK. Because I don't know how it's physically possible.'

'I'll keep you posted.'

'Thanks.'

Anna laughed and took another sip. They were silent for a moment and then she asked, 'Does it have to be of the hit-and-run kind? The sex?'

'It's all I can manage,' said Cordelia. And she looked away.

Chapter Ten

'I've got an opportunity, Anna,' said Peter as they sat in bed that evening, reading books open on their laps.

'Oh?'

She wanted to say *What's an opportunity?* because the language sounded so alien, but the shadow in his eyes stopped her.

'It's a start-up.'

As Peter explained the idea he licked his lips and ran his fingers anxiously through his hair.

A group of engineers he knew were planning to manufacture products designed to stop water evaporation in hot countries. They needed a mechanical engineer to contribute.

'But that's wonderful,' she said and leant across the bed to take his hand.

'It's not in London,' he said.

'Where is it?'

'Sheffield. A colleague at the university is leading it but it's an independent venture.'

'Sheffield? But when will we see you?'

'On the weekends.'

'No.'

'No is what you say when you have money in the bank.'

She looked at him and saw that his skin had turned from peach to grey.

'Then we can all move to Sheffield,' she said.

'No, we can't,' he whispered. 'You know that.'

They couldn't take Luke out of the local school he had only just begun to settle into. And what would they do with the grandmother, the dog, the cat, the snake and the girl who needed to come home when the adult world shook her too violently?

'It's only a trial position and there's no money, but it could go somewhere.'

'Oh,' said Anna softly.

'I thought I was too old to be scared,' he said.

Anna whispered, 'I love you.'

'Yeah. I know,' he said quietly.

Anna reached for her husband. He took her hand and kissed her knuckles one by one. He lay on the bed. She put her head on his chest then pushed her nose into his neck and breathed in his smell. He let her do it.

She slipped a hand under his pyjama top and glanced at him. He shook his head.

She withdrew her hand and rested her head on his chest. She felt the booming vibration of his heart.

The edges of their ribs settled, one row of bones against the other, until Peter's breathing evened out and he began to snore. Anna longed for sleep. She felt Liebe's nose nudging her as if to say, *I know you are awake so what are you waiting for?*

She slipped out of bed and down the stairs.

The night was warm for that time of year and the air moist. Anna and Liebe walked around the park and up the deserted high street. She would've found comfort in seeing the Arab couple moving about. Even more to have him bless her as he'd done before, *Baraka Allah fiki*. But the house was dark.

Anna woke dry-eyed from lack of sleep, and immediately threw herself into the task of straightening out the chaotic order of events in Cordelia's story. It took some doing. Lunchtime came and went. Only dread of the blank page of her own story kept her at her desk for the hours it took to wrangle a structure that did the story justice.

Anna was beginning to sense the pleasure of that finally working when the espresso machine behind her let out a sudden hiss. She jumped.

'Shit! You snuck up on me, Nonna.'

'I don't sneak, child, I glide,' said her grandmother.

She wore a hat on her head for afternoon prayers at the Catholic church around the corner which held services in Italian on Wednesday afternoons and on Sundays at eleven. She always rewarded her piety with a good strong espresso.

Anna hoped that her grandmother would take her coffee into the living room and leave her to her labour, but it was not to be.

'So, what did you make of my book?' said Nonna when she saw *The Sheikh* on the kitchen table.

'I'm hoping mine will be better.'

Nonna snorted. 'You want to write rubbish like that?' she asked. 'Even while the storm clouds gather?'

'What storm clouds are these, Nonna?' asked Anna with a sigh. She was as disturbed as anyone else by the increasingly divisive goings on in Europe and America, but her nonna had a way of claiming primacy over everyone else's anxieties.

'These English fools have forgotten what a divided Europe is like,' said the old lady, 'and how much worse with that dangerous *pazzo* in the White House. If your grandfather was here he would pull the hair from his head.'

Anna had never met her maternal grandfather but she'd heard stories of his exile by Mussolini on the island of Salina just before the war.

He'd been tortured by the blackshirts for his involvement with the anti-fascist league until fear for his life had driven him and Nonna to stow away on a fishing boat headed for Southampton in the fourth full year of the war. Anna couldn't quite conjure the two young people hiding amongst the olive barrels in the bottom of a boat as her grandparents.

'He was twice the man of these fool politicians,' said Nonna as she sat at the table.

Anna said nothing. She could feel her grasp of Cordelia's story falter.

'He was also more of a sheikh than that idiot with eyeliner,' said the old lady, pointing at the painted actor on the cover of the book.

'I bet,' said Anna, and she planted her fingers on her keyboard in one final attempt to return to the work. A row of random letters bloomed on her screen. 'Got to get this done, Nonna, OK?'

'Did you know your grandfather was the best kisser in all of the Aeolian islands?'

'I didn't know that . . . in fact.'

Nonna reached for a biscotti. 'He had very light brown eyes, like a lion.'

'Eyes like a lion and lashes like a cat,' said Anna – she'd heard that before.

'And muscles in his arms like ropes from a big ship. He was a runner, you know.'

Nonna dunked the biscotti in her coffee and took a bite. With her mouth full she said, 'Of course, we were virgins when we met. If my father had found out what went on in that ferry waiting room he would have cut my Pietro's throat before we made it to the altar.'

Anna felt Cordelia's story vanish into the undertow of her grandmother's tale.

'Start at the beginning, Nonna,' she said.

Her nonna laughed. 'It is not for you to know, my child. You need to tell your own story.'

'I don't think I have one,' said Anna quietly.

'Such things are sent by God, *cara*. It was he who sent my Pietro to the ferry building on the night of the storm.'

'Was it a bad storm?'

'Bad enough so they stopped all ferry crossings. I couldn't get back home from my job at the haberdashery in Palermo.'

'Go on.'

'Because he was a "political", Pietro was obliged to register with the authorities there once a month. It seems everyone else in the world was warned about the storm and kept away, so it was me and him, led there, *come ho detto*, by the creator.'

'And?'

'And it was the time of the curfew so we couldn't walk the streets trying to find a place to sleep. We had to stay there, in the ferry building.'

'Alone?' said Anna.

'Alone.'

'And?'

'The first part of the night we were on either side of the room. He ate his bread and cheese. I ate my boiled eggs. We made polite conversation,' she covered her mouth with her hand, 'but by the morning we were one, body and soul.'

'You had sex?' Anna asked, aghast.

Her nonna shook her head. 'We had our wedding night, in the company of God and the angels.'

'Good Lord! You married him then and there?'

Her nonna placed her hands on her belly and said, 'That night I married him here,' and then she touched her heart, 'and here. And for that feeling, that communion of his body with mine. For that feeling, I would have given up my soul.'

Anna sat at the kitchen table long after Nonna had shuffled out and up the stairs for her afternoon nap. A troublesome new companion joined her there. She couldn't quite place it; only later did she come to know it as regret.

Chapter Eleven

Cordelia came over with a bunch of flowers and a bottle of wine to thank Anna for her help on her story.

She had taken most of Anna's suggestions on board and after a cathartic tussle with her self-confidence had, that very afternoon, submitted the finished story to the publishers.

'Ah, my papa had a cow with a ring through its nose,' said Nonna as Cordelia followed Anna into the kitchen. 'What's yours made of?'

'Silver.'

'Lucky you.'

Cordelia grinned. Nonna patted the young woman's cheek, a gesture of unusual warmth for so recent an acquaintance. *Well*, she would always say, *you know a good one when you see it.*

'Come, help me chop,' she said.

Nonna, in her red satin dressing gown and a shower cap on her head *for the curls*, was busy with early preparations for dinner. She positioned Cordelia in front of the low, wide-lipped wooden bowl on the table and showed her how to use the mezzaluna.

Cordelia whistled. 'That's a grand way to chop stuff.'

'Do you know what you are chopping?'

'Capers?'

'*Sì. Capperi di Salina.* They come from our island. This dish I can still cook, *grazie a Dio*,' muttered Nonna.

Anna watched them work for a while and then she said, 'Cordelia's written a good strong soup of a story, Nonna.'

'With a lot of help from you,' said Cordelia and then she paused. 'But is soup a good thing?'

'Strong soup is high praise,' said Anna. 'We live by food metaphors around here.'

They chopped until the capers were a mush and the olives added. Nonna threw them into the pan with the sizzling garlic and chilli.

'And when are we going to see *your* story-soup, Anna?' asked Cordelia.

'That is the thousand-dollar question,' cried Nonna. 'Soon! Or we'll have only stale bread and water next time you come to dinner.'

Anna looked at her grandmother, angry at this betrayal of their condition. How dare she?

'Straight talk breaks no friendship, *cara*,' said Nonna. She turned to Cordelia, threw basil and oregano into her bowl and said, 'Chop, chop, chop.'

There was no spoken invitation for Cordelia to join them

for dinner, just an assumption that she would. She and Luke laid the table for five. Peter called to say he was having a drink with old colleagues so they cleared one away again.

'Did it hurt?' asked Luke as he pointed at Cordelia's nose ring.

She scraped her plate clean with a crust of focaccia and said, 'No, but my da's lashing did.'

'He hit you?' asked Luke, horrified.

'Well, I was only thirteen when I got it and he thought it a very bad idea.'

'I like it,' said the boy.

'Thanks. To be fair he did try to make up for the thrashing.'

'How'd he do that?' asked Anna.

'He sat on the step outside my bedroom and played "Danny Boy".'

'What did he play it on?' asked Luke.

'Saxophone. And very badly.'

'Did he teach you?'

'Only to sing while he played.'

'You sing?'

'I do. You play?'

'I'm learning.'

Cordelia sat at the piano. 'You know this?' and she played the opening bars of 'Summertime'.

Luke blushed. 'First song I ever learnt.'

'Well, go on then,' said Cordelia.

And so they played together as Nonna and Anna cleaned up. Cordelia sang in a voice that was rich and soulful. Luke glanced across at his mother and his eyes shone.

After she said goodbye to Cordelia at the front door, Anna came back into the kitchen to find Luke had gone to bed and Nonna was sitting at the kitchen table, ready, Anna could see, to drive her point home.

'If this . . . this . . . lovely child . . .' said Nonna as she waved her hand in the direction of the front door.

'Cordelia?'

'Cordelia.' And she smiled. 'If she can do it, so can you.'

'Maybe I don't want to . . . no, I mean, you know, it's possible that I just can't write sex . . . at all.'

'Anna, when you're in a leaky pot you learn to swim.'

Nonna's sayings never failed to do a disservice to both their meaning and the language itself.

'Argh, bloody hell, Nonna,' said Anna. 'I know all about the leaky pot. And just so you know, not everything is what it seems with Cordelia.'

'*Che cosa, cara?*'

'I mean that she might be able to write about lust and love but she can't bring herself to go anywhere near it in real life.'

'What are you saying?'

'She's celibate, OK, apart from the odd fling with a stranger.'

'Oh, poor girl,' said the old lady. 'Why?'

'I don't know!' Anna threw up her hands. 'I'm going to make tea and try not to think about it.'

'I'll have a *marteeeni*,' said Nonna.

'That you can make yourself,' said Anna. 'I've got to get some sleep.'

*

But Anna didn't sleep. She lay in the bay window of her bedroom with her knees pulled up to her chest until she heard the front gate open and Peter's tread on the path up to the door.

She went downstairs.

'You're still awake,' he said as he pulled off his coat.

'I've got to write a sexy story,' she said.

'Why's that?'

'So that I can make some money.'

'Do they make money?' he asked.

'I hope so. Will you help me?'

'What do you want me to do?'

'Kiss me.'

'OK.' He leaned forward and he pecked her cheek.

'Not like that.'

'Oh Anna, my head.'

She followed him into the kitchen and hovered as he filled a glass of water and then downed it. Her moment of truth in the fifth-floor loo at Waterstones came back to her. Now she asked herself if her own stories might deepen the charge between her and her husband if she found a way to write them?

She watched him drink another glass of water.

'It might help me to get a little spiced up,' she said when he had finished, and she was aware that the words did not sound like they'd come from her mouth. She tapped her fingers on the sink.

'Heaven help us if you get any spicier,' he snapped.

She stopped moving. 'What do you mean by that?'

'I believe it's something to do with the Southern European in you,' he said, and his words had a bitter ring to them. 'I'm surprised there isn't a line of men at the door as we speak.'

Whoa, what?

She stood in the middle of the kitchen and wished, more than anything, that she'd stayed upstairs.

'You've been drinking,' she said quietly.

'A bit,' he said.

Anna was back at the beginning of her life with Peter; her first book soaring on the fondness the world has for offerings from the young and gifted. The money flowed without her even trying. Money made by accident, *the only dignified way to do it*, said her Swiss father, who found the whole subject distasteful. Peter watched and imagined that life with her would always be this way.

Dinner with her new and powerful agent was billed as the night she would meet his family, but when she arrived at his private club there was no wife, only her, and him, and a bottle of very good red.

When she felt his hand on her leg it seemed like someone else's leg. She found herself thinking, *No one will believe this.*

His fingers were damp on the back of her neck as he led her into the toilet. Sour breath, soft, aging belly against her back.

'No one writes sex like you do.'

My fault, my fault, crowed her inner voice.

Peter was waiting up for her when she got home that night. The toothpaste already squeezed out onto her toothbrush.

It revealed the gap between her night and his, *her life and his*. As she washed her body she imagined him saying, *Why didn't you just push his hand away? Tell him to fuck off?*

And her paltry reply: *I didn't tell him to fuck off because I work from the back foot of doubt.*

Now she would add, *I'm to blame, don't you see? Too pretty, too sexy, too Southern European.*

Silence was preferable to that. Surely.

Chapter Twelve

'What have you done, Anna? You look like shit.'

Anna looked across the lunch table at Lisbet's peroxide blonde hair and ruby red lips and laughed, 'Thanks.'

Lisbet could wear leopard skin stilettos; she had that kind of scale as a human being. Years ago, Anna had tried to weave Lisbet into her tight circle of friends, but her brash straightforwardness earned her the nickname of the 'The South African Savage', which quickly became just 'The Savage'. None of Anna's efforts seemed to soften the bruising effect Lisbet had on their small community, and before long Nadia had declared, 'It's her or me.'

The wave of Lisbet's terrible divorce broke just as she and Anna were finishing work on the manuscript of her third book – *he's a fucking bastard, he's a pig* – so for about half a year they spoke almost every day. Anna did her best to shore Lisbet up as her life shifted from one shape to another.

Lisbet had survived. She had made a new life of friends and travel, children, and the occasional date. She had grown as a person, buoyed by her intelligence and her grace, to say nothing of her irascible Boer intelligence.

Their phone conversations since then had settled into a reassuring calm of friendly gossip, word counts, and delivery schedules until Peter's job loss threw them this new challenge.

'Seriously, where has my beautiful author gone?'

'I'm OK, really.'

'So, what's the fucking plan?'

Anna took a deep breath and said with a confidence that belied her struggle, 'I'm going to write erotic fiction . . .'

Lisbet stared at her, silent.

'. . . that will make me, and you, a lot of money.'

Still no response.

'Lisbet?' said Anna tentatively.

'You?'

'Me.'

'You know the people who read those books require a happy ending?'

'I don't think I can do those.'

'That's what I thought. Go back to work on my book, OK, *your* very good book about Boubakar and his mother.'

'Like I said, I've run out of time for that.'

Lisbet took a swig of her tall Bloody Mary. 'Hand it over then.'

'What?'

'Your sexy story.'

'Oh, but I haven't written it yet.'

'Jesus, Anna! Nothing at all?'

'An idea . . . maybe.'

'Have you got something for us to talk about or have you not?'

'No . . . I do,' Anna sighed. 'I mean I will. I will have something to show you.'

'And I will read it, but you should know that, at best, it will appear in a crappy erotic anthology and sink like a stone.'

Anna took a deep breath. 'Lisbet, if this doesn't work I'm going to have to live in a ditch with my children and my grandmother.'

'What about your husband?'

'He'll be in Sheffield, in a different ditch.'

Lisbet polished off the last mouthful of her Bloody Mary. 'I know this is the last thing you need to hear but you're going to have to pay back the advance on the Boubakar book.'

'But I can't. I need more time.'

'It is out of the ordinary.'

'But you could ask?'

'I could but I won't.'

'Why not?'

'It's embarrassing and I don't think it'll be good for our friendship.'

'If I don't fix this, I will lose everything, Lisbet. Please.'

'I can't help you, Anna.'

*

Anna's insides were in the spin cycle of her washing machine. When Luke got home from school he played Charlie Parker's 'Yardbird Suite' on his saxophone for three straight hours. Any other day she would have loved it, however imperfect his rendition, but not today. She tore open his door and said, 'Lukey, if you don't shut up I am going to have to tear the ears off the side of my head.'

He looked up at her and blinked. 'Oh . . . OK . . .'

Then Nonna got stuck in the bathtub. 'Oh, come on, Nonna, pull up on my arm.'

'I don't have the power, *cara*.'

'Oh, bloody hell.' Anna took off her shoes and jeans, climbed into the bath and hauled her bird-boned grandmother to her feet. Then she dried her with a towel and dressed her in her pink pyjamas. She wished she could have been more gracious as she did it.

She spent an hour on the phone with the council to try to talk them into installing a pull-up bar above the bath. No, she did not have the money to do it herself. Yes, she was a British citizen, and apparently now a full-time carer. Yes, the old person in question was also a naturalised English person although you wouldn't think it listening to her speak. It will take how long to process the application? About a year? Oh, oh, oh.

Anna forgot that it was her turn to host her book group. The book in question lay unopened on her bedside table and she had nothing in the fridge. All that, and then Peter phoned to say he'd be late. He sounded drunk.

Anna emailed everyone in her book group, a pathetic note begging forgiveness: *My children call me Dory from* Finding Nemo *and now you know why. Next time at mine, P. Sherman, 42 Wallaby Way, Sydney. Just kidding. Sorry, sorry, sorry.*

She got a few wry replies and then a message from Cordelia popped up on her screen.

OK, so how many words today, Anna?

No words.

That's not good.

I'm up shit creek.

The next thing Anna knew Cordelia's face appeared on her screen like a hallucination and said the words, 'Get out of there, Anna, and get to work!'

'I just can't fucking do it,' said Anna. 'I can write dark literary shit any time of the day or night . . . but not this.'

'So, make someone up.'

'What?'

'Invent someone who can write it.'

'Don't be ridiculous.'

Cordelia would have none of it. 'What's her name?'

'Um, OK, um, Janet . . . Jessica!'

'Jessica what?'

'Don't know. I'll think of something.'

'How old is she?'

'Thirty-one.'

'Younger!'

'OK, twenty-five.'

'Born?'

'Maine, born and raised. But she lives in London . . .'

'Yes . . . ?'

'And her husband is from . . . Brazil, via Barbados.'

'Christ! Why can't they both just be from Sussex? OK, OK. Does she love sex?'

'Of course.'

'Well thank goodness for that.'

And so Jessica was born and it was clear straight away that she didn't give a tinker's cuss who she offended or appalled.

'Now get out. Go to the pub or something!' said Cordelia. 'And take your computer with you. Everyone will survive without you! GET! GET!'

Chapter Thirteen

Anna stood in the rain with the umbrella over her head. It was a flimsy contraption and drooped on one side where a spoke had snapped.

She walked past the home of the Arab couple. A glow from the back of the house, a candle perhaps, was burning. She wondered if they'd failed to pay their electricity bill and if so, how they kept warm?

Anna turned towards the pub.

She ordered a martini in Nonna's honour and downed it in two gulps. She ordered a second one to take more slowly and sat in the corner.

The air around her took on a blistered sort of quiet. Then she opened her computer and got on the ferry.

Hooked

By Jessica De Paul

Hand on heart, neither me nor the Englishman would

have dreamt ourselves capable of what happened in the waiting room of that ferry building in Casco Bay.

I mean, truth was, we both came into that stormy night with a trail of heartsickness a mile long, but that still doesn't explain it, nor why I remember all the succulent peaks but none of the gentle slopes leading up to them.

I know that time passed, and ordinary human things were said and done which drew us closer, but I swear it seemed like one minute he was Thomas, the well-bred Englishman, and the next he was closing in on me with a sound I'd never heard a man make before.

And when he kissed me, a sweet, hot, liquid raced up from my feet to my head. It burnt as it swept into my muscles and soft tissue. It even had a sound, a beat, a fluttering riff. I'd never heard the like, and I was lost.

But wait, let me start at the beginning because, even though it doesn't feel that way now, there was a time when the Englishman and I were not acquainted.

I wasn't looking forward to spending the night in the falling-down waiting room at the ferry, and it felt extra cruel after four years away at college, but a storm is a storm and it waits for no man.

At least it was *my* sky above my head and the pier was mercifully deserted apart from one lone man standing at the far end looking down at the water. I remember thinking to myself that this was Maine and so he probably didn't have murder on his mind.

I looked closer, just to be sure, and I noticed an unusual

stillness in the angle of his head as he stared into the water. I thought to myself, that's a beautiful, dark-haired, fine-necked, long-limbed, melancholy man.

I lay down on the wooden slats of the dock and stared up at the high openness of the sky and even the threatening indigo cloud seemed to stretch out its arms toward me and say, *I know you.* And the belonging brought me such rare peace. I have no idea how long I lay there before the screaming kid dragged me back to the moment.

Oh, yeah, one glance was all I needed to get his measure; a tough island kid, been sailing since he could walk, only today the sea was choppy and he'd lost his dog overboard. He was in a meltdown, turning his tender in ever-smaller circles around the dog's bobbing head. Didn't he know his propeller was dangerously close?

'Wait!' I shouted. I don't know what good I thought that would do but I shouted it again anyway. And I ran. But someone beat me to it.

The melancholy man was in the water and heading towards the boat.

As he swam, the clouds opened and the rain pelted its small silver daggers onto his melancholy head.

He grabbed hold of the boat, calmed the boy, and then he pulled the boat to the dog and scooped the creature up in his arms. So burdened, he made his way slowly to the shore where I waited.

The boy and I pulled the small boat onto the shingle and tied it up. He and his dog shivered on the sand.

'You OK?' I asked.

The boy nodded.

'Pretty big storm, huh?'

He nodded again.

'Want me to call your ma?'

He shook his head.

'Your pa?'

He shook it again.

I waited and then he said, 'I'll get a whipping.'

And he looked at me to see if I was going to rat him out. Then he pointed at the water and he said, 'That's my chicken.'

Your what? The man was back in the water swimming after a *chicken*! I would not have risked life and limb to save that bird. The sea was pretty high, real live waves crashing over the rocks.

I didn't know it then but the Englishman had no choice but to save what he could.

How he snagged the chicken and got himself back to the pebble beach in one piece I don't know, but as he stumbled out of the waves with that bird under his arm he held out his hand to me and said, 'Freeman, Thomas,' as if he was reciting a school roll call.

I swear something in my stomach shifted when he touched my hand.

All I could manage was, 'Who?'

I mean he must have thought I was an idiot, with the freezing child on the sand beside me and the heavens opening above our heads and all I could say was, 'Who?'

He handed the chicken over to the boy and he and his dog took off over the rocks.

The big storm hit as darkness fell. I watched the tempest it brought with it through the window of the ferry building and I guess I sort-of-sang to myself, the melody hanging by a thread.

At the end of the song there was quiet. I turned to see him looking at me with that pin-eyed-pupil gaze that came with longing.

'You have freckles,' he said.

'I do.'

Neither of us said anything more. He simply came to stand beside me in the window, kind of sentinel-like. He didn't look at me, or reach out, or turn away. He just paid attention. He did it like no one had ever done it in my whole life. He even listened with his skin.

That's when he took a towel out of his backpack and handed it to me to dry my hair and I mumbled, 'Thank you.'

'My pleasure,' he said, with unusual lightness. His fine, intelligent face smiled at me. It led me on to say, 'I'm Lily Littlefield.'

When I looked into his tired eyes I saw a kind of tenderness in the soft, blue pools.

That's when he kissed me and the liquid ran up to my head.

Then he remembered himself, stepped back, ran his fingers through his hair, and muttered, 'I'm so sorry, sorry, sorry.'

What just happened? I thought to myself. I don't *ever* do this. And yet, and yet . . .

'I'm so sorry,' he said again.

And being from this island world and feeling like a sinner to boot, I replied, 'No, *I'm* sorry . . .'

But the truth was neither of us was sorry and neither of us was in any kind of state to let the other go.

I took his fingers and led them to my lips. As you would expect of someone who had just emerged from the freezing sea, he was shivering. I said as much, so he pulled off his sopping shirt.

I looked away from his muscled body. *Strong enough to save you*, were words that arrived unbidden into my mind. They made my stomach lurch again and the beat came back, that fluttery, enveloping rhythm that beckoned.

He undid the buttons of my shirt, one by one, with trembling fingers. I could tell he was expecting me to be wearing a bra, but I was on my way home from a four-year college marathon in New York City with a suitcase of dirty laundry. I didn't have any clean clothes apart from the ones I stood up in.

So, no bra.

I saw a small patch of liquid bloom on the zipper of his pants as he looked at my breasts, white and full, and then heavy in his fingers.

My nipples went from soft to hard in the space of a breath. I tore off my shirt. He pulled off my jeans.

The bloom of wet widened on his pants, I undid his zipper to free him and, without thinking, licked the wet off with my tongue. I could hear him grind his teeth. He told me later that that was when he bit his tongue and blood spurted into his mouth.

He pushed my head away. I could see what it took for him to keep himself together but I wanted more, and lapped at him like a cat.

He pushed me off again; this time I lost my balance and fell onto the floor with a bump. I could hear myself grunt as I landed. Then I looked up into his eyes, his light blue, dilated eyes, *oh man*, and something in the face-to-faceness of that moment reminded me again that *I don't, won't do, never did*, this kind of thing.

So, I grabbed my shirt from the floor beside me and did my best to restore my modesty. A bit late, I know, but I knelt there with a sleeve over my button nipples and the rest of it between my legs.

He watched me, still as stone for a moment, and then he knelt down and said, hoarse, almost a grunt, 'Show me.'

I shook my head.

'Show me.' He said it deeper. I could see that he was beyond hearing.

'Now.'

And I did. I put the shirt back on the floor.

'More,' he said.

So, I opened my legs a bit; I was pink and blood thick.

'More,' he said again.

I tilted my hips so he could see the slippery wet that I could feel. He ran his fingers slowly across the wet, just once. I couldn't believe the sweet heat of it and cried out, 'More.' Now it was my turn to say that.

'Don't move,' he whispered.

But I followed his fingers. I had to press myself against him; open-legged, even if it meant that I left a trail of silver on his skin like a snail.

'Don't move!'

But I moved.

And he pushed into me with his long fingers, hands wrapped around my bottom until he held me entirely. The whole of me, balanced on him, light, so light and quick.

Later, he told me he knew I would feel like that. But I didn't, I never knew that anyone walking the earth ever felt like that.

The beat in my blood was big-band-size and I followed it where it led. *Scary-hot-crazy.*

He flipped me over and pulled me onto him. And I wondered if he was real, the way he got me started all over again and filled me up.

I felt the heat, and the future, wave after wave of it, like the storm water rising outside the window. It was all beyond me but I didn't care.

For this feeling. This communion.

For this, I would give up my soul.

When it was done, Anna blinked. She finished the last of her martini, sent the story to Cordelia, closed her computer, and walked out into the rain. This time she didn't bother with an umbrella. When she got home she peeled off her clothes and took a long, hot shower. She stood under the almost scalding water, one foot up against the wall, until her own orgasm poured out of her primed, husbandless body, just as Lily's had for the Englishman. Then she leaned against the wall and closed her eyes.

In the morning, she was woken by a text from Cordelia:

It's a sizzler Miss Jessica! A sizzler!

She put her head in her hands and whispered, 'Oh thank God.'

Chapter Fourteen

When Wednesday yoga came around Stokely the teacher looked at Anna and said, 'There are apples in those cheeks, Anna.'

Bouchra looked at Anna and said, 'I see them.'

'Oh yes, oh yes, me too,' said Nadia.

Anna looked at her friends and said, 'Enough chatter.'

The yoga was easier for her than it had been for months. She began a gesture and her ligaments and muscles finished it effortlessly. In her handstand she felt as if she might lift off the floor altogether. Stokely murmured, '*Funktionslust*.'

'What?'

'Pleasure taken in doing what one does best.'

'Like dolphins swimming?'

'Or you doing a handstand today . . .'

If Anna hadn't invited Bouchra and Nadia over for tea after yoga they would've showed up at her house anyway, they knew something was up.

'Now, what about these apple cheeks, Anna?' said Nadia as she sipped her tea.

She shrugged. 'I've got a story, I think.'

Bouchra and Nadia waited for more. They glanced at Nonna, who turned away from their inquisition.

'Well?' asked Bouchra.

'Will it make you any money?' asked Nadia.

'I don't know,' said Anna. 'I submitted it to the publisher.'

'What's the title?'

Anna took a breath. '"Hooked".'

'Oooh, it's a romance,' said Bouchra.

'She's not talking romance, ladies, she's talking the red-hot chilli peppers,' said her grandmother.

'That's a band, Nonna,' murmured Anna.

'Not the band,' said Nonna.

'What? You're writing pornography now?' asked Bouchra.

'No.'

'Pornography! Really?' asked Nadia.

'Erotica.'

'Whatica?'

'Short stories about sex, but imaginative ones, I hope, with character and context and all that.'

'Dear God in heaven,' said Bouchra. 'My ancestors are turning in their graves. They're saying get out, get out of the house now while you still have a chance.'

'Yours and mine both,' said Nadia. 'But I want to read it. Can I?'

'If you must.' Anna looked down into her lap and said, 'I just hope it works.'

'*Con la volonté de Dio*,' murmured Nonna.

There was silence a moment and then Bouchra added, '*Inshallah*.'

They all looked at Nadia.

'Really?' she said. 'Must I?'

Nadia was the most virulent agnostic among them. 'OK,' she declared. 'If my mother were here she'd say *Bhagwan ki kripa se*, and it means: if it happens it will be down to the mercy of God.'

'I'll take mercy from wherever it comes,' said Anna.

Nadia lifted her glass. 'Here's to you, my friend. Plain and simple, you and what you can get done.'

'Thank you.'

The drive up to Sheffield was almost silent apart from the sound of Peter shelling pistachios, *rustle-click-flick*, followed by the crunch of his teeth sinking into the green nut-flesh. Comfort eating, he did that when he was scared. The sound built up in Anna's ears until it seemed that she shared the car with a full percussion ensemble.

The soft hills around the town were blurred by mournful drizzle. There was no let-up to the rain as they carted cardboard boxes of books into the desolate warehouse that was to be Peter's new place of work. A young intern with striking red hair hovered, anxious to help. A sharp exchange of static, finger-to-finger when she and Anna shook hands, unnerved Anna, although she had no idea why.

Anna drove most of the way back home with her stomach in a knot. Her recent writing breakthrough had come too late to make it possible to keep Peter with the family and she still didn't know whether it, and the stories that followed, would bring him back again.

The rainstorm hit as the Midlands gave way to the plains on which the vast city of London spread itself.

Into this maelstrom, courtesy of Bluetooth, came Cordelia's northern voice.

'How's it going there, Anna?'

'Argh, driving home in a storm, feel like I could just close my eyes and carry on right into the sea.'

'Yeah. Don't do that.'

'Sorry.'

'I just got a response from you-know-who. Can I read it to you?'

'Yes!'

And she began, 'Thank you for submitting the partial manuscript of *Back In The Hunter's Bed* for our consideration.'

Anna guffawed. 'That was your title?'

'Shush.'

'Sorry.'

'Whilst we appreciate the care and attention that has gone into this story, regrettably we feel that this submission isn't suitable for publication on the series romance lists you are targeting. While our series readers are looking for romantic, intensely couple-focused stories . . .'

'I don't think I like where this is going . . .' said Anna.

'. . . we have always prided ourselves on our good taste and we feel your story exceeds those boundaries by some distance.'

'Oooh, shit,' muttered Anna.

'And if that were not enough, the use of the present tense narrative makes it . . .'

Anna shrieked, 'Ah, not that chestnut.'

'They obviously haven't read *Ulysses*.'

'Or Martha Nussbaum.'

'The huge amount of work needed to bring this story into line with series expectations would, we fear, be beyond the writer's ability.'

'Whaaaaaat?' shouted Anna. Cordelia's stories may be on the edge but they ushered in the winds of change and illumination. This kind of voice needed to be defended, for Pete's sake.

The rain hit the windows and the windscreen wipers clicked back and forth. It felt to Anna as if the world beyond her, the rain and her car had stopped moving.

'If you are interested in submitting a fresh proposal,' continued Cordelia, 'please note that up-to-date writing guidelines for this series can be found at blah, blah, blah.'

'Jesus, you don't need to write one of those watery soups,' declared Anna.

'What I need is to make a living,' said Cordelia and her voice sounded tight.

'Yes,' said Anna. 'I know. And there must be readers like us out there.'

'Maybe. But how do we find them?'

'We'll have to self-publish,' said Anna brightly.

'Right. Like we know how to do that.'

'If you can master that maudlin fellow Kierkegaard, nothing is beyond you. Seriously, I'm not taking that rejection lying down and neither should you.'

And that, all of a sudden, became part of Anna's mission.

'We are going to have to write under pseudonyms,' she declared, 'especially if you insist on writing that kind of smut.'

Cordelia laughed. 'Kierkegaard wrote *Fear and Trembling* under a pseudonym,' she said.

'He wrote something called *Fear and Trembling*?'

'And he called himself Johannes de Silentio.'

Anna laughed.

'Also, Anti-Climacus, and, perhaps best of all, Hilarius Bookbinder . . .'

Anna hooted. 'Why don't you borrow that?'

'Because there's a limit, Anna.'

'Is there?'

'What about Kikki Marsh?' suggested Cordelia.

'Maybe ditch the Marsh?'

'Yeah. Kikki Feelgood?'

'No! That's heavy porn. How about Kikki Hunter?'

'That's the one!' said Cordelia decisively.

'You can lure them in with the Kikki and then blow their

minds with the rough stuff; whips and fisting and whatnot,' said Anna.

Cordelia let out a howl. 'Oh, bloody hell, Anna. I need a writing buddy who can make me laugh.'

The rain was still bucketing down, windscreen wipers swishing back and forth. Then Anna heard Cordelia say the magic words, 'OK. Self-publishing it is.'

Chapter Fifteen

When Anna reached the outskirts of Milton Keynes she phoned home to make sure Luke had found the cannelloni she'd left out for his dinner. Nonna was attending the all-night vigil commemorating the first anniversary of her friend Ruby's death. If she'd been home she would almost certainly have been saying, 'Come on, Lukey, let's go out for pizza.'

'Yeah, I got it, thanks. Everything OK with you?' asked Luke.

'Yes. I'll be home soon.'

'Is it raining where you are?'

'Pouring.'

'It's bad here. The wind's howling, just like last time.'

Sudden alarm filled Anna's stomach.

'Hold up the phone.'

Anna could hear the high-pitched whistling of the wind. There was something about the way the houses in Carlyle

Road were built, just on the brink of the rise and facing due east, that meant they caught the brunt of the gales that blew in off the sea and up through the Thames valley.

She and most of her neighbours had lost the roofs off their houses about once every five years. The last time it had happened they'd had to be evacuated. It took six months before they could move back into their homes, now with dramatically spiked insurance premiums.

It occurred to Anna then that she'd taken a stupid risk cancelling the monthly payments on her insurance. Too late now.

'Lukey, stay inside, OK?'

'Yeah.'

'I'm going to phone Bouchra or Nadia to see if either can come and be with you.'

'No, don't do that.'

He said it with such feeling that she understood he needed to manage this without an auntie sweeping in to save the day. Yet Anna could hear that he was afraid.

'Just stay on the phone with me then, OK.'

'Yeah.'

In this way, Anna made her way through the pouring rain towards the outskirts of London and then through the city to their home. Afterwards, she could barely remember what she and Luke had talked about but as the screech of the wind rose in the background, the anxious clattering of her heart rose with it.

'Mama, the lights are flickering.'

'I'm nearly there, Lukey.'

When Anna pulled up outside her house she could barely get her car door open. She was fully drenched in the seconds it took to reach the front door. It opened to receive her and Luke fell into her arms.

'You OK?'

He said nothing, just held on tight. As they stood there Anna could hear the wind howling.

'It's a bad one, Lukey.'

'And Dad isn't here.'

'No.'

They stood poised in the hallway and then Anna said, 'Let's batten down the hatches and try and get some sleep.'

'Can't see that happening.'

'It's worth a try. Tomorrow is a school day.'

Luke's lip trembled. 'First answer me one question.'

'OK.'

'If you had a job would Dad have had to leave us?'

She turned to face her son. 'Probably not.'

'OK then.'

'Not if it was a halfway decent job.'

'Would you put up with that?'

'With what?'

'Someone who didn't earn any money,' he asked quietly. 'Would you?'

'No, I don't believe I would.'

'But it's OK for you to do it?'

Anna looked at Luke's pale, exhausted face. It was the unravelling of his family that made him rage. It would burden him further to hear her say, *My job has been the care of you and Sofia, so you wouldn't have to be raised by a pack of wolves like Mowgli.* And it didn't even approach the whole story, so she said nothing.

'Maybe it's you, Mama?' Luke said. 'Maybe Dad left because he's running away from *you*!'

He picked the towel off the floor.

'And I don't blame him.'

He stumbled away into his bedroom and closed the door.

Anna stood in the silence for a moment. Then she began to walk down the stairs.

She opened the fridge. She pulled out the spinach, the broccoli, the carrots and the red onions, some bacon too. She hauled her favourite chopping board onto the counter and she began to chop.

My fault.

Of course, in a sense, it was. All of it.

Anna cut and shredded, she chopped, diced and sliced until she had three piles of vegetables on the board.

And all the while winter claimed the house, floor by floor, until outside and inside were as cold as each other.

The storm blew itself out as the late winter sun was rising. Anna woke to the touch of Nonna's hand on her arm. The old lady had just returned from the vigil to find Anna fast asleep on the sofa and the house as cold as a grave.

'Coffee, *cara*?' she asked.

Anna sat up, blinked the sleep out of her eyes and repeated

the question she'd asked herself all night: 'Do I work hard, Nonna?' she asked. 'I mean, do I work hard enough?'

'Ah, my Anna, you know the answer to this question,' said Nonna and she sat on the sofa beside her.

'Tell me again.'

'Two jobs!' said the old lady, holding up two fingers. 'For twenty years, you have raised the children and written the books. You work hard.'

Why then had Anna's working self not been more visible to her children? And then it came to her that she had always worked in the cracks, when she wasn't needed elsewhere. She worked, and then behaved as if she did not.

She remembered a conversation with Peter from the early days of their marriage.

'What are you doing?' he'd asked.

'I think I might be writing a book,' she'd said.

'A book?'

'Yeah, maybe.'

'Can you pick up my dry cleaning before ten on Monday? Oh, and my mother's coming to stay on Friday. Probably be with us a month, we can put her in your office.'

Peter taught in America most summers when the children were growing up. Anna begged him to take the summer off so she could work more and so his children would know their father better.

'But what about the money?' he would say.

While he was away, she and the children went with Nonna to their crumbling ancestral house on Salina. There, over the years, Anna wrote her first two books and watched her children turn nut brown, and learn to swear in perfect Sicilianu. If it hadn't been for Nonna, and her brother Stefano, Anna would've walked into the sea from exhaustion.

'In my day, all that was asked of me was that I should be a mother,' said Nonna. 'One of the hardest jobs in the world, I know, but at least my only one. And my Pietro was a good papa. But Peter was never there, Anna, and when he was, he did not understand how to be with young children.'

Peter's lack of involvement with his children had always bewildered Anna. Could it be that loving them was simply beyond his capacity? Or worse, that he found himself completely sufficient in that regard?

And was her own delusion that she was a writer with something to say?

Anna scrambled off the sofa. She sat as close to the space heater as she could get and dialled Cordelia on FaceTime.

'Whoa, did the storm goblins get you?' asked her friend when she saw Anna.

'You could say that,' she said but she didn't linger there. 'So, are we going to start a small business today?'

'That's an excellent idea,' said Cordelia and she put her glasses on for emphasis.

'Good. I was afraid you'd changed your mind.'

'I might've, if I had any sense. But I've never shown too much of that.'

Chapter Sixteen

It became clear to Anna as they spoke that Cordelia had put quite a lot of thinking into the *how* and the *what* of self-publishing.

'I think it's going to have to be a blog,' she said.

'What blog?'

'We'll make one, on WordPress or Tumblr.'

'And that's where we post our stories, right?'

'Right. And our books.'

What books are these? thought Anna but she didn't want to ask a difficult question right off the bat.

'Then what?'

'Then you can send people there by telling them on Twitter or whatever, like Hello there, I haven't seen you for months but during that time I've become a writer of erotica and if you are interested you can find it on my blog . . . See? You get lots of comments and votes from readers, so instant feedback.'

Anna let her finish and then she said, 'That doesn't sound like a very ambitious start for a kickass company, Cordelia.'

'I'm just learning here, Anna. You got any better ideas? You could ask your agent.'

'My agent and I are not speaking,' said Anna.

'OK then,' said Cordelia. 'If I'm all you've got, give me your credit card number.'

When it was done, Anna said, 'Watch out, world. Here come Kikki Hunter and Jessica De Paul.'

Cordelia posted the stories then and there. They sat in silence for a moment.

'Well,' said Cordelia, 'I don't know what it means or where it's going but if you congratulate me I'll congratulate you back.'

'Congratulations, Cordelia,' said Anna.

'Yeah, you too.'

They fell silent again.

'The thing is,' murmured Cordelia, 'I'm not entirely sure how we actually make any money.'

'Well, shit.'

'What I do know is that we've both got to post another episode in the next few days. Tomorrow, actually.'

'Shit, shit, shit.'

Anna waited for everyone in her household to make their way to bed, then she poured herself a glass of wine and got back on the ferry. To her great relief, Lily Littlefield was waiting for her.

Hooked

by Jessica De Paul

Part Two

The Englishman and I must have been asleep for a good few hours because when I woke the wind had died down and the night rang with the sound of katydids. They weren't that plentiful in Maine that early in the summer but these guys sounded like they were having a clan reunion.

You didn't have to speak cricket to hear them freely passing on the news that the girl in the ferry building, that native of the fine state of Maine, was nothing but a harlot and a slut. *Har-lot-slut.* I heard it loud and clear. *Har-lot-slut.*

I lay there and what was left of the decent person in me watched the Englishman sleep and vowed to warn him off.

'You don't want to get too close to me,' I murmured when he opened his blue eyes.

He ran his finger across my lips but didn't speak.

'I'm trouble,' I said.

'That so?' he asked, finally.

'Yeah.'

But what I didn't say was, 'I have a boyfriend.' And that we grew up together. I didn't say that I hadn't seen him for a long time and I had no idea what was left between us but he still called himself that, and so did I. I didn't say it because I didn't want to scare him off.

He lowered his head to listen further, as if there was a voice speaking inside me that was truer than the one that reached my lips. It made me shiver.

'Cold?' he asked.

He led me to the tiny shower around the back of the ferry building and peeled off my clothes one by one. Then he hosed me down with warm water. Tenderly, as if he could repair me. As if he must. I couldn't help weeping. He believed I was crying from shame at what had happened between us but it was not that. It was the thought of it never happening again, now that I knew the bold bliss of it, that made me weep.

He kicked off his clothes and stepped into the shower with me. He kissed me until I whimpered and he lifted me up in his taut English arms and slipped me onto him. I was tight, he insisted, gently. I clung to him and wept some more.

He breathed into my neck as he pushed inside me and said, 'I'm coming to the island with you.'

That's when I slapped his face. Hard. And hissed, 'Don't say things you don't mean.'

'I mean it!'

And he pinned me to the wall to make sure I understood and then he shook an orgasm out of me like sugar cubes from a jar.

Actually, it felt more like a warm grass fire that began in my feet and spread up my legs, gathering force, until I pushed my feet into his waiting hands and cracked myself open like a crab. His fingers, his penis, and his mind, bore down on me, insistent on *more* - and I gave it. All my father's dumb-assed talk of saving myself for Mr Right revealed itself for the fuckery that it was. Mr Right was inside me all the way up to my pagan heart even though I'd first laid eyes on him just hours before. I didn't know his family, nor did I care, and I damn sure didn't know if he was a believer. But he was the one for me, if only for this one, blinding, moment.

I felt the spurt of his liquid hit the walls of my insides and gave myself over to the flame of my own orgasm. We barely kept ourselves upright as we rocked. I held on to the sturdy shower pipe above my head and he on to me.

He ground his teeth when he came. And rested his head on my chest.

'I'm afraid my boyfriend will kill you,' I said, because he was way too decent to lie to any more.

He looked at me then and whispered, 'Do you love him?'

'I did once. A long time ago.'

'Now?'

'Not any more.' And I wanted to cut my tongue out of my mouth. It was the truth; but only since Freeman, Thomas came into my life.

He smiled then, broader than a cat.

Oh, I got just about everything wrong about *Freeman, Thomas*. The most important being that he wasn't deciding, along with the katydids, that I was a harlot and a slut.

As he said later in his own beautiful way, 'I don't much care for the role of judge.'

He told me that even as a small boy he had climbed into the apple tree at the bottom of his garden to hide his younger brother from the neighbourhood boys, intent on giving him a beating for cheating at soccer. *He just wanted to be worthy of the game, beyond his ability, don't you see?*

When our second bite of each other was over and we were limp as wet rags, he made a bed for me out of his dry clothes. I lay down and closed my eyes. I heard him settle nearby and I could feel him watching me. I forced my breath into an even pattern, easy-going, like a swing tune, slow and sweet.

He moved a little closer. I could tell that *thinking* was Freeman, Thomas's normal way of doing things, but that night wasn't normal.

Later, he told me he had no idea what was happening to him but as he watched me sleep he knew it was his turn to cry. Maybe he had just filled up with sadness at the human wreckage he tried, and mostly failed, to save. He told me he was a doctor at a London clinic specialising in addiction and he'd lost two teenage patients in a row.

Who knows, maybe he had propelled himself, blindly, into the eye of this storm so that he could look down on the lost soul that was me, and finally weep?

I'm not proud of what I did next but I wasn't going to let him cry himself dry without a reminder that he wasn't alone in this world. I groaned, and I stretched my legs out, so the line of my body would call him back. I heard him shift and sigh. I murmured as if in a dream, and I let my legs fall open.

I could hear him stop breathing, and I knew I had him. I rolled over and lay my leg over his.

He told me later that he had never, in all of his English life, seen anything like the provocation of my body in sleep.

He says that it came to him, via his flesh and bones, that such a creature as me needed a protector. And he decided in that moment that he would guard my plentiful body and defend me from whatever danger might come my way.

Now what can you say to that?

Chapter Seventeen

The story was as finished as it would ever be by lunchtime the next day. Anna sent it off to Cordelia with a note: *Well, who would've thunk it. Now I can't shut Jessica up.*

The doorbell rang. Farhad was on the doormat with a bowl of soup in his hands and a fedora on his head.

'It's happened,' he said.

'What's happened?'

'He's left me.'

'Oh, Farhad, why are you bringing *me* soup when it's *your* heart that's broken?'

'Because this boy needs soup and who knows what the comfort-food situation is around here.'

'If you only knew,' said Anna, thinking of the huge pot of soup her chopping had produced.

Liebe prostrated herself at Farhad's feet, stomach in the air, beseeching to be taken outside.

'Oh, Liebe,' Farhad said. He put the soup on the entrance hall table and crouched down to scratch the dog's stomach. When he'd finished, she bounced up onto her feet, wagged her tail and barked, little, half-articulated yaps that said, *What about a walk? Huh?*

'Flirt,' Anna said.

'Me or her?' Farhad asked with a grin.

'It takes two . . .'

The frisbee swept through the air, low and steady. Farhad whistled in admiration.

'So, what happened?' Anna asked.

'He got tired of climbing in and out of the window. I mean, who wouldn't?'

Anna knew how hard it was for Farhad's traditional Pakistani family to embrace his sexuality.

'Have you ever talked to your mum about it?'

Farhad raised his hand to stop her, as if to say *Don't go there.*

'Come with me to yoga on Wednesday,' she said instead.

'Me? Do yoga?'

'It reduces stress.'

'What I really need is a flat of my own. But I can barely keep this place going, let alone set up a whole new household.'

Anna looked at him for a moment. 'Can you write?'

Farhad stared at her. 'You mean can I write a shopping list or can I write, like, beautiful prose?'

'I think this is somewhere in between.'

Anna told him the whole story and he listened attentively.

When she was done, he sat back on his haunches and said quietly, 'You want me to write gay pornography?'

'More like erotica.'

He cocked his head. 'How about romance? I used to watch my mother's Bollywood bodice rippers when I was a kid . . . swoonworthy.'

'Romance is good too, as long as there is plenty of sex.'

'Moist lips and fluttering eyelashes.'

She laughed.

'A young boy is at the well drawing water and the gorgeous spice trader arrives on a camel . . .'

'I think you might have a knack for this,' she said.

'It's better than real life, on days like today.'

Anna made him no promises about the money, or how it might all work out.

'Can I share the story-writing gig with a few others?' Farhad asked her.

'As many as you like.'

'You might regret saying that.'

'I think I'm on my way to becoming a publisher, Farhad, and, right now, we need to be building up until we're posting a story a day.'

He clapped his hands. 'It's sort of like Al Qaeda.'

'Hmm . . . how so?'

'A loose connection of cells, you know, all working to the same end.'

'And you're commander-in-chief of the gay erotica division!'

'Which, lucky for us, does not involve martyrdom.'

They were almost home. Anna heard Nonna calling from her kitchen door, 'Phone for you, *cara*!'

'Got to go.' She pecked Farhad on the cheek. 'Come and get your soup. You'll need it later.'

Cordelia was on the phone to say their stories had been noticed by Scarlet Blazer.

'Who?'

'Scarlet Blazer, I'm told she's a taste-maker in the sexy story universe.'

'She reviews erotica?'

'She writes it too. She has a blog and she's followed by over two hundred thousand people.'

'Wow. So, what'd she say?'

'"People!"' Cordelia read. '"Something new is cooking in the sexy story kitchen. Two fresh new voices, Jessica De Paul and Kikki Hunter, write about love and sex with the juice of literary scribes – you will not regret taking a nibble of these wonderful writers. A tryst between two strangers in a ferry building in Maine will have you wishing you'd made different holiday plans. Ms Hunter takes on the fetish vocabulary that has grown old and tired and gives it a whole new twist. You think you know who goes for the rough stuff? Think again. Beautiful language, people, and a savvy and original style. You better hope these two writers put out regular instalments or we'll all be a little less alive."'

There was silence for a long time, then Cordelia said, 'Might be a game-changer for us, Anna.'

'Amazing.' Anna shook her head. 'And what a strange world.'

'We've got to build on this quickly.'

'Right,' muttered Anna. 'How are we going to do that?'

'We can serialise. Write in instalments and publish them one at a time. Like Dickens.'

'But can we write them fast enough?'

'We'll have to call in the troops.'

'What troops would that be?'

'Well I could marshal a load of philosophers . . . some waiters . . . my sister . . . though who knows what fruit that particular tree will bear.'

Anna laughed. 'I invited my neighbour Farhad to write for us, and he said he'd gather some others. I could also ask Bouchra and Nadia.'

'And they are?'

'My oldest and dearest, but honestly, I haven't the slightest idea if they'd be up for it, especially Bouchra.'

When they talked about it afterwards neither could remember who started giggling first.

'Anyone else?' Cordelia asked.

'Well, the man at the dry cleaner has always had a bit of a twinkle in his eye.'

'The DHL delivery man, now that's a trope.'

The trickle of laughter became a helpless flood.

'Your nonna,' said Cordelia, 'I bet she's seen some firecrackers.'

'The ferry building idea for "Hooked" came from her.'

'Did it now? Can't see my grandmother giving that one up. Who else?'

'The Carlyle Road Allotment Association, especially the peony club.'

It went on until their stomachs hurt. If Stokely had seen it he would've had a German word for the release it brought them from their cares.

Anna swept up the stairs to Luke's door. He was practising when she knocked.

The music stopped.

She asked softly, 'Lukey, are you hungry?'

'Mama,' he said quietly, 'come in.'

She pushed open the door.

He held out his hand to her. His long-fingered hand, it felt to her like a shoot of green unfurling in a slow-motion film of a plant growing.

'Sorry,' he murmured.

'No. *I'm* sorry.'

He laid his head on her hand.

She fought hard not to cry.

Luke got up and hugged her awkwardly. Lightly.

Then he gently shepherded her to the door and out into the carpeted hall. He touched her head with his hand, stepped back into the room and pulled the door closed.

She stood there for a moment and she then heard him say, 'I love you, Mama.'

She paused a moment – she on this side of the door, he on the other. 'I love you too.'

Chapter Eighteen

Peter and Anna spoke on the phone most evenings that week before they retired to their respective beds.

'The work is really exciting,' he said. 'I mean, we've got a chance to make a difference to the problem of water evaporation that is turning parts of the world into a desert, can you imagine?'

By the second week their bedtime chats were much less frequent. On Thursday Peter sent Anna a text to say he wouldn't be able to make it home for the weekend. He had too much to do.

Come home, Peter, Anna texted back. Please.

Worry that he was slipping away pinned her sleepless to her bed through that long night.

Friday afternoon came and she heard the key in the door. Her first thought was, *He's come!* The next, following hot on its heels was, *Oh shit, he's here, now what?*

Still, she walked into Peter's arms and the two of them held tight to one another for a long time. It brought puzzled looks to Luke's and Nonna's faces.

Sofia showed up when they were all sitting down to dinner. She was always starving on her first night home. Anna fired up the last of the vegetable soup to bolster their meal.

Luke smacked his lips and grinned at his gathered family.

'Is there chilli in here?' asked Peter, taking a spoonful.

Nonna shook her head. 'I taste rage,' she said, matter-of-factly.

Anna looked at her grandmother and asked herself, not for the first time, how she came to know what she knew and, by implication, what form of witch she was.

Peter looked unduly long at Anna. 'Have you had a haircut?'

Anna shook her head.

'She's written a story,' said Nonna as if the two were the same thing.

Peter looked at her. 'Really?'

Anna glanced up at him. 'It's nothing really.'

'It's not nothing!' said Nonna.

Sofia looked up at her mother and said, 'What's it about?'

Her grandmother answered for her. 'Sex.'

Peter's head shot up. 'You did it?'

'Eventually. And now we've published it online.'

'Who did?'

'Cordelia and I.'

'Who's Cordelia?'

'She's a cool philosopher with a ring in her nose,' said Luke. 'Sings too.'

'I met her at the romance-writing workshop.'

'Wow, Mama, you went on a romance-writing workshop?' said Sofia.

'I did.'

Sofia clapped her hand over her mouth. 'My mother writes erotica!'

'Yeah, kind of,' said Anna, uneasy at the flurry of feeling around the table.

'How cool is that?' said Sofia.

Luke looked at his mother in blank consternation. 'Love stories, or, like, actual sex?'

'A bit of story but mostly sex.'

'It's my worst nightmare,' he muttered.

'You and me both,' said his father.

Farhad took Anna's advice and accompanied her to yoga on Wednesday. She introduced him to Stokely as they laid out their mats and waited in child's pose for Bouchra and Nadia to show up.

'I read "Hooked",' announced Nadia as she walked in the door.

'Where's Bouchra?' asked Anna.

Nadia shrugged. 'She didn't message me. Did you hear what I said?'

Anna groaned.

'What's "Hooked"?' asked Stokely.

'Anna's sexy story,' said Nadia.

'I'd like to read it,' said Stokely.

'No, you wouldn't, cookie, trust me,' Anna said. 'You can write some though.'

'Me?'

'Or just give me the idea and I'll write it?' Anna saw his face clam up. 'Stokely?'

'Mmmm. It's not really my thing,' he said, and he ran his long fingers through his hair. 'I mean, to be honest, I left sex on the side of the road a few years ago.'

'You talking celibacy?' asked Anna in surprise.

'Yeah.'

'And such a beauty!' murmured Farhad mournfully. 'Pity.'

'Actually, there's a lot to be said for it,' said Nadia, boldly. 'For having a little bit of peace.'

'But you're married,' said Anna.

'Even more reason,' she said, and she turned away from Anna's gaze.

There had been times over the years when Anna had heard Nadia talk about her attempts to avoid sex with her husband. She offered him an extra whisky before bed to encourage sleep, fennel tea, a foot rub.

If she could swing it, she would engage her children in a useful task to delay having to go to bed at the same time as he did. If the young ones were out, she might find herself some long, slow, domestic task to keep her downstairs, like her attempt to bake sourdough bread, which so far had produced bricks rather than loaves.

In this way, Anna knew, she mostly managed to avoid sex, but not always. Sometimes, despite her efforts, she'd find him sitting up in bed in the pitch dark when she tiptoed in.

Aalim was a good man, and in the early years of their marriage she'd adored the lust and affection he had lavished on her voluptuous body. He had loved their children and kept a secure roof over their heads. He'd put up with Nadia's insistence that they not huddle with the expat subcontinent bankers and their wives in Kensington and St John's Wood.

He had even taken her back when she'd had a fling a few years ago. For all of that, Nadia was grateful.

'But, for the life of me, Anna,' she told her friend, 'I just can't find it in my heart to desire him.'

'So, no sex at all?' Farhad asked looking first at Nadia, who shook her head, and then at Stokely.

'Too hard on the heart,' said Stokely and he patted his muscular chest.

'Where the hell is Bouchra?' asked Anna again but nobody answered.

'So, are these stories going to help you keep a roof over your head, Anna?' demanded Nadia.

Anna sighed. 'I don't know. You really have to churn them out to build your base.'

'How are you going to manage that?' she asked.

'Farhad's going to help for starters.'

'Ah.' Stokely turned to look at Farhad. 'So, you're one of this band of troublemakers?'

'Just written my first,' said Farhad.

'He's a natural,' said Anna.

'OK,' said Nadia, 'so the team so far is Farhad . . .'

'And my posse,' said Farhad.

'How many in your posse?'

'Five . . . and counting.'

Nadia counted on her fingers. 'So six, and Cordelia, and you . . .'

'She's not me, actually,' said Anna. 'She's an imaginary front-woman named Jessica who steals stories from friends and family and claims them as her own.'

'Tell Jessica she's not getting mine,' said Stokely.

'That suggests that you have one to give away,' said Anna.

'Did I say I'd *never* tasted the fruit?' he said and he smiled.

'OK so that makes at least eight people writing for you or contributing ideas,' said Nadia.

'Yeah, that's true,' said Anna in surprise.

'How are you and Cordelia going to manage all that and write your share?'

'Long days, I suppose.'

Nadia cocked her head. 'I think you might be looking at your new online manager.'

'Really?'

'You need me, Anna,' she said.

'I'm sure I do, I'm just not sure I can afford you. And you have a job already, kind of . . . don't you?'

It was true that Nadia dabbled in the markets. She was a better analyst than her husband and a much better trader, but it was not *work*. Sometimes, when she woke at three in the morning to the sounds of Aalim conferencing with the office in Karachi, she wanted to shout out, 'Short the Chinese on the drop in steel, that's the next big story,' or whatever. But she didn't for fear of making him feel diminished.

'I don't expect to be salaried,' Nadia said, 'I'll work on a percentage. Were you planning to pay PAYE and all that hoo-ha?'

'Um . . . I don't know,' said Anna and she shrugged. 'Right now I don't know very much at all . . .'

'Oh, shut up, we can't have any of that scaredy-cat talk if we are trying to make a business work,' said Nadia. She got majestically to her feet. 'I'm happy with a percentage of earnings.'

'And me,' said Farhad.

'OK then,' said Anna.

'Right, so now that that's sorted, everyone in child's pose,' said Stokely and he clapped his hands like a bossy school-teacher.

Chapter Nineteen

Anna and Nadia found Bouchra in bed with her head under the pillow, her grand, obsessively pristine bedroom sullied by an anthill of dirty laundry in the middle of the floor.

'This is not a sight I ever thought I would see,' said Nadia as they took in the mess.

Anna and Nadia sat on the bed.

'Go away, you two,' came a muffled voice from beneath the pillow.

Anna felt something under the sheets and pulled out a bottle of single malt whisky. It was half finished. 'You drank this?' she asked.

Bouchra emerged from hiding and gripped her head. 'Ow, ow, ow,' she moaned.

'Oh shit,' said Nadia. 'The teetotal is a soak.'

Bouchra looked up at them both and, out of nowhere, asked, 'Did you go to Bhavin's without me?'

'What? No!' said Anna.

'Never,' said Nadia.

Once a month, after Wednesday yoga, the three friends made the pilgrimage to Bhavin's, the great Indian grocery store in South London, to buy spices and the sweetest mangoes in the city.

The last time they'd visited, Bouchra had gone, unusually, into the shop next door, stacked floor to ceiling with roll upon roll of fabrics, and settled in amongst the silks, saris and fine hijabs.

Anna had found her there, holding a length of transparent silk up against the light.

'Bouchra?' said Anna.

Her friend had looked up, startled.

'Nadia wants to know if you want a box of mangoes?'

'It looks like how I am, Anna.'

'What?'

'Invisible.'

Bouchra let the silk fall.

'I don't know what's happening to me. I feel like someone has taken out my insides with an ice-cream scoop.'

Bouchra's children had long ago left for university in America and her empty nest filled her with a bewildering vertigo. At first, they'd come home in their holidays, but of late the other calls on their time won out: internships, boyfriends, work.

Some days, if she was alone too long, Anna could tell that her friend found it hard to string a sentence together, as if her brain was softening like an underused thigh muscle.

To Anna, Bouchra and her husband Majd had a somewhat mysterious relationship. It was evident that they colluded in the business of rising-up in the world, but if you asked her what he did for a living she would shake her head and say, 'There are some things I need to know and others I need not to know.'

At a dinner party, not long after they first became friends, Anna had asked him, 'So, what do you do, Majd?'

He had glanced at her and said, 'I steal from the poor and give to the rich. You?'

'I write books nobody reads.'

'Ah, then we are both selfish bastards.'

It had stuck in her gut, that phrase.

Once, in an unguarded moment, Bouchra had said, 'He used to find me *soulful*, *delicate*, and *true*. He said so, in my ear.'

'And now?' Anna had asked.

Now he never whispered anything, she'd said, not even when he dressed her in lurid Syrian lingerie festooned with bees and open-mouthed orchids, pressed her face into the bathroom counter and pounded into her from behind.

'Bastard,' Bouchra had whispered.

Now Bouchra sat up in the bed, looked at Nadia and said, 'Majd didn't come home last night.'

'Oh shit,' said Anna.

'Did you have a fight?' asked Nadia.

'I may have been raised in a cornfield in Iowa,' Bouchra said, 'but I'm still more Syrian than American.'

Nadia shrugged. 'Of course you are.' And she pointed

at Anna. 'And she's more Italian than anyone in Italy even though she was born in Kensal Rise.'

'No, I wasn't, I was born on Salina.'

'OK, but you grew up here, Anna, and there's no mistaking it.'

'And Majd is Lebanese,' Bouchra continued, 'so he doesn't feel the same way I do about Syria, but the least he can do is give some of his money to help these poor refugees.'

'Damned right,' said Anna.

'He says it is not his war, nor his country.'

'But we are who we are through the people we love,' declared Nadia. 'We belong where they belong. I'm local to Lahore, to Delhi, and to Kensal Rise and nobody can tell me otherwise.'

That Nadia's husband was a Muslim Pakistani, and she a secular Indian, gave her words their sting.

'Well there are no locals left in Syria,' said Bouchra.

'And that sucks,' said Anna, borrowing a word Bouchra used frequently but out of her mouth it sounded more like *sooks*.

Panic fluttered in Bouchra's face. 'Now I wish I hadn't laid down the law like that.'

Anna kicked off her shoes and climbed into the bed on one side of her, Nadia took the other, and they all three sat in a row, in silence.

Finally, Anna said, 'You can come and stay with me if you don't want to be alone.'

'Thank you,' said Bouchra, 'but I need to be here, you know, for when he comes home.'

'Oh.'

'Right.'

Long after the inhabitants of Anna's household had settled into sleep she heard her nonna shuffling around in her room.

She knocked on her grandmother's door.

'*Avanti*.'

Nonna was sitting up in bed – knitting.

'You knit?' said Anna. 'I didn't know.'

'I *don't* knit,' murmured Nonna, her needles clicking against one another. 'I found it in the bottom of Sofia's cupboard. Gives me something to do with my hands.'

Anna sat on the bed beside her grandmother.

'I have lived through a war, Anna.'

'Yes, you have.'

'And if the bombs are falling and you fear for your children or you are watching them starve, you *must* flee. How can we not help these Syrians, especially the children?'

'I don't know, Nonna.'

'It could just as well be your grandfather and I, sailing for England in the bottom of a boat, bleeding and sick and scared.'

Anna stared at her grandmother. 'Why were you bleeding?'

Nonna shook her head.

'Why, Nonna?'

Her nonna lay her head back against her pillow and she looked a thousand years old.

'Just after we were married the blackshirts came for my Pietro.'

Anna knew that the blackshirts had kept him poor by forbidding him to work and that soon after, when Nonna's father went to market to sell his capers, no one would buy his produce for the first time in fifty years. He was the father-in-law of a communist and so he was shunned.

'I didn't know they arrested him.'

'They didn't call it that. And nobody asked. They just had the power to do what they wanted and so they came. This time they kept him for three days. I went every day to the police station to ask about him. I saw people there I had gone to school with and I begged them for help. They did nothing. On the third day, the commandant said I should come back that night and he would give me my husband. My father said I should not go but I climbed out of the window and I ran into the village.'

Nonna fell silent.

Anna waited.

'That same commandant invited me into his office and closed the door.'

'Oh no,' whispered Anna.

'In the morning, they gave me my husband. They had cut the tendon on the back of one of his feet so he couldn't walk. He had no skin on the palms of his hands. He was almost blind from the blood dried over his eyes.'

Tears washed down Nonna's cheeks. 'He never asked me about the blood on *my* body. He showed me that grace.'

'Nonna . . .'

'My father found a way to get us on the boat leaving that night.'

Anna reached for her grandmother and held her tight. It was a long time before the old woman spoke again, and when she did, it was in almost inaudible Italian.

'*Le persone che sono fuggite dalla Siria, hanno visto de peggio.*' The people who fled Syria, they've seen worse than that.

Chapter Twenty

You would have thought Lisbet had brought tidings of life and death the way she pounded on the door and shouted to be let in.

'Hello!' she bellowed into the letter box. 'Anna? Someone? Anyone?'

Anna froze. 'Oh shit.'

She and Cordelia were in the kitchen, polishing and then posting the stories submitted by Farhad, as well as the second instalment of 'Hooked'.

Anna heard Nonna open the front door. Of course, she had told her nonna about the bust-up with Lisbet and now she prayed she wouldn't let her in.

'Hello, Nonna,' Anna heard her say.

'You know I used to defend you,' Nonna said, 'when they called you the South African Savage.'

There was a moment of silence and then Anna heard Lisbet say, 'She called me that?'

'Not Anna, the friends did. Anna called you something much worse.'

Anna put her head in her hands. There was a moment of silence then Lisbet said, 'I've just got to use your loo, can I?'

Anna could hear Lisbet's footfall cross the entrance hall, bypass the loo and then it was only a matter of time before she came pounding into the kitchen. The first person she saw was Cordelia.

'Who are you?' she barked.

'Who's asking?' said Cordelia, eyes wide as she took in Lisbet's flamboyant fake fur coat and her shock of silver blonde hair.

'I'm Lisbet, Anna's agent.'

'Cordelia, Anna's publisher.'

'Really?' Lisbet's eyes narrowed and she turned on Anna. 'I've left a thousand messages,' she said.

'Yes, but we were having a fight so I didn't listen to them.'

'Oh, grow up, Anna. I think you want to hear what I have to say . . . I mean, I hope so because I went way out of my comfort zone to ask them for this. Not something I wanted to do, like I said, but I did—'

'You're babbling, Lisbet,' said Anna.

'Yes, I know,' she said without skipping a beat, then she looked at Anna and told her that she had, in fact, asked the publisher if they could give her more time to repay her advance.

'And?'

'As long as you need. And they hope you'll go back to Boubakar and finish his story when the time is right.'

'They said that?' she asked with a pang – Anna so missed the lively Malian child.

Lisbet looked down at her feet. 'Sorry I was such a prick.'

'You were a prick.' Anna saw the regret in her old friend's face and she softened. 'Now take off that bearskin or you'll roast.'

Lisbet began the arduous process of freeing one arm from her coat, and then the other.

Nonna didn't often lose her rag but she stomped down the stairs into the kitchen, hands on hips, and announced to Lisbet that she didn't like liars.

'I'm sorry,' said Lisbet, 'but you weren't going to let me in otherwise.'

'True,' said Nonna. Then she told Lisbet that Anna had just written a very good story and published it herself and therefore didn't need her help any more.

'I wouldn't go that far, Nonna,' said Anna.

'Of course, I gave her the idea,' said her grandmother and she rubbed her knuckles on her puffed-up chest as if to say *It's all about me really*.

'Is it a romance?' asked Lisbet.

'More the red-hot chilli, than the romance,' said Nonna.

'Don't start, Nonna,' said Anna.

'How many people die in this one?' asked Lisbet.

'Nobody dies!' shouted Nonna victoriously.

'Well, everyone dies a little bit when they have perfect sex,' said Cordelia, and when all three looked at her in consternation, she said, 'Freud, that's what Freud said. Sort of.'

Nonna giggled. Cordelia followed suit.

'Stop it, you two,' said Anna.

'How do you know what Freud said?' demanded Lisbet of Cordelia.

'She's a doctor of philosophy,' said Anna.

'Almost,' said Cordelia.

'She knows about love from A to Z and her sexy story is like a rich soup,' said Nonna.

'Can I see it?' asked Lisbet.

'No,' said Anna.

'Why not?'

'Because we publish them ourselves.' She looked at Cordelia.

'On our blog,' said Cordelia.

'Oh, come on!' hooted Lisbet.

But no one laughed with her.

'What do you know about publishing, really?'

'We don't have to, Lisbet. Welcome to self-publishing and the Internet.'

'Oh Anna,' Lisbet shook her head. 'That's what all my young writers say when they feel the first flush of that possibility. And then I watch them starve.'

The quiet, uneasy silence that followed her words sent Anna skittering for the kettle.

'For starters, what do you know about copyright?' asked Lisbet.

'Nothing,' said Cordelia.

Lisbet looked at Cordelia as if she had at last found someone in the room who had some sense. 'So, which are you? A philosopher or a writer of rich soups?' she asked.

'More a writer, of late.'

'Jesus, another one.' Lisbet sat heavily down at the table.

Cordelia glanced at Anna in alarm.

'Just know that publishing good books,' she said, 'is like trying to stuff yourself into a hosepipe and walk all the way to China.'

All three women watched despair wash over the South African's face.

Nonna leaned over and spoke softly in Anna's ear. '*Siamo sulla terra per nutrire gli affamati e l'acqua laccata.*'

Anna looked up. 'Nonna wants us all to eat some leftover soup and polenta.'

'*No*, Anna!' said Nonna emphatically. 'What I said was . . . we are on earth to feed the hungry and water the parched.'

'Well hallelujah,' said Cordelia.

Lisbet raised her hand and whispered, 'Parched.'

Chapter Twenty-One

After lunch Anna and Cordelia showed Lisbet their material; the review by Scarlet Blazer, and the archive of posted stories.

'I need to read them somewhere quiet.' Lisbet picked up the computer and took it outside.

The enduring chill of early spring meant she once again had to bundle herself in her brown coat. She sat on the bench in the garden and took out a cigarette.

'Is she clearing her throat? She always does that if she's pissed off,' asked Anna, too anxious to look.

'No,' murmured Cordelia. 'She's not moving. She hasn't even lit her cigarette.'

'Really? That means it's going down extremely well or extremely badly,' said Anna.

When Lisbet finished reading she stared up into the sky for an inordinately long time. Cordelia peered out at her and murmured, 'She's like one of Wagner's divas.'

'Without the singing,' said Anna. 'If you asked her, she'd say it was the desert where she grew up that made her what she is.' She was suddenly aware of how much she'd missed her friend.

'What desert is that?'

Lisbet came from South Africa's Northern Cape. She always said there was nothing there but space and back-breaking struggle, but Anna knew that for her it was the loveliest place on earth. She went there every year to visit her mother and was always calmer when she returned. For a while, anyway.

When Lisbet finished reading she got up, still oblivious to the gallery of eager faces watching her. She sailed into the kitchen, threw her unsmoked cigarette on the table and announced:

'There is money to be made here, ladies. You have a blog, but there are blogs and blogs. Scarlet Blazer will help, she's a player, but that's only one of many things that must happen. So, I shall send you Tekkies to sort out your position on Google search and the rest . . .'

'Who the hell is Tekkies?'

'My cousin. Master of the Internet and rock-and-roll drummer. He's in between jobs.'

'Oh, that's great, your unemployed cousin with the weird name . . .'

'Stop before you say something you'll regret!' snapped Lisbet.

Anna waved her hands in surrender.

Lisbet continued more quietly, 'And here is the deal-breaker – when we are good and ready, I reach out to everyone I know: the bloggers, the newspapers, the magazines and the PR people. I send them a beautiful missive to say I am consulting on this sexy new venture and no one, and I mean no one, should let these stories get away from them because they lead to a pot of gold.'

Anna stared at her agent. 'But Lisbet, they aren't your stories.'

'No, but I'm saving the asses of the greenhorns who've written them.'

'But we already have Nadia.'

'Who?'

'Nadia is going to run the office.'

'Fuck me, another greenhorn.'

'Stop it, Lisbet,' said Anna.

'OK, so, granted, you'll have enough staplers and your spreadsheets will be gorgeous but you won't be any closer to knowing how to publish anything, nor how to protect it.'

'So, tell us,' said Cordelia sharply.

'First step is to get a lawyer to register your trademark in whatever territories you'll be trading in.'

'We don't even have a name yet,' muttered Anna.

'I mean, tell us how the money is made?' snapped Cordelia.

Lisbet looked up. 'You post great stories on your blog for a couple of months, for free,' she explained, 'and when you have your audience desperate to know what happens next or to read more of a particular writer, then you say hang on a minute, you'll have to cough up for that on the closed part of the site.'

Anna had to admit that it sounded like Lisbet was on firm ground. Cordelia took notes, frantically.

'You widen your net every day and then the advertisers start to nose around wanting to buy space on your platform; cost per click, or you feature a link to some gorgeous underwear for sale on another site and get a percentage of that action. When Lovehoney or Ann Summers wants to advertise on your site, that's when you know you've got a chance.'

'That's a lot of stories to write before you earn a penny,' said Anna.

'Oh, it's all about volume. Good-quality volume,' said Lisbet.

'And are you?' asked Cordelia.

'What?'

'Saving our asses?'

'If you'll have me?'

Anna and Cordelia exchanged glances.

'Oh please,' said Lisbet in exasperation, 'you need me like your teeth need your toothbrush. That Internet shit will only get you so far.'

'Blasting everyone in your address book does sound like it would be useful to get things rolling,' said Cordelia tentatively.

'I don't know—' began Anna.

'Ah, *cara*, don't start,' Nonna chipped in. 'Say thank you very much, we could do with the help, and get on with it.'

Luke clattered into the room at that moment. The

headphones in his ears stopped him from hearing the ruckus as he approached.

All the women in the kitchen looked up at him in surprise.

'Did somebody die?' He looked startled.

'No, love,' said Anna. 'And you've got to stop asking that! Auntie Lisbet is giving us her two pennies' worth on our publishing business.'

He raised a hand and said, 'Homework is calling,' and turned to flee.

'Whoa, since when do you get away without a hug, Mister Luke?' said Lisbet.

He turned back into the room, blushing. 'Hello, Auntie Lisbet.'

Auntie, when he said the word he was ten years old again. He avoided his mother's gaze and made himself weather the storm of fur and perfume that constituted an embrace from the South African Savage.

Anna could tell that today he took secret comfort from Lisbet's cheer. They'd always had a soft spot for one another.

As she hugged him she said, 'Are you ever going to stop growing?' She turned to measure herself against Luke, back to back. 'Bugger, he's a good four inches taller than me, and I'm a giant.'

She kissed Luke on the cheek. 'Your mother and her friend here are going to make a shitload of money, my boy.'

Luke looked at Anna. She smiled faintly.

'Blast! Look at the time.' Lisbet held out her arm for Luke. 'Get me out of this house of ill repute, my boy,' she said, and together they left the room.

Chapter Twenty-Two

It took Nadia just three weeks to get the writing team scheduled and running smoothly. A board went up in the kitchen with a colour for each writer and their story responsibilities marked out for the week.

Farhad and his crew produced a steady stream of material. Some of it was great, but some was beyond the help of even the world's finest editor. Only the writers who passed the first hurdle of Anna and Cordelia's approval were taken into the fold.

Anna edited for content, Cordelia and Nadia for punctuation and grammar. Lisbet popped in when she could and still, somehow, lorded it over them with her comments. 'More of that,' or 'I don't think so,' or 'They do that to each other, for real, really?' And her eyes would widen in surprise.

The first workplace encounter between Lisbet and Nadia took place at the coffee machine. Anna's failed attempt to integrate Lisbet into their friend group all those years ago hung in the air.

Both women lived on a diet of coffee until six p.m. and Pinot Noir thereafter. So, when Nadia used the last of the Sumatra beans for her mid-morning espresso, it did not go unnoticed.

'Oh, coffee's finished,' muttered Lisbet.

'So it is,' said Nadia.

'Are you popping out for more?'

'No, are you?'

'I thought you were managing this office, Nadia.'

Anna's heart sank.

Just then Cordelia looked up from her computer. 'I've got five new stories for you to look over, Anna.'

'You've written five more stories?' asked Anna. *Merda! How did she do it?*

'I wish. Did I ever tell you about foreverstudent?'

Foreverstudent? Anna had met a few of those, young people who flowed from one degree to another until they sprouted grey hair. But what Cordelia referred to was, in fact, a Facebook group she had started that gave her and her university friends a platform to share their dark poetry and personal non-fiction with one another.

'I posted a call for stories,' she said, 'with a spiel about erotica as our liberator . . .'

'And?'

'And I've already got five stories. They need work but they're promising – another three are coming.'

'You are a magician, Cordelia.'

And she was, because although her foreverstudents were a bunch of nerds, collectively they were hot-wired into the feminist student population in London and beyond. And those women read erotica.

Over the next couple of weeks editing ate up most of Anna's time and the pile of publishable stories began to mount up. There were some differences of opinion about style and content but between writers and editors they hashed out an agreement that gave everyone enough freedom.

An Ikea delivery truck stopped outside the house ten days later and offloaded three desks, all of which went into the living room. To make space, one of the sofas and Anna's favourite chair-by-the-window had to be moved out. The sight of her old sofa waiting in the rain for the council collection truck unnerved her and so did the desks.

'Who paid for these, Nadia?' she asked.

'I did.'

'But that's nuts.'

'I'll claim it back, trust me. Now shut up, I've got work to do and I don't want to do it on my lap.'

'You know,' said Cordelia, 'if we are going to be the classy kickass company we want to be, we're all going to need to get up to speed on current thinking about desire.'

'What current thinking?' asked Nadia.

'Actually, it's the beginning that matters most,' said Cordelia. 'We'll never understand unless we know the roots.'

'How far back is that?'

'Plato.'

They all looked at Cordelia as if she had lost her mind.

She threw up her arms. 'You can't do an interview with the *New York Times* about our effort to upend the genre when you don't have the faintest idea about Freud, now can you?'

'Why the hell not?' asked Lisbet.

'Who's upending what?' asked Nadia. 'Looks to me like we're doing what everyone else does, only better.'

Anna thought they both had a point but she shut her mouth.

'So, come on then,' said Cordelia, 'what is desire and how is it different from want?' She looked around the room. Not one of the group dared answer.

'Well,' she went on gamely, '*want* means you can choose – to eat a bowl of noodles, say, or to smooch a stranger when the lights go down in a plane. Desire, on the other hand, *real desire*, controls you.'

There was silence.

'Now you tell me we don't need to understand that.'

Nadia sighed. 'OK. Just make it snappy.'

Cordelia told them about Plato's *Symposium*, starting with the idea that people began by desiring material things, *stuff*, the kitchen sink, and then when all that was in place, they longed for a lover, and then when that was satisfied they discovered a desire for God.

'How come God is last?' demanded Nonna.

'I can't answer that,' said Cordelia, 'but I can tell you that the God stuff was sorely tested when Plato imagined a conversation between Socrates and his lover Alcibiades who argued that people were only driven by lust and basic sexual attraction.'

'It's like a game of skittles,' said Anna.

'Yeah!' said Cordelia. 'Actually, even before Plato, Homer was shouting about the dangers of blindly following one's desire. He famously told the story of Calypso seducing Odysseus into her love lair and keeping him there for seven years.'

'Lucky boy,' said Farhad.

'Yeah, and that was only one of his many erotic adventures,' said Cordelia.

'OK, everyone,' said Nadia, getting to her feet, 'enough talk, more work.'

She looked at Cordelia over the top of her glasses and said, 'You're going to have to do this in instalments, and it would really help if you turned it into a musical.'

Luke seemed comfortable enough with the comings and goings of the workday in the house. Nadia was always first to arrive. 'Good morning, rug rats,' was her call to arms. 'Put on the coffee!'

He was most often sitting at the kitchen table chomping his way through a bowl of crunchy cereal when Farhad dropped off the week's stories on his way to work, and he and Luke always exchanged greetings.

When Lisbet thundered into the kitchen, she kissed Anna and then Luke. He took it without complaint.

'What did you do this weekend, Lukey?' Lisbet questioned him as she helped herself to a slice of toast.

'I went on a date.'

Anna stopped pouring the coffee.

Lisbet blundered on, 'Was it nice?'

'Yeah.'

'What's her name?'

Luke hesitated and then smiled a devastating smile. 'I'm not ready to divulge that piece of information.'

'OK, Big Guy.' Lisbet eyed him with a twinkle and said, 'Is she an actual girlfriend?'

'Yeah.'

'In that case, it is a family matter and I must now insist on knowing her name.'

'Mama, she's killing me,' Luke said to Anna.

Anna recovered herself. 'No need to badger the boy, Lisbet. We'll just withhold food until he tells.'

Luke groaned and went back to his breakfast, eating quickly.

Lisbet filled her coffee cup and swished up the stairs, saying, 'I'll get you, Lukey.'

After years during which at least part of every day was spent in quiet reflection, Anna was now surrounded by constant noise.

People quipped, chided, jostled and sparred. There was plenty of laughter too, but sometimes Anna stopped herself in the middle of what she was doing and wondered who the hell she was and when these people were going to give her her house back.

Some mornings she purposely stayed out in the allotment so that she didn't have to hear all the chatter.

It was getting light earlier now, and the cold was giving way to milder weather. Anna threw the frisbee for Liebe until her arm ached. Then she sat on a plastic bucket someone had left there, with her back to the wall.

She heard the window of Farhad's bedroom opening, which likely meant someone was leaving.

She would not look. It was not her business. Then she heard someone say the word '*Namaste*' – spoken ironically, and with affection.

What? *Namaste* was the Hindu word they routinely said to their teacher at the end of their yoga classes to thank him for his guidance.

She peered over the wall and saw, tripping gracefully over the grass, Stokely, the so-called celibate.

She sank lower so she would not be visible and hoped with all her might that Stokely would put up with arriving and leaving via the window for longer than his predecessors.

The mud produced by the warmer April weather meant that Liebe had to be hosed from head to toe before she was allowed into the house. Anna was busy doing that when she saw a stranger, a large male stranger, seated with his back to her at the kitchen table. He was deep in conversation with Cordelia and Lisbet.

They didn't hear her come in. Liebe sniffed around the stranger's feet for a second and then sank her nose onto his lap. The stranger looked down and caressed the dog's head.

'Who the hell are you?' asked Anna.

Chapter Twenty-Three

The man got to his feet, and as he did so he seemed to fill the room with his scale. He extended his hand and said, 'I'm Tekkies. How do you do?'

Who on this earth still said *How do you do*?

She nodded her head. 'Anna.'

'Anna!' He made a small bowing movement. 'I've heard a lot about you.'

He spoke with a broad South African accent, all rolling r's and flattened vowels. And his name sounded like a mechanical car part. 'Tekkies?'

'Running shoes, in Afrikaans,' explained Lisbet. 'With a Cape twist.'

'Right . . .' said Anna, still lost.

'The boy was the only Jew in Port Nolloth,' Lisbet explained further. 'He had to run away from a lot of people when he was a kid.'

'So, they named you after a running shoe?' Anna asked him.

'They did.' He grinned, lopsided, and added, 'Sadly.'

'But when he became a coding wizard he only had to lose the "s" to become Techie,' said Lisbet.

'Lisbetjie,' he said. '*Jy hoof nie my lof te sing nie.*'

'*Jammer*,' said Lisbet. She looked at her friends. 'He says I can stop talking about him now, which really means he will chop off my head if I don't.'

Anna had never seen Lisbet so proud of anyone. Neither had she heard Afrikaans spoken in her house. It boomed and rumbled pleasantly.

'Tekkies is helping us with the Google thingy,' said Cordelia.

'What Google thingy?'

'You know, to make sure we come up first when someone Googles erotica, romance, etc.'

'Oh.'

'It's bloody tricky,' said Cordelia and she went back to work.

'Age limits are next on the to-do list, people,' said Lisbet. 'We don't want any underage visitors stumbling into our world.'

Anna clattered around the stove as they worked, somewhat out of joint to find yet another person in her kitchen.

'Luke will be home soon,' she said after they'd been at it for a while. Tekkies was skimming a text Anna couldn't see. She found herself hoping that it wasn't one of hers.

It wasn't long before Lisbet brought things to a close. 'Tomorrow is another day,' she said, as she led her cousin to the front door.

Anna waited for Lisbet to come back into the kitchen and before she could say anything she mumbled, 'Sorry.'

'What the hell was that about?' asked Lisbet.

'I don't know.'

'Oh, come on, Anna, don't fuck with me!'

'OK,' she said. 'There are too many people in this house. Your cousin is a very nice man but when he opens his mouth what he does to his vowels makes my ears ring.'

The lie fell out of Anna's mouth like a toad.

Lisbet stared at her.

Cordelia ran her fingers through her hair. 'Oh, Anna, you didn't just say that.'

'I did,' she snapped. 'Is it not possible to find a techie who doesn't talk . . . like that?' Digging herself deeper into the mire.

'Not someone who has his powers,' said Cordelia.

'What powers are those?'

'He's a master coder, Anna. Genius, actually.' Cordelia gathered her papers off the kitchen table. 'He's done most of the difficult work already and tomorrow he starts building the pay site.'

'What's that?'

'The mechanism that enables you to make a bloody living, you idiot,' snapped Lisbet.

'I didn't know he was so skilled.'

'You didn't ask,' said Lisbet.

'Sorry, I know he's family.'

'Yes, and I love the boy, so don't mess with me. And spill the bloody beans on what's really bothering you.'

Anna knew Lisbet would hound her to the end of time to get her answer – but how could she say, even if she could nail it down for herself, that what had disturbed her about Tekkies was his *maleness*.

And what's more, she was uncomfortable with this almost-stranger poring over their sexy stories. What would he make of them all?

Of her? What would he make of her?

That's why you write this stuff under a pseudonym, she thought, *so that perfect strangers from Port Nolloth don't confuse you with the character in your stories.*

'OK, here it is,' she said. 'I don't like him reading our stories.'

'What?'

'I know, I know.'

'You know he's volunteering his time, for free.'

'Well that's plain wrong,' said Anna.

'Oh really? Tell me, missy, where are you going to find the money to pay him?'

'If he's unemployed, Lisbet, you absolutely can't exploit him.'

'He's loaded, Anna. *Loaded*. And he's got a lot of time on his hands. I offered him this work because he needs it even more than you do.'

'Why?'

'He's getting over something, OK? He'd string me up if I told you,' she said. 'And in the process, he's turning your sow's ear into a silk purse and all you can say is that you don't like how he talks!'

Lisbet got to her feet, her outrage rising with her. 'Oh, and you're shy about someone reading your sexy stories. It's a bit late for that, don't you think?'

Lisbet grabbed for her handbag and knocked over a cup of tea. It splattered over the floor and across the kitchen cupboard. 'Oh fuck,' she said.

Cordelia got up to help, dug in the cupboard under the sink and found a cloth.

Lisbet turned on the tap. Water thundered into the sink. 'Maybe he thinks you sound like a donkey too?' she said, more to herself than Anna. 'You ever thought of that?'

Anna had to smile at her ferocity.

They heard the front door open and Luke shouted, 'Hello.' He poked his head into the kitchen. 'Hi, guys.'

Cordelia managed a smile for Luke.

'Are you hungry?' asked Anna.

'Nope, homework.'

He waved, and was off. Anna saw him glance back into the kitchen as he went. He never missed a ripple of unease.

Lisbet finished cleaning the tea spill off the floor. 'Maybe he thinks he's never seen a house as dirty as yours?' she said, holding up the now blackened cloth. 'And he'd be right. No offence, but he would.'

Anna took the cloth from Lisbet's hand and helped her to her feet.

'Sorry. I'm an ass.'

'Yes, you are,' Lisbet said. 'A first-class ass.'

Anna was waiting the following morning when Tekkies knocked at the front door.

'I'm sorry if I was rude yesterday,' she said. 'I'm just not used to working with so many people, day in and day out. Makes me tetchy.'

The corners of his eyes crinkled and he said, 'Tetchy?'

Later, Anna overheard Cordelia ask him in a roundabout way if he was comfortable with their 'material'. He looked at her and he said, 'What do you mean?'

'Well, you know, the sex.'

'They're beautiful stories,' said Tekkies. 'If they help a person get through the night, or remember something about themselves that they have forgotten, it's more than most people can do in a day's work.'

Later that day, when Cordelia, Lisbet, Nadia, Farhad and Anna were seated around the table, Tekkies opened his computer and said, 'Ready to look at some numbers?'

Anna blinked. 'Must we?'

All her life she had dreaded the moment her school report was delivered, or her blood tests were sent through by her doctor. Usually it was good news but there was always a chance that some awful fact would have to be faced.

'You've got to toughen up, girl,' said Lisbet.

'Sock it to us, Tekkies,' said Nadia.

Anna held her breath.

'Well,' he said, 'Google search generated . . . oh wow . . .' and he stopped talking as his eyes flicked over the screen.

'Is it bad?' asked Anna.

'No . . . it's . . . um,' he said as he skimmed, 'hang on . . . nearly there.'

Nadia leaned over his shoulder and whistled, 'Twenty-two thousand two hundred and sixty hits.'

'*What?*'

'Yeah.'

Lisbet sat back in her seat. 'I'm not going to say I told you so because I'm much too classy for that.'

'But the real point is,' said Tekkies, 'in the five hours since I got it set up, the pay site has had seven hundred hits.'

'Fucking hell,' said Lisbet.

'In just five hours?'

'Oh, thank you,' whispered Anna under her breath.

'Now we really need a name, people,' said Lisbet.

'*Ja*, a really good name,' said Tekkies.

'Wait.' Anna looked around the table. 'Shall we check those numbers again, just to make sure it wasn't a mistake?'

Chapter Twenty-Four

'I know you have to make a living, Anna, but in the name of all things holy, could you not have found something more dignified to do?' said Bouchra as she lay down on her yoga mat with her knees pulled into her chest.

Anna and Stokely exchanged glances.

'Did you read my story?' asked Anna.

'Yes. And that Hunter woman's!' Bouchra bounced back up like a jack-in-the-box. 'Why would anyone want to do any of *that* to someone they loved?'

Anna opened her mouth to say something but Bouchra stopped her.

'Actually, I don't want to know. And neither does anyone else.'

'The stories are fantasies, Bouchra,' said Anna.

'Oh please,' she said. 'So why write them?'

'Because if they can help a person get through the night, or remember something about themselves that they've forgotten, it's more than most people achieve in a day's work.'

Anna clapped her hand to her mouth. She had just quoted Tekkies, the abuser of vowels, *verbatim*.

'Enough, please,' said Bouchra.

Anna lay down on her mat. There was a faint knock on the door and Farhad entered. He waved at everyone and rolled out his mat.

'I mean really,' continued Bouchra, 'is it not outrageous? The whips and the shackles, and that's not the worst of it!'

Farhad looked startled.

'Who are you?' asked Bouchra, noticing him for the first time.

'Farhad, hi, I think we might have met before . . . at Anna's.'

'You have,' said Anna and she turned to Bouchra. 'He lives next door, you've been to his peony party.'

'Oh.'

'And he's the commander-in-chief of the gay/romance/travel division of our small enterprise.'

Bouchra lay down again. 'Oh, good Lord.'

'And actually,' said Anna, 'according to Martha Nussbaum, nothing is disgusting if it brings two people into communion.'

'Who the hell is Martha Nussbaum?'

'Philosopher,' said Stokely, 'of the very cool and very moral kind.'

Anna would have loved to ask Stokely where he had encountered Martha Nussbaum, but just then Nadia arrived. She did not look happy.

'All good?' asked Stokely.

'I took my car to have a service this morning and got a taxi here.'

'O . . . K?' said Bouchra, clearly lost.

'Want to know what the taxi driver said to me?'

'Yes,' said Anna tentatively.

'He said, so when are you people planning to leave? So I said, what do you mean? Then he said, I mean when are you going home? I said I am home, I've lived here for twenty-three years. He said, it's not going to be so easy for you any more, is it? And I said, what do you mean? He said, I mean we aren't all going to bend over whenever you tell us to, no matter how much money you have. I said, my children are English, sir. And I've paid a shitload of tax in my twenty-three years. He said, doesn't matter, the party is over for you people.'

'Bastard,' said Bouchra.

'I said, you can let me out on the corner. He said, whatever you say, love. I said, I'm not your love. Not even remotely. And I handed him the money.'

Nadia stopped and looked at them all. 'What is happening to our city?'

Anna wanted to say storm clouds are gathering but those were her nonna's words, so instead she took Nadia's hand and kissed it. 'Sorry.'

'We'll do an extended warrior sequence as a big *fuck you* to the taxi driver bigot,' said Stokely quietly.

They were dripping with sweat by the middle of the class.

But they felt better. Bouchra bolted as soon as they had completed their final *shavasana*.

As the others rolled up their mats Nadia said, 'What's with *her*?'

'She read the stories . . . mine and Cordelia's,' Anna told her.

Nadia nodded. 'Oh shit.'

Before she could stop herself, Anna muttered the words, 'Beware the clever woman rendered vicious by lack of purpose.'

'What did you say?' asked Nadia.

'Yeah, what was that?' said Stokely.

Anna repeated the phrase, this time more slowly, 'Beware the clever woman rendered vicious by a lack of purpose.'

The words hung in the air.

'Hmm,' said Nadia, 'I think that might have been me.'

'Me too, sometimes,' said Anna.

'Quite a few of the vicious ones do yoga,' said Stokely, 'lots of yoga.'

'I feel for you,' said Nadia.

'I keep my head down,' said Stokely.

In an effort to tackle the mounting pile of stories assigned to her for editing Anna worked late into the night for the rest of that week and into the following one. Nadia often stayed with her, dabbling with spreadsheets and production schedules. Anna's pile of stories remained dauntingly large.

'I'm going to be here all night again,' she said on Tuesday.

'I'll hang with you,' said Nadia.

'No, you don't have to do that. Go home to your family.'

'Pria left me a note this morning saying she was going to Santorini with Pedro,' said Nadia.

'Who is Pedro?'

'The new boyfriend. She'll be back in ten days. And Moni is in the dorm this year, remember.'

'Is Aalim travelling?'

Nadia shook her head. 'It's Tuesday night.'

'And?'

Her friend looked down at her hands.

'Nadia?'

Something was amiss.

'Don't move,' said Anna. She got up to open a bottle of red wine and threw some cheese and crackers on a plate.

'A couple of months ago, he came home from the office,' said Nadia, 'and asked me if I knew where his cricket jersey was because he was playing with the Citibank team on Sunday and did I want to come?'

'And you said no.'

'I said no. But I made him chapatti and okra.'

'Yum,' said Anna.

'He said I made him a happy man, except for the sex.'

'Oh,' said Anna.

Nadia downed her glass of wine in one gulp. 'I can't sleep with him. I mean I just can't . . .'

'I know,' said Anna.

'Then he reached for me. I said, I'm so sorry, Aalim, and I hugged him and he said that if I wasn't going to give him what he needed the only decent thing to do was let someone else do it.'

'What?'

'He asked for my blessing to find sex somewhere else.'

'So?'

'So . . . I thought about it and I said yes.' She looked up. 'It's every Tuesday night.'

'Nadia, what if you lose him?'

'I'll lose him if I don't.'

Anna refilled Nadia's glass but she didn't touch it.

'I cried all night the first time. And then he came home as sweet as ever, and life went on.'

'Oh, my friend.'

Nadia looked at Anna and asked, 'What's wrong with me?'

Chapter Twenty-Five

The rat-a-tat on Anna's bedroom door woke her. She pulled herself up against the pillows, blinking to adjust to the bright spring light streaming onto the foot of her bed.

'What?' she asked of no one.

Her bedroom door opened and Nonna and Luke appeared, faces shining.

'Oh shit,' she said, 'I'm late.' And she began to reach for her dressing gown.

'No, Mama, stay,' said Luke.

Liebe bounced over to her bed. Anna could see that she had been fed and exercised. What on earth was going on? She heard a soft voice in the doorway behind them, 'Happy birthday, Mama.'

She had forgotten her own birthday. Who, ever, did that?

Anna turned to see Sofia come in, grinning. She carried a tray on which was balanced a coffee cup, a bowl of berries and a cake tin tied with ribbon. They all burst into 'Happy birthday to you, happy birthday to you . . .'

Anna watched them gather at the foot of her bed; the little old lady and the two luminous young ones. Her people.

Luke darted out of the room and returned with his computer under his arm. He and Sofia piled cushions at the foot of Anna's bed and propped the computer on top of it. They set a chair next to the bed for Nonna. Then with a lot of bickering and laughter they snuggled either side of their mother, opened a file, and clicked play.

Anna recognised the strains of Charlie Parker, the very music she had insisted Luke stop practising just a few weeks ago. It was her son's own imperfect, beautiful rendition. 'It's you, Lukey,' she said. She smiled and kissed his hand.

The music formed the soundtrack to a series of photographs, edited together to make a snapshot of their lives. The words were written, she knew, by her daughter.

Pai attenzione!

This is the story of a beautiful and intelligent mother
And her equally beautiful and intelligent daughter
Ditto her son
And her grandmother
And her dog,
Especially her dog
Most of all we like to eat your food
And hear you laugh
And, also cry. That's OK too. If you must. Sometimes.

Thanks for being our mama.

Buon compleanno!

When it was over Anna wrapped one arm around each of her children. She put her head down, determined not to cry. 'Sorry, sorry . . .'

'Is Dad coming back to celebrate with us?' asked Luke.

'He said he would,' said Sofia.

'Probably stopped somewhere to get a present,' said Luke hopefully.

Anna didn't dare open her eyes.

When her father phoned to wish her happy birthday, he asked her to put the phone on speaker and he greeted everyone in the room. Then he played the Brandenburg Concerto in G Major on the piano. It had been her favourite piece growing up.

All her birthdays from twelve to forty-three, had begun with the fact of her mother's loss. Not only for her, but also her brother, father and grandmother – no one ever mentioned it but they started every important day accompanied by loss.

Nadia and Bouchra surprised her with champagne and sweet kulfi at teatime. Her brother Stefano phoned from Salina while they were there. He sang happy birthday in Italian and melted all of their hearts.

It was early evening by the time Peter got home. He walked into the kitchen carrying an Amazon book parcel. He pecked Anna on the cheek and put it down on the table.

'Happy birthday, Anna.'

'Thank you.'

'And get dressed for dinner, we are going out.'

'Let's do that when we have some more money, OK?'

'Just get dressed.'

She stopped talking when she saw his face.

'OK.'

'Now open your present.'

Anna smiled at him and tore open the parcel. The book that lay in its crisp brown folds was a complete mystery to her. She read the title: '*The Power of Self-Transformation* by Swami Pakradesh?'

'Oh, shit, sorry,' he said and laughed. 'That's for me. Weird, I ordered them at the same time. Yours will come tomorrow.'

Something about the way this was unfolding was all wrong. She shook her head to ward off the feeling. 'Who is Swami Pakradesh?' she asked.

Peter looked at her. 'I'm told he knows something about . . . peace. I think that's what someone said.' And he turned away from her gaze.

The local Italian was packed so Anna and Peter had a glass of wine at the bar and waited for their table. In the heat and shuffle of the restaurant Peter began, suddenly and without provocation, to cry. Anna was so surprised that she didn't know what to do.

'I'm sorry,' he said.

The sight of this quiet, generally reserved man so overcome filled Anna with dread.

'Peter, what is it?'

He shook his head as if to say *I can't answer that.*

'Are you sick?'

Again, he shook his head.

'But you're sad? I know that what is happening to us has been hard but we'll get through it.'

He lifted his hands to stop her talking, and in the quiet that followed, the question she had to ask pushed its way into her mouth.

'Are you in love with someone else?'

He looked away, and then back at her.

'Don't be scared,' he said.

'I am,' said Anna and she felt a flipping of her stomach. 'Scared of what you are about to say to me.'

Peter sighed. 'It's been a long time coming.'

Oh, no, please no.

'I've always wanted you, Anna . . . like I've never wanted anything in my life.' He touched her cheek, his eyes bored into hers. 'I don't claim to understand you entirely, but I do know that you've made me more than I was.'

'Don't.'

'But time is running out for me.'

'Oh,' Anna whispered under her breath. 'No.'

'I'm so sorry to do this on your birthday, Anna, but I have to leave.'

She looked at him.

'I just want a chance to have something simpler before it's too late,' he said.

'What do you mean?' she asked.

'Fern.'

'Her name is Fern?'

He didn't answer.

That was it.

'Do you love her?'

Peter did not dignify her with an answer.

All Anna could think just then was, *Air, I need air.* She knew if she stayed there any longer she would smash something. She stood up so swiftly that her chair fell over. All the while Peter looked down at his hands. *Was this it? Really?*

'Do you love her?' she asked again.

Peter lifted the napkin to his mouth as if he was going to throw up. He nodded.

Anna turned from him and walked out of the restaurant.

Chapter Twenty-Six

She walked without seeing anything at all until she found herself sinking onto the inhospitable metal shelf at the bus stop that stood in for a bench. She seemed to have temporarily lost control of the muscles in her body.

She might have made it home with her dignity intact had Peter not emerged from the restaurant at just that moment. She saw him take a huge gulp of air and reach inside his jacket for his phone.

Anna saw him dial a number and then lower his head to talk, no, not to talk, but to *report* the events of the evening to Fern. She knew it.

This person named Fern.

Fern. I mean, come on. Jesus.

She heard Peter laugh, it had a hook in it – that sound – and before she could stop herself she was striding across the concrete pavement that separated them. She ripped the phone out of his hand and threw it onto the road.

'Are you mad? That's my bloody phone.'

She could see he was scared. It had gone so well, he'd been so relieved.

She was shaking at the seams.

A father and his two teenage boys stopped on the pavement. Being a decent person, the father asked Anna if she was all right.

'Fine,' said Peter. 'Sorry.'

'He's not sorry at all,' said Anna. She turned to the man. 'He's fucking someone named Fern.'

'Stop it, Anna,' hissed Peter.

'But thank you for asking,' she said to the man.

'It might be an idea to go home now,' said the man to Anna.

'Yeah,' she said, 'in a minute.'

The decent man and his sons took their leave. Anna saw him glance back at her once and then they turned the corner and were gone.

Peter was on his knees with his shattered phone to his ear. 'Hello, hello,' he said.

'Hello,' said Anna.

He looked up at her and said, 'You've broken it.'

'It doesn't matter.'

'I'll send you the bill.'

Anna laughed, and then shuddered. 'Are you coming home to tell the children?'

The bastard coward that had been her husband shook his head and looked away.

'Oh, you can't leave me!' Anna howled.

'Is that so?'

'You don't have the imagination. Or the courage. That's why I chose you.'

Peter took in her vitriol and her fright. Then he got to his feet and said, 'Just watch me.'

And he walked away.

Anna opened the front door of her house. She stood in the hallway and glanced into the living room. The TV was on. Nonna was asleep in the one remaining armchair while her two children lay on the sofa watching a movie.

Her children, *ah no*. She would have given her all so they wouldn't have to know this.

They chattered and laughed as they watched.

Anna made herself enter the room.

Sofia looked up. 'Good dinner?'

She found she could not reply.

Sofia asked, 'Where's Dad?'

Anna shook her head.

'Mama?' said Sofia.

Luke pulled himself away from the screen and asked, 'What did he give you for your birthday?'

'A book . . . actually it wasn't the book he meant . . . to give . . . me.' Anna couldn't say any more.

'What happened, Mama?' asked Sofia, anxious now.

'Well,' said Anna and she was aware that the words she was about to say could've come from a soap opera, and that she didn't know how to change them. 'It looks like Dad won't be coming back to live with us.'

Luke's head shot up. 'You mean not until his project is over?'

'No,' said Anna gently, 'I mean . . . I don't . . . he doesn't plan to come back at all.'

The colour drained out of Luke's face.

'I'm so sorry.'

'I don't believe you,' he said.

'Shut up, Luke,' said Sofia.

'You shut up.'

'I believe her name is Fern,' said Anna. 'Just so you know.'

Their house remained still and dark for the rest of the night and half the following day. If any of them moved it was quickly, like unwelcome ghosts. Nadia came over and cobbled together a lunch from leftovers in Anna's fridge. Then she called Sofia and Luke to the table. As they ate, she tried to engage the children in conversation.

'Try it with a little extra coriander, Lukey,' Nadia said as she saw him hesitate.

'Do I have to?'

'He's not so keen on the green,' murmured Sofia.

'Blast it with chilli pepper if it needs a lift,' said Nadia. 'Did you see the Arsenal game?'

'Yeah,' said Luke, and he smiled faintly. He didn't like playing but he was a crazy-keen Arsenal fan.

Anna sat on the edge of the conversation, still stunned to find herself in the strange land of husbandlessness.

She read the faces around the table.

Sofia and Luke did their best but they looked hollowed out. As soon as lunch was over, they both asked to be excused.

'This is hard, my friend,' said Nadia when they had gone.

Anna nodded.

'It will get harder still.'

Anna shuddered. 'Don't say that.'

But she was right.

The rain started in the late afternoon just an hour after Sofia had left to go back to university.

Anna had held her daughter close as they'd said goodbye. Sofia was still badly shaken, her eyes were as big and dark as a cave pool.

'Ti voglio bene, mamma,' said Sofia as she left. *I love you.*

The wind followed soon after, and by the time darkness fell, it was as though banshees were shrieking at the window glass.

Luke walked out of the bathroom in his pyjamas with his toothbrush in his mouth. He glanced up and, just then, the skylight flipped back like a bottle top. As if in slow motion, the rest of the roof followed, peeling back and over with a groan – deep, and oddly lifelike.

Anna found Luke standing in silence, watching the raindrops begin to hit the walls on the inside of the house, sprinkling the carpet with perfect polka dots of wet.

'Oh, dear Christ in heaven!' she whispered, just as she had

as a child when things had overwhelmed her. She stood beside her son looking up at the open sky. A raindrop landed on her forehead and it felt like a slap. Neither of them seemed to be able to move. Finally, she said, 'Put something warm on, Lukey. It's going to be a long night.'

Anna phoned the fire brigade and the police. As she stood on the pavement watching the firemen assess the safety of the building, she saw the Arab man watching from some distance away. She waved to him and he waved back. Then he put his hand on his heart as if to say, *I see your hardship*.

A few minutes later Anna felt a tap on her arm. She turned to see the Arab man's wife, head covered, offering her a plastic container of food.

'Oh, thank you. That's very kind.'

'*Mansaf*,' she said quietly.

'Oh.'

'Lamb with rice.'

'How lovely.'

The woman smiled and turned away.

This time they were the only house in Carlyle Road to lose their roof.

When the fire brigade had left and calm returned to the road, Anna went inside and began to carry boxes down from the now roofless attic storage area.

'What are you doing, Mama?' asked Luke.

She hadn't heard those words spoken in that way since Luke was a little boy. Then, he would ask her that all the time. It was his way of interrogating the world.

'I'm moving all the photos and memory boxes so they don't get ruined by the rain.'

Silently, Luke joined her. It was back-breaking work and took them hours. By the end, Anna could barely lift the boxes.

Luke was dogged but Anna could see his strength was failing him too.

'Go to bed, Lukey.'

'No.'

'I can manage, there's not much left.'

'Did you tell Dad?'

'No.'

'Are you going to?'

'No, *caro*.'

Luke was silent.

The rain lessened as they worked until only a light drizzle fell onto the soaked carpet.

At last, they were done. Anna sat on the boxes on the landing, wet and exhausted. She wiped her face with a bath towel and then handed it to Luke. He would not take it.

'You hungry?' she asked.

'No.'

'Try to sleep if you can.'

'You have to get him back, Mama.'

Anna reached for Luke's hand to comfort him. He pushed it away and stood up. He was trembling. 'Just get Dad back.'

'Lukey . . .' said Anna.

'No,' said Luke. 'Just do it, OK? OK?'

Nonna's bedroom door opened and she took in Anna and Luke poised amongst the devastation. Her capacity to sleep through anything had always amazed Anna.

The old lady looked up at the open sky above her and blinked. '*Dio, quello che è successo qui?*' Dear God, what has happened here?

'Trouble came, Nonna,' said Anna.

Chapter Twenty-Seven

Nadia and Bouchra sailed into Anna's house like a crisis delegation from the United Nations.

Nadia sat at the kitchen table and hauled out her cheque book.

'We're doing this as a team, Anna. We've talked about it.' She indicated herself and Bouchra. 'So, how much do you need?'

'For what?'

Nadia looked at her in exasperation. 'You'll pay us back,' she said, pen poised.

'How will I do that?'

'From the stories we publish, you idiot.'

'We don't know how that's going to go yet, Nadia.'

'Anna, you are my sister,' said Nadia. And it was indeed the way they sometimes referred to one another.

'And uninsured apparently,' said Bouchra sharply.

Anna glared at her grandmother. She must have told them.

'I raised you to be a gracious person, Anna,' said Nonna and she elbowed Anna in the ribs as she passed. 'Say thank you to your friends for their kindness.'

'Have you all gone mad?' asked Anna, and she sat at the table, bone-weary.

'She's worrying about me,' said Bouchra.

'Damned right I am.'

Bouchra would turn on her one day, Anna knew it, especially since she could see that Nadia was strong-arming her into helping.

Everyone around the table remembered that neither Bouchra nor Anna had managed a prior loan, given to Anna years ago for the treatment of Sofia's deadly viral meningitis, with anything like the necessary maturity. Bouchra had resented how long it took Anna to repay her – Anna had thought Bouchra's impatience cruel, given her sick baby. What had begun as an act of love and friendship had led to resentment and distrust.

And that was *before* Bouchra's grief over the loss of her husband's love had further poisoned her well.

Beware the clever woman made vicious by lack of purpose.

'For pity's sake, don't be such a white person, Anna!' cried Nadia.

'What?'

'She means a self-sufficient, Anglo Saxon icebox,' snapped Bouchra.

'My Anna is not an Anglo Saxon,' declared Nonna.

'Oh whatever!' said Nadia. 'Last week I shorted the pound and I made enough for ten new roofs.'

'Good, well, that's something,' said Anna.

'And I've got nothing better to do with my spoils. I can't even tell my husband about them because it will make him feel like shit, and I won't give it to my kids because it will ruin them for ever. So please, my friend, let me pay for your roof to be mended and your carpets replaced.'

Anna hung her head.

'I can't, I know better, I just can't.'

She ignored Nonna's gasp of exasperation.

'That is your final word?' asked Bouchra.

Anna nodded.

'Well, at least we don't have to pretend any more,' she said. She picked up her handbag.

'Pretend what?'

'That we are sisters.'

Bouchra walked out of the house without saying goodbye.

Nonna didn't talk to Anna for two days.

The rain continued to fall until the tarpaulin, dragged by the fire brigade over the gaping roof, began to hang down between the rafters, heavy with water.

Anna sat on the stairs looking up at the ominous bulge growing with every raindrop. She phoned the roof man. The quote he gave her to fix it was three thousand, one hundred pounds.

'When can you start?' she asked.

By so doing, she ensured that her shrinking savings would run out two months earlier than she had planned.

Anna felt like crawling into her Wednesday yoga class on her knees.

No husband.

No best friend.

Two children who, until their father started earning again, depended on her absolutely.

No roof over her head.

It felt to Anna that she wanted, just for a day, to be back somewhere she recognised, but she had sailed out to sea and there was nowhere to go but ahead.

Stokely, Farhad and Nadia had the grace to let her cry, and the wisdom to keep her moving. They did the whole sequence from beginning to end as Anna sobbed into her T-shirt. Tears dripped onto her mat in downward-facing dog, and into her nose in back bend. She concentrated so hard in headstand that they ceased entirely but started up again the moment she was back on her feet.

The session left them all wrung out. All Anna wanted was to go home to sleep for a long, long time.

When she got there she found Nonna, Sofia and Luke standing in the hallway.

'We're going to Salina,' said her nonna.

'No,' said Anna. 'Oh no, I have . . . Cordelia, and all the others. I have work to do.'

'No, Anna, it is time for *di riposo.* You need rest.'

'They all chipped in to pay for the tickets,' said Luke. 'One for Liebe too.'

'That's what I was afraid of.'

Nonna said sternly, 'Anna, the good Lord says grace is about receiving as well as giving.'

'Maybe the good Lord doesn't know Bouchra.'

'Bouchra didn't do it. It was the others,' said Sofia.

'And Nadia says there are too many chiefs in the tepee right now so she wouldn't mind if you became an Indian until they get their systems sorted,' said Nonna.

Anna smiled faintly.

'Lisbet even took Liebe to renew her pet passport,' said Luke.

'Give them a chance, Anna. If those two warships, Lisbet and Nadia, find a way to work together,' said Nonna, 'there'll be no stopping *le donne di amore*.'

Chapter Twenty-Eight

The port at Palermo saved up its first and most ferocious spring storm for the arrival of Anna and her battered clan. The uncharacteristically violent lightning and rain seemed to take Anna's married skin off, layer by layer.

It drove Liebe under the bench for safety. She'd always mistrusted lightning.

In the calm between gusts of wind and rain, Nonna and Anna took the dog for a calming walk in the port. She led them to a little wooden ferry building, now forlorn, on the end of the old pier.

They approached it carefully. The planks of the jetty were old and partially decayed. They pushed open the door and found the interior almost empty apart from a few ropes, a stack of tinned olives and a pair of child-size wellington boots. They freed Liebe to sniff every corner.

Anna watched Nonna walk tentatively into the centre of

the room and then across to the window. The storm outside cast cold white light on the old lady's delicate frame. It wasn't necessary for her to confirm that this was where Nonna and her Pietro had found one another. Anna could see it in her grandmother's face.

A lifetime ago, and yet so close, her nonna as a young woman, entirely unbowed, bold enough, even in those times, to seize the moment that led to a long life of love.

She couldn't tell whether her nonna's trembling hands were a result of the temperature or the passage of memory through her old body. Either way, she could see that her grandmother needed more time there.

Anna was grateful for the chance to turn away from her and to picture Lily Littlefield from Maine and her Englishman, who, thanks to Nonna, had found one another in a building such as this. Maybe she would meet them again? Maybe she would write herself a great love story and in that way know it too?

When she was ready, her nonna took her arm and the two women made their way out of the small room and up the jetty to rejoin the children.

After the customary brief stop at Lipari, they found her brother Stefano waiting for them on the dock at Salina. He held his sister close. 'You've known worse, sissie,' he said, kissing her forehead.

Then he hugged the children and Nonna in turn, and swept them homeward.

Stef had prepared their favourite pasta with capers and olives and made up their beds.

They all finished their dinner with a little of his home-made Malvasia wine and then stumbled towards sleep.

The stone walls of the house, unchanged for more than six generations, held their ancestral marrow; enough for Anna's children to say, when asked where they came from, 'The two islands of Salina and Britain.'

These walls had never embraced Peter in spite of all the Christmases he had spent there. He refused to visit in the summer because the sun blistered his skin and old island friends of the family were not moved to love him.

Anna lay in her childhood bed and listened to the wind. It had once been her mother's bed, and Nonna's before that. It was also the bed in which Luke had been born. None of that brought her much comfort tonight.

When Anna woke, the house was quiet. The storm had blown itself out in the small hours. The early morning sun shone as she walked out onto the stony beach at the bottom of the road. She saw Stefano's boat already out in the bay and the tiny shapes of her brother, her children and her dog moving on it as they fished. She was grateful for him and his capacity to love them all.

Anna walked down to the black pebble beach. She felt the warm stones beneath her bare feet, and the muffled blankness that was her true state rose up from her feet into her head.

Every so often snippets of imagined conversation played in her head.

What do you see in her that you didn't find in me?

Desire.

Really?

No, Anna, I see hope.

Oh, fuck off.

Anna sat at the far end of the beach.

I'm not a monster, Anna. I just have a new erotic life.

Well, fuck that too.

The waves lapped at her feet. The sun grew hotter and bore into the top of her head and the stones burnt the soles of her feet.

When she was sure no one was near she lifted her head and bellowed 'Fucker!' The sound flipped up into the sky.

Thank God for wild places and the fury they let loose in us.

Stefano and Luke fished every morning and fixed the broken tiles on the roof in the afternoon. Hard work in the company of another man made Luke steadier. Anna joined them when she could, working long and hard at his side to reassure him that the centre held.

Sofia found peace with her nonna. They cooked and gardened in the small allotment on the hill above the village where Stefano had planted vegetables. Anna worked alongside them too, weeding and turning the soil.

When she wasn't working, Anna trod the beaches and the

dusty paths above the village. If the heat overwhelmed her, she swam.

She also visited the small village shop, owned and run by Natalia, a friend from Anna's childhood summers.

Natalia had three children and four grandchildren and she knew everything about everyone on Salina. In the afternoons, she made Anna a double espresso and pulled up a chair behind the counter so they could talk.

As each customer left with their shopping, Anna would ask, 'And so?'

And Natalia would fill her in on whether the person in question was happily married, or not, in love, or not, tormented by their spouses, or pining for another.

She heard about Antonio who everyone, apart from his father, knew to be gay. The old woman, Carmela, widowed twenty years earlier and lonely ever since; young Giulia cavorting with the son of the mechanic known to be in the pay of the Cosa Nostra.

As the days passed Anna began to feel less done-in. Now, when people asked, '*Come sta andando*, Anna?' she could shrug and say, 'The days are passing.'

It was enough for now.

Chapter Twenty-Nine

A week or two later a very small boat washed up on the island and brought with it new challenges.

Anna was walking on the high mountain path above the village when she first saw the flimsy craft in the swell just beyond the harbour.

It drifted sideways, onto the rocks beyond the black pebble beach, unmanned, it seemed. It snagged there as the swell broke onto its flimsy hull.

Anna patted her pocket: no phone. Shit!

Nothing happens in the sea off Salina that is not seen by a hundred eyes: it is the thing they look to first when they wake and last before they sleep.

Within minutes, Pietro from the boatyard and two island policemen were hauling the boat onto the stony beach. Pietro lifted a woman out and then a child. Even from this distance Anna could hear one or two words of Arabic.

She saw two figures running to help; one had Luke's long strides and the other Stefano's shorter gait.

A man clambered out of the boat, his legs could barely hold him; he had a bundle in his arms. A baby!

He handed the bundle to Stefano. As Anna's brother looked down on the infant, the woman began to wail. Stefano said something to her that Anna couldn't hear and then he turned and ran towards the police car. 'Saline, sugar water . . . *proprio adesso*,' he shouted.

Anna watched the baby's mother stumble after him across the rocks. Luke took her arm to steady her. As they ran her keening filled the sky.

It was almost dark when Anna found Luke on the black stone beach. The sun had set and his face was in shadow. He didn't look up at her as she arrived.

She sat nearby but not too close. Neither spoke.

'Is the baby alive?' he asked, eventually.

'Yes. *Grazie a Dio*,' said Anna, sounding just like Nonna. 'Stefano says she's responding well to the saline drip.'

Luke reached for Anna's hand. She took it.

'They were so scared, Mama.'

She nodded.

'So thirsty. So thin.'

'Yes, I could see that, even from up on the pass,' she said. 'But they are alive, *caro*.'

*

From then on the talk in Natalia's shop was of little else. The travellers had started their voyage in Gao in Mali, headed for Catania; or Tunisia headed for Lesbos. He was a doctor in Bamako; no, a Kurd. A Sudanese farmer. Clearly a Tuareg jihadi.

'We have to help them, Mama,' said Luke.

'We will do what we can,' said Anna.

'We must do more!'

'Oh, Luke, we don't have much to spare.'

'They have nothing!'

Of course, Luke was right. And his concern occupied her sleep.

Anna woke before it was light. She made a strong cup of coffee and sat at the table by the window. She opened 'Hooked' on her computer and began to translate it into Italian. Her mother tongue gave the prose a levity that she found surprising.

When she had finished, she made photocopies at the post office in the village, and went to persuade Natalia to put a small stack of stories on the counter of the shop.

'But what kind of stories are they, Anna?' she asked.

'Sexy stories.'

'Are you mad?'

'Sell them for me, Natalia, and give the money to the new family.'

'The boat people?'

'*Sì*. It won't be much,' said Anna, 'but not much is still something.'

Natalia shook her head. 'If this causes me any trouble, I'm sending it straight to your house.'

The first person to buy a copy of Anna's story was eighty-year-old Carmela, head to toe in widow-black. She sat at one of the small tables outside the shop and read with the aid of her thick glasses. Before leaving she popped her head into the shop and asked if Natalia had the next instalment.

Natalia sent her grandchild over to Stefano's house to tell Anna she needed more. Carmela must have spread the word because all the copies were gone by the end of the day.

That night, Anna translated part two.

It flew off the shelves.

The following morning, she texted Cordelia.

Translation . . . Translation. Translation!

It was so obvious now that she thought about it, and yet it had not occurred to her what an impact translation could have on the reach of their stories.

It took only seconds before she heard the ping alerting her to the arrival of a text.

Anna! How are you? We miss you.

Miss you too.

Anna explained her plan to support the Syrian family with food from Natalia's shop and within minutes the team in London had agreed to her using their stories.

When she'd translated Cordelia's latest, which, by the way, made her ears burn, she dropped it off in Natalia's shop.

'This one is a hot chilli pepper,' she said.

Natalia grinned. 'Quality control,' and she began to read. She was so engrossed that she barely looked up when Anna took her leave.

As Anna walked slowly through the village, she caught a glimpse of the immigrant child playing in the square. He could just as well have been Boubakar. His mother sat on the stone steps of the church watching him, with the infant in her arms.

Anna took the path up through the caper bushes into the hills above the village. On the trail ahead she saw not one, but two vipers, coiled like rope together on the sand. She stopped to watch them.

An approaching goat and its raucous bell sent them slithering back into the scrub and cleared the path for her to walk on.

It was, she decided, time to go home.

Chapter Thirty

The dawn rose pink and lush over the allotment garden. Farhad's peonies were the first thing Anna saw when Liebe led her out on their first morning back – breathtaking blooms, from white to pink, from red to deepest black.

Anna needed the solace their beauty offered. Peter had cleaned his books and clothes out of the house while she was away. The finality of it tugged at the peace Anna had found on the island. When she got dressed after her shower she noticed her jeans were loose. She looked as if someone had run off with her muscle and flesh.

They'd arrived back late the previous night to find – to Anna's amazement – the roof repaired, the walls freshly painted and on the stairs, a new grey carpet. It had been too late to phone, but Anna texted Cordelia, Lisbet, Farhad and Nadia to say, Thank you, treasured friends. Thank you. Thank You!!!!!!!!!

It was after midnight when Lisbet texted back, Did you

thank Tekkies too? (FYI We've all been paid back from your royalties as instructed!)

Yay. No, should I have thanked him?

Yes, you idiot. He did all the work! It's 07734086672.

Anna wondered what that meant. Was he the project manager tasked with returning Anna's devastated house to a place of shelter? If that was the case, she was grateful, and hoped it had successfully distracted him from whatever godawful thing he was trying to forget.

It also made her think of Boubakar. She had to stick her hands under the cold water tap to stop herself from opening her computer and clicking on the archive folder for his company.

Instead, Anna wrote, Dear Tekkies, thank you for helping to fix my roof, Anna.

When everyone gathered for what they had come to call Friday-night-fess-up, there was a new face in the group, not in the room exactly, but on the computer screen on the table.

'Anna, this is Samar, coming to us from Nablus in Palestine,' said Tekkies. 'Courtesy of Skype.'

Samar waved.

'Hello, Samar,' said Anna.

'*Marhaba*, Anna, I'm glad to meet you.'

She spoke English with the lilting, rolling 'rrr's' of her Middle Eastern tongue.

'Samar is a professor at An-Najah National University,' said Cordelia.

'But now I'm on an unpaid sabbatical for a year,' said Samar.

'Why is that?' asked Anna.

She smiled sheepishly. 'Well, the Women's Studies course I was teaching went a little too far, too fast.'

Cordelia laughed.

'So the administration thought I needed a cooling-down period.'

'How did you find us?' asked Anna.

'I follow Scarlet Blazer,' said Samar as if it was the most obvious thing in the world. 'I saw the rave review she gave your work.'

'May the Lord bless that woman,' said Nonna, 'and keep her safe.'

'Samar wrote into the comment page on our blog,' said Cordelia, 'and I noticed, so I wrote back. Long-story-short, lots of toing and froing, and we now have a new writer.'

Anna made a mental note to remind Cordelia that any new collaborators needed to be agreed by them both before being invited into the fold. It made her feel slightly queasy, as if her absence had shifted her grasp on things.

Sofia wandered into the kitchen in her mismatched pyjamas, her skin the colour of acorns from the Aeolian sun. She blinked at them and said, 'Don't mind me. I'm just in need of . . . a sandwich. A salami and mozzarella sandwich.'

She brought something guileless and young into the room that lightened the atmosphere.

Lisbet clinked her fork against her glass. 'I have an announcement, people.' She got to her feet and cleared her throat.

'Apart from the great news that our commander-in-chief is back and looking like a million dollars . . .'

Liar, thought Anna.

'. . . it gives me great pleasure to tell you that today was a bloody big day in the life of our little company . . .'

She held up her glass. 'At three o'clock GMT, reader number one hundred thousand visited our site.'

The room exploded in whistles and applause. Anna gasped.

Sofia turned to look at her mother, her face alight.

'It's a love factory, Mama,' she said.

A Love Factory.

'*Ecco qua!*' said Nonna. 'It is *The* Love Factory.'

'That's it!' said Cordelia.

'We have a name!' said Lisbet and she immediately turned to Tekkies and said, 'Quick, *bokkie* . . .'

'*Ja*, the domain name. We've got to buy the name!' he said, and he opened his computer.

'We have a name, everyone!' said Anna and she raised her glass to Sofia. 'The Love Factory.'

Sofia held up her sandwich in salute and added, 'A global badass love factory!'

And she was right. Almost every one of them was from somewhere else. Between them they covered most continents, five time zones and an ocean or two.

And then there was Cordelia.

'I'm from the north of England. If Westminster had their way they'd sever us from the mainland.'

Anna laughed. Something real was being made here;

something imperfect, perhaps, but a living thing that bound all their lives in shared endeavour.

And now an Arab academic had joined the ranks of their Love Factory and brought a whole new part of the world with her.

Chapter Thirty-One

Later, when Nadia had opened the bottle of champagne she'd been saving for just such a moment, and everyone had toasted the name, the milestone, and the sweet fact that they were together again, Samar invited Anna to come closer to the computer screen.

'I need to show you something,' she said.

Anna peered at the screen. Samar held up a page covered with neat Arabic script.

'What is it?'

'"Hooked" in Arabic.'

Anna felt the heat of a blush colour her cheeks.

'What?'

'I translated it into Arabic.'

'What for?'

'So you could publish it in the Middle East. It works well

set in the fishing dock in Fez. And I made it so that the girl is running away from an arranged marriage.'

'But . . .'

'Anna, you yourself have been talking about translation!' said Cordelia, catching onto the conversation.

'But not for publication in the Middle East!'

'Why not?' asked Samar.

'Because I haven't the faintest idea what we would be dealing with there.'

'But I do,' said Samar quietly.

'OK, so you tell me. From where I sit it seems like there are a lot of men raging against the basic emancipation of women. These stories go a lot further than that, in every imaginable way, and I have no desire to rile anyone.'

'Yes, there are,' said Samar, 'more every day. But we can't let that rule us.'

'But will it be safe for you? I mean, if the wrong people come to know that you're working on these kinds of stories?' insisted Anna.

'I hope so. I have three children to feed.'

'Surely they can be traced to you?'

Anna saw Cordelia glance at Nadia. They both looked uneasy.

'Tekkies is helping me cover my tracks pretty effectively, but it's possible, I suppose,' said Samar.

'Not much comfort in that,' said Anna.

'Until then,' said Samar, 'it matters that we talk about love in a place like this.'

'Yes,' Nonna sighed and walked over to the sink. 'I'm not a learned person like my husband was, but what I do know is that if you want to save the world, you must begin in the bedroom.'

'That sounds about right to me,' said Nadia.

'And me,' said Sofia from her spot in the corner.

Samar laughed gently. 'You know, there are times when I read Hafiz for pleasure, and Faulkner is a favourite. But when terrible things happen I go to a site called *Jamilat that Ash'ar al Aswad* . . . the Raven Haired Beauties. Their stories are in Arabic, of course, and posted from Beirut. They give me such peace.'

Anna sat back in her chair, thoughtful.

'It is true that we read things like this to get away from how things are,' said Cordelia.

Anna leaned in to the screen. 'You can translate anything I write, Samar.'

The new member of the team nodded graciously.

'This is your risk to take.'

'You can have mine too,' said Farhad.

Cordelia raised her hand. 'And mine.'

Stokely raised his hand too.

'Thank you,' said Samar quietly, 'and I will give you mine.'

When everyone had left, Anna sat in the single remaining armchair in the overcrowded living room. The children were in bed and she could hear Nonna shuffling her way through her nightly ritual.

Anna leaned her head back and closed her eyes.

It was true that, together, the members of The Love Factory made up a veritable Babel. Samar wrote in Arabic, Farhad was fluent in Farsi, she in Italian. Even now, Natalia wanted more stories to sell in the small shop in Salina. Anna asked herself, why not sell all over Italy? Then there was Nadia, not a writer, but fond enough of language to translate into Hindi. And Lisbet into Afrikaans. But who would translate Samar's Arabic into English?

She knew that if she asked Nadia, she would say 'Bouchra, of course!' She'd asked Anna just that afternoon when she was planning to visit her old friend.

'I don't know,' Anna had said. 'How is she?'

'She's sad.'

Anna had turned away.

'Holy shit, Anna, are you going to let a stupid fight over nothing destroy years of friendship?'

Anna shook her head.

'Then go and see her, dammit, you can't wish away all the difficult things. And talking of which, here's another. We need new offices and we need them soon.'

'Where the hell did that come from?' asked Anna.

'I don't want to work in a corner of your living room any more,' said Nadia. 'I want a glass desk and an assistant called Herman. And we can afford it too.'

Anna looked at her. 'Really?'

'Really.'

Anna hesitated. 'How's that?'

Nadia hauled out the spreadsheet showing their collective earnings for April, May and the first week of June. It showed a steep curve upward. Anna, Cordelia and their partners, Farhad, Stokely, Lisbet, Nadia, and now Tekkies by dint of his hard work on the tech interface, were sitting on earnings of over three hundred thousand pounds. Of course, that didn't mean that all of them would want to invest in a shared property, but the possibility was there in black and white.

Anna was gobsmacked. 'Shit, am I the only one who missed this?'

'You were away, Anna,' said Nadia, 'and recovering from a horrible break-up. Give yourself a bloody break.'

'And I'm still not sure. I mean, aren't we all supposed to sit in a lovely location somewhere and conference in? Isn't that the way people work these days?'

'Not with this lot,' said Nadia. 'We all seem to want to huddle together like lemmings. And how would we have as much fun alone?'

'Think big,' Anna,' said Nonna. 'Nobody is too old for these stories . . . too young, maybe, but not too old. And it might be better for Lukey if he didn't have to live with it going on in his house every day.'

'He is a teenage boy,' added Nadia.

'So?' asked Anna, alarmed.

'So how weird is it to be surrounded twenty-four seven by people cranking out erotica?' asked Nadia. 'Quite aside from that, we're bursting at the seams! Every one of our markets is going nuts: gay, straight, lesbian, fetish . . . and everything in between.'

'Really?'

'We are going to have to take on more support staff too. Tekkies says he's found a great unit in an old building near King's Cross that needs a lot of work but has room for all of us.'

Anna got up to put on the kettle. This was going much too fast.

Later that evening, when she had calmed down, she reached for the story on top of the pile waiting for editing. It was a collaboration between Farhad and Stokely and it took her just a second to see that in the alchemy of their combined minds, they had conjured a startling story.

Chapter Thirty-Two

Farhad and Stokely's Story

My boys tell me I've got the swagger. I tell them I get the good stuff because I'm a clever, gay, brown-skinned boy who is going to be a doctor. People love a doctor.

I turn up on the first day of third year pathology as I mean to continue, top of the class and up for anything that comes my way. One glance at my professor tells me that the neuropathologist who everyone says is super-clever is also gay, and YOUNG, and a beauty; long-necked, fine-fingered, lean-limbed – but there's a nuance to that, you know, a texture. A something . . . ? I'm keen to know more.

Pathology is straight after lunch on a Wednesday, and he always arrives with cheeks glowing and water dripping off the ends of his long, dark hair.

Our microscopes have two sets of lenses so student and teacher can look at the same cell and swap diagnoses. Well, I'm wise enough to shut my mouth and just listen to him telling me what's going on in those cells. Beautiful stuff. We're close enough to kiss and I smell this diffused green scent coming off him that makes me want to dive into a cold lake – it's like grass, and cardamom, and maybe some ginger? Ah . . . it's the smell of my auntie's horse chestnut orchard in the Himalayas that I haven't smelt for a decade or more.

It leads me to wonder about the provenance of my lovely professor. Has he traced his DNA? It's an exercise we all did in first-year medicine and I, who'd always had a soft spot for my Punjabi roots, discovered the startling fact that I'm sixty per cent Welsh, and probably as much coal miner as high mountain prince.

How cool would it be to know the origins of my professor's olive skin, pale yellow eyes and, most beguiling of all, his full, ripe mouth. There are days when just listening to his voice raises my penis from its slumber. It prods against my trousers and makes it hazardous for me to stand up. It's not a polite kind of prodding. It's urgent, so I excuse myself and get relief in the john while the visual of the back of the professor's petal ear runs through my head.

I work like a madman to keep up my lead in class and he invites me to shadow him on his ward rounds at the Royal Free. The guy is a crackerjack diagnostician;

kind, funny, generous, the patients love him. I concentrate so hard my head is throbbing but it's worth it because I spot the Epstein Bar when no-one else even considers it, and when the bloods come back, I am right. He shakes my hand and smiles. I want to come right out with it and say *I'm sorry, I know you are my teacher, but all that bally-cock shit about power imbalances between teacher and student just doesn't hack it with me. Please, let me kiss your cherry of a mouth.*

They say that the big room at the Turkish baths in Bayswater has always been a gathering place for Arab women from the community and that the tradition continues, but I happen to know that almost no one uses the smaller bath. When a space opens up in London there's always someone waiting to fill it. I'm lucky enough to be in the loop when our trickle of enthusiasts begins to show up in those very same clouds of steam.

It's always bloody freezing when you first take off your clothes and I shiver all the way from the changing room to the old brass doors that keep in the heat. Ah, but then that same soft, sweet heat gathers you into its arms.

Truly, the hours that follow are full of promise. Even if I don't find a willing partner in the hot clouds, I live on the pinprick of that possibility and it keeps the heart pumping. I'm told that a long time ago cleansing rites of passage happened in this bath; I'm thinking of young maidens on the night before their wedding, or Jewish boys before their bar mitzvah, the washing away of all the sins of those Catholic novitiates before their final confirmation.

Now there's just me and the black-eyed lad, Turkish, I think, who has sat down beside me and who promises to be generous with his delights. It's he who leads me to the hidden corner where gifts can be given and received out of the view of others. Delicious, cock-sucking gifts, that leave me as limp as a puppy.

Sadly, the weeks that follow the encounter with the gentle Turk are lean. I still go to the baths because I've got work to do and sleep to get, and it's just way more pleasurable than the nightclubs and cruising spots that once filled my nights.

Now it's late on a Friday and the baths are due to close in a couple of hours. I lie back on the marble, resigned to solo pleasures tonight, and the heat settles in, softening my knotted back, lengthening the muscles. Then, all of a sudden, I feel someone at my side.

He's a beauty with a long, lean face and strong arms. And as he lies down next to me his arm brushes across the small white towel that covers my penis.

Christ. Maybe I wasn't so sanguine about all that solitary pleasure after all. I feel him take my hand and I follow him along the low passage billowing with steam to the hidden corner beyond it. And I'm thinking that Dickens would've loved the steam as thick as pea soup and the grumbling of a distant pump. I don't have time to ask where we are before the lad kisses me full on the mouth, the neck, the stomach, the groin and then he lifts that little towel and he takes me into his mouth. Oh . . . no words. Really, no words. I just close my eyes and thank my lucky stars.

Then I smell it, the green, the ginger, the horse chestnut. How can that be? I feel a hand over my eyes so I can't look, even if I want to, and then fingers circle my nipple, pinch it. My eyes flick open, I push the hand away and there, in all that heat and steam, is my beautiful bloody professor.

'Hello,' he whispers.

'Yeah,' I say, cool as a cucumber, but my whole body, legs, cock, arms are shivering with excitement.

My prior companion slips away into the steam and I wonder if he was sent in to set me up. And then I forget what I was wondering. Oh Christ, the professor's mouth makes a spurt of white billow from my tip, because he is wearing lipstick! Finely drawn coral on his fucking incredible mouth – edible, pluckable, bold.

That kiss I will never forget. I slip my fingers behind his perfect ears and I can feel him respond . . . easily, naturally . . . my kind of man.

Weird what happens to time when you are so in your body you forget there's a world of clocks ticking out there somewhere. I don't know how long we stand there reaching for each other, but I can tell you that every single second is like nothing I've felt before, even his fingers running over my vertebrae, one by one, turns me to lava.

I'm pleased to say that I too bring something to the table. I'm not only the student any more. I'm on my knees with his incredible cock in my mouth when I slip my thumb inside his opening to find that beautiful, slippery knot of synapses, that web that sits behind his rod and as I massage it I can feel him spill into my mouth with a shout of surprise. 'Oh, oh, God!' he says and he takes my face into his hands and mumbles, 'Thank you.'

I laugh from my belly. I'm happy. That would've done it for me. I could have taken his hand and walked out into the night and been content but the professor has something else in mind. I feel him turn my slippery body to face the wall. He puts my hands above my head and he borrows a little of the come seeping out of my cock to wet my opening. He leans over and whispers, 'I'll go slow.'

And I feel his cock, full again, jeez, that was quick, against my legs, fuller even. I swear.

And he bends me over and he pushes into me. A light goes off behind my eyes and I push against him – my hands on the wall for power, he kicks my legs open and pushes deeper. Completely fills me up, like utterly, and I can feel my orgasm spreading down from the top of my head to the bottom of my feet and then I feel a mouth close over my cock and I think, fuck me, what's that? and I look down and see it's my first companion back belly side up with what feels like my whole life in his mouth.

I groan and I've not heard that sound come out of my mouth before, bliss it was.

And then he comes, my professor, great waves of him shoot against my insides and I just can't hold on any more and I join him and I swear the two of us could light up the skies of London with our blind, bloody pleasure.

Anna closed her eyes and was glad. Stokely and Farhad's passion for one another was what drove their story and made it sing. That, and the reach of their cultures. Anna imagined that Stokely, only just back in the sexually active fold, probably baulked at writing the sexy bits, but he would have loved the set-up and the tropes of gay erotica which were the story's building blocks. Farhad would have taken over when it was time to bring it home. What a duo.

The night was warm and the clouds low. Liebe pulled Anna into the park for a longer walk than usual. As they passed the mini-golf course Anna saw the woman walking ahead of her on the path hesitate and then stop altogether. She did so, it seemed, to watch the approach of a young white man and his Staffordshire terrier. The man bounced onto the balls of his feet as he walked in a gesture of confrontation, or was it jest? Not even Anna, long familiar with the ways of the English, could fathom its intention.

The woman glanced over her shoulder, nervously. It was only then that Anna recognised her Arab neighbour, the woman who had so kindly cooked her *mansaf* the night the wind blew the roof off her house.

Anna quickened her pace. She could see two more men, jittery, rough boys, join the man with the dog.

The parties were still some distance apart when Anna caught up with the woman. Anna handed Liebe's lead to her and said, 'She'll warn us if there's trouble, she knows everything before I do.'

The woman looked somewhat startled but she said, 'Yes, thank you.'

Anna stroked Liebe's face. 'Stay with her, Liebe.'

They walked on in silence. It seemed to take a long time but when they did finally pass the men the dogs paid each other no heed. When Anna glanced back she could only just make out the shape of the man bouncing away into the night, his two accomplices on either side of him. Anna heard her neighbour suck in a ragged breath.

'I'm Anna,' she said.

The woman gave her a fleeting smile. 'Reem. Thank you for walking with me.'

It began to rain gently as they reached Reem's building. The front door of the flat was open and her husband was waiting on the walkway.

When he saw Anna and Liebe walking with his wife he called out his usual blessing, '*Baraka Allah fiki*,' and came down the steps to meet them.

'Good evening.'

As he approached, Reem's hands flew to her bare head. A kind of frantic patting followed. Her face was stricken.

Her husband took her hands in his. 'She forgot her hair cover,' he said to Anna by way of explanation. 'At home they used to flog women for that.' He put his arm around his wife. 'I tell her the only thing to fear here is the winter cold.'

'And maybe the park at night,' said Anna.

The man looked at Anna for a long moment and then nodded his head. 'Like all dangers, it must not be underestimated.'

Chapter Thirty-Three

Although she'd never found the right moment to tell him so, Anna loved the grey carpet Tekkies had chosen for the stairs and landing in her house. She liked to lie on the floor outside her bedroom in the afternoon when the sun fell on it. She put a pillow there to rest her head when she was reading and then a blanket in case of a chill breeze from the open window. She'd never imagined that this functional corner of her house could be so beautiful.

Luke found her there as he stomped up the stairs on his return from school. 'It's a colour match, Mama,' he said.

'What?'

'You and the carpet have the same colour hair.'

What? Whoa! What?!

When the first grey streak had appeared in Anna's hair a few years ago, she'd yanked it out. Every time a new one came in she did the same. Then the day came when there were just too many to manage in this way.

The following week her hairdresser returned her to her original smoky auburn, and then again six weeks later, and again every six weeks after that until Peter lost his job.

Anna had never met a hairdresser so uninterested in hair. She'd followed her to four salons over the years, not because she thought her so skilled, although she was, and effortlessly so, but because she knew how to tell a good story and she made Anna laugh.

When Nadia had told Anna, just back from Salina, that she should have 'a bloody haircut' to match her suntan and her shrinking waistline, Anna had ignored her. But no one wants to look like a grey carpet, however luxuriant.

When she walked into the salon her hairdresser looked up at her and said, 'I said to my husband just the other day, I said, I wonder if Anna, the nice writer lady, has died.'

Anna laughed. 'I wondered that myself.'

'Sit down. We've got to vanquish that grey,' and when she said the word 'vanquish' she twirled her hands in the air.

Anna emerged two hours later looking not unlike her younger self and not at all like somebody who'd recently had her entire universe turned inside out.

She took a roundabout route to the Tube station. It had been a long time, she realised, since she'd window-shopped the swanky streets of London. She and Sofia did it sometimes, to pick up ideas on how to put together a new outfit or refresh an old one, but they never imagined actually buying.

A blue coat hung in the window of the white-stone boutique on the corner, luminous with colour and possibility. It beckoned Anna inside, where more garments hung in pools of light.

A voice behind her made her jump.

'Can I help you?'

Without much conviction, the young sales assistant shepherded Anna and the blue coat into a changing booth. They had a nose for the modest spenders.

The blue made Anna's eyes shine. The coat was cut so it fell closely against her body and was made of the lightest cashmere. The shop assistant sent her out to look at herself in the larger mirror.

A man and his teenage daughter who were surveying the boots on sale nearby glanced up at her – Anna could tell that with her new haircut and the blue coat she had caught his eye.

The girl handed the chosen boots to her father, and said, 'Thank you, Dad. Got to go.' She picked up her schoolbag, pecked him on the cheek and darted out of the shop.

The man paid for the boots and stopped behind Anna on his way out. 'It looks good, you should get it.'

She turned to look into his startling eyes, one blue and the other brown, like David Bowie. It gave what he said an unsettling weight.

'The coat,' he said quietly, 'you, and the coat.' His attention was razor sharp. Anna's heart beat a little faster.

'It'll look even better with that.' He pointed to a silk dress.

'And those.' He indicated a pair of shoes. He had an eye for beauty.

'Oh.'

No one could say Anna wasn't bold. She tried it all on. His flattery was like rain in a desert. And, good Lord, when she looked in the mirror it wasn't herself that she saw any more. It was the story, layer on layer of glamour and disguise. She smiled at the man.

'Would you have lunch with me?' he asked. 'Please.'

Anna paused and the words, *Who, me?* came into her mind. Then she looked at him and said, 'You've made me feel lucky, thank you. But no.'

Lucky to have had the chance to put it all on, and to be, for a moment, someone else. Then she headed back into the dressing room, took it all off, and made for the door.

As she pounded along the pavement she said to herself, 'WTF, Anna, you've been writing too many stupid stories. Who the hell do you think you are?'

Before the trip to the hairdresser that morning, Nadia had convinced her to at least come and see the building that Tekkies had found as a potential office. She had also made a pitch for the benefits of owning office space over renting.

'Oh bloody hell, all right,' Anna had said. Now she was late because of the man with the Bowie eyes and the blue coat.

The young man at the entrance to the building site gave her a neon yellow waistcoat four sizes too big – 'sorry, miss, health and safety regulations'. He also insisted on boots that felt like buckets on her feet, and a luminous hard hat that came down over her eyes every time she moved her head.

Nadia seemed to manage the safety attire much better than Anna did as they ventured into the not-at-all-safe sixth floor of the old factory building.

'The estate agent said this floor was probably once a marmalade factory, or maybe a small flour mill,' said Nadia.

'It hasn't been anything for a long time, by the look of it,' said Anna.

This kind of undeveloped space was a rare find in a city like London, especially near the hub of two bustling stations and the city's most dynamic art school. Nadia explained that the left-leaning Camden Council had refused the developer planning permission in the nineteen eighties on the grounds that the area was in need of small cooperative business development, not the swanky corporate offices he imagined. Then the old bugger had gone and died intestate, leaving his heirs to fight over it for another five years. Now, finally, that was all sorted, the council were satisfied that the building would be a modest hub for small businesses, and the heirs were ready to sell.

The building was situated on the slope behind King's Cross Station near Regent's Canal. It had been built in the Georgian period when large panes of glass were first produced. So, despite its industrial purpose, it had beautiful dimensions – tall windows, although many of them had been painted over – and high ceilings.

No way would they buy this, thought Anna. It was a bloody ruin.

'Good haircut,' said Tekkies as he strode across the large space towards them.

'Thank you.'

Lisbet pecked her on the cheek. 'Thanks for coming.'

'Anna, I found a good place for your desk,' said Tekkies.

'Really?'

'Come see.'

Anna followed Tekkies to the very front of the open factory floor and onto an ancillary landing that extended out over the street below. The original windows had been removed and the new ones not yet installed. Someone had put up flimsy yellow tape to mark the edge. Anna hesitated, heart pounding; *Jesus, there is not one thing to stop me if I fall.*

'Come,' said Tekkies, and the way he said it made her brave.

She followed him right up to the very edge and heard him say, 'There.'

And my God it was beautiful.

The way the building sat on the rise situated it midway between east and west and facing south. Tekkies confirmed that by pulling out the compass on his phone.

'Sun rises there, sets there,' he said as he pointed. 'With floor-to-ceiling windows you'll see the light move across the city from dawn to dusk without taking a step.'

Anna had never seen anything quite as open to the passage of the day in London before. It felt like the city was holding her in the palm of its hand.

Tekkies stood by her side in silence. He seemed to intuit that she needed a moment of quiet to grasp it.

Lisbet shouted from the far back corner of the room, 'Tekkies, *kom kyk*!'

She was kneeling on the floor, her red fingernails picking at the old linoleum floor coverings. Tekkies knelt down and lifted the plastic further.

'*Sien jy?*' she asked.

He tucked his fingers under the covering. Anna peered over his shoulder to see what Lisbet had found.

'There's wood underneath,' he said.

He positioned himself, Anna, Lisbet and Nadia at each corner and talked them through the lifting of the linoleum.

'Gently, we don't want to split the wood underneath.'

'This wood doesn't split,' said Lisbet.

'Are we even allowed to do this?' asked Nadia. 'We haven't bought the place yet.'

'Maybe they'll take a low-ball offer,' said Lisbet. 'Not everyone will want to do the necessary work.'

'Do we?' Anna asked.

'I do,' said Tekkies as he lifted one side of the linoleum sheet. 'Keep the pressure even, Anna.'

'We could always rent some of it out to cover our mortgage for the first year or two,' said Nadia.

'A bit higher,' said Tekkies as he scratched at the sticky bits with his penknife. Anna had the sense that a bomb could've gone off outside and Tekkies would not have heard, such was his focus on the task. She abandoned all thought of staying clean and crawled under the linoleum to help him. As they worked she smelt the smoky grass odour of his body. She noted that it made her think of open space and a not-too-distant sea.

Finally, the linoleum lifted off and Tekkies and Lisbet looked at one another.

'*Bloedhout*,' said Tekkies.

'*Ja, kiaat*.'

'Oh, bloody hell, will you two speak English!' said Nadia.

'*Ag*, sorry,' said Tekkies, 'but just look at this.'

He licked his thumb and ran it across the wood. It went from dark and dusty to a glowing gold. 'It's a protected tree in South Africa. Bloodwood, also called African teak or *kiaat*.'

'I've never seen planks like these,' said Lisbet and she felt the wood with her fingertips. 'They were probably laid at the turn of the century from old-growth trees, shipped all the way from the indigenous forests of central Mozambique.'

Tekkies looked closer. 'The planks were cut from the heartwood.'

'*Ja*, the sapwood's redder.'

'It doesn't burn so people in southern Africa build houses with it,' said Tekkies. 'It gets no termites or dry rot. That's probably why the floor is so sturdy.'

'How do you know so much about this bloody tree?' asked Nadia.

'My mom grew one in our garden,' said Tekkies. 'It shouldn't have been possible in that stony ground but she dug in compost and tea bags and bonemeal and anything else she thought would help it grow. And she watered it even through the droughts.'

'The birds loved it, we built a treehouse, remember?' said Lisbet.

Anna could imagine the two of them climbing up, hanging on, hiding out. That he and Lisbet were sidekicks meant that Tekkies was old enough to know the value of a good tree.

'I kissed Karina van de Vyfer in that treehouse,' he said.

'*Ja*,' said Lisbet, 'and then her father fed you to his ridgeback.'

'I was five.'

'A perfect dog snack.'

'A Jewish dog snack. *Ek onthou die vrees*.'

'He remembers the fear,' said Lisbet to Anna and Nadia. 'How many stitches did they leave you with?'

'Eighteen.'

'After that he hid out in the treehouse,' Lisbet continued. 'He read books and fixed broken electronics. The only nerd in Port Nolloth.'

'That's me,' he murmured.

'Well, now we have to buy the bloody building, don't we?' said Nadia and she slapped Tekkies on the arm. 'Since the nerd has ripped up the floor.'

Tekkies turned to Anna. 'What do you think?'

She opened her mouth to speak but a German word arrived in her head instead – she'd first heard her father use it to describe a piece of music. The closest she could get in English was *soulful*, but the way her father used it implied something both sharply intelligent, and full of feeling. *Seelenvoll*.

Tekkies was *seelenvoll.* It felt as though she might have seen him as he truly was for the first time.

'I think it sounds . . . plausible,' she said, finally.

'Thank God for that,' said Lisbet and she let out a laugh.

Chapter Thirty-Four

'Take a deep breath, Anna,' she said to herself that evening. And she packed the South African and the word she had found to describe him away in her backpack of future possibilities and got on with the here and now.

There was Luke, after all, and Nonna, and Sofia to attend to. And she had stories to write.

But she had no power over the smell of him. It arrived when he did and lingered after he'd left at the end of a day's work.

Anna watched him go after the acquisition of the King's Cross property like a terrier. Offer and counter-offer flew back and forth throughout the week. He took meetings with the surveyor and the mortgage assessor. He worked late every evening and he was the first to arrive in the morning.

Anna trapped him at the coffee machine midweek and she said, 'Milk?'

'*Ja*, thanks.'

She poured milk into his coffee and asked, 'Why are you here, Tekkies?'

He looked startled, and then he shook his head. 'What?'

'Fixing my roof? The beautiful carpet? Everything you are doing for The Love Factory?'

He didn't look at her.

The minute hand on the clock on the kitchen wall moved around its old-fashioned analogue face.

'I don't know,' he said, 'I just see what's there.'

'What?'

'I see you.' He paused. 'Nothing I can do about that.'

The first time he turned up at the crack of dawn she said to him, 'If you show up at this hour you're going to have to put up with me in my pyjamas.'

He grinned his lopsided grin. 'Fine by me.'

'Coffee's on,' she said, before wandering out to the allotment to give Liebe a run before the work day began.

The next morning, she wore her nice pyjamas which did good things for her cleavage. She could see his eyes widen at the sight of her in the doorway.

Towards the end of the week Anna invited Tekkies to eat breakfast with Luke.

'Do you like oatmeal?'

He proceeded to demolish a large bowl in a matter of seconds. She watched him get through a second bowl and two slices of toast.

'I never thought I'd meet anyone who could out-eat me at breakfast, Tekkies,' said Luke.

'Happy to oblige,' he said. He looked up at Anna. 'Sorry. I've got an empty leg.'

Luke laughed.

'It's hollow, isn't it?' Tekkies blushed. 'A hollow leg.'

By the end of the week he and Luke were exchanging music, having discovered that Tekkies played drums for a small band of renegade jazz musicians. He invited Luke to come to one of their gigs.

Along with her visit to the hairdresser, braces for Luke's overbite, and a replacement for Sofia's broken laptop, Anna reinstated the household insurance and the morning delivery of fresh milk as well as the newspaper to her door. She did all this using a monthly spreadsheet with tutoring from Nadia so she could get a grip on her finances. It didn't come easily.

'I don't think you like numbers, Anna,' Nadia noted.

It was true that Anna struggled, almost nightly, to understand the fiscal reports Nadia generated for The Love Factory.

'You get your sevens and your nines mixed up and you write your fours backwards.'

'I know that,' said Anna, 'but it doesn't have to stop me from understanding what's coming in and going out, does it?'

In the end, Nadia prepared a simple rubric for Anna's domestic budget and a slightly more complex summary for the business. Before long Anna had mastered both.

*

July arrived with a heatwave. Anna watered the beds in the allotment earlier each day to stop the plants drooping from the heat, especially the perpetual spinach and the carrots she'd seeded in the winter. Farhad's peonies, approaching the peak of their glory, needed a good drenching too.

On the seventh straight day of record temperatures, when Tekkies had once again arrived early to start his working day, Anna heard the kitchen door burst open and his voice call out, 'We did it, Anna.'

Anna looked up to see him barrel though the gate into the allotment. 'We exchanged!' he said.

As he ran between the beds towards her, Anna noticed how differently he occupied his body than most English men she knew. He moved with a hot country sort of ease.

'Say that again?' she asked with the hiss of the hose in her ears.

'We got it. We own the sixth floor!'

'*Mavala!*' She laughed. 'Really?'

It seemed the most natural thing in the world that when he reached her he would scoop her up in his arms and swing her round. She opened her mouth and laughter bubbled out.

Tekkies set her back on her feet.

'You OK?'

'I want to tell my mother.'

'Then tell her.'

'Can't.'

'Why not?'

'She died.'

It was as if that fact was new to her too.

The bright, smoky, sea-grass smell of him that Anna had become so familiar with seemed to deepen as they stood there close enough to kiss.

'She would've loved the view.'

Tekkies took the hosepipe from Anna's hand and turned it off at the tap.

He kneeled next to the bed of carrots she'd just watered. Anna watched him feel the top of each carrot with his long fingers.

'May I?' he asked.

She nodded and watched him pull at the green top. A carrot emerged out of the ground.

Anna wondered if she'd ever seen anything quite as vividly orange before. Tekkies washed the carrot clean at the tap and snapped it into three pieces. He put one into Anna's mouth to spare her having to use her muddy hands.

'Sweet,' she said.

They both watched Liebe take her piece in her soft, bird-catcher mouth, then turn away to crunch and gulp.

'Let's take some in for Nonna,' said Anna as she crouched beside the bed to harvest some more carrots.

They worked alongside one another in silence. He was careful, she noticed, not to disturb the younger carrots as he harvested.

'We had a dog named Jessye,' Anna said as she shook the dirt off a carrot and added it to the growing pile on the grass. 'She was a pointer, like Liebe, a hunting dog.'

'Jessie,' Tekkies said, and smiled.

'After Jessye Norman, the opera singer. She loved going to the reservoir at the Welsh Harp because it was wild and full of squirrels. We loved it too because my brother and I could have our mother all to ourselves there.'

Anna fell silent. It occurred to her that she had not, for more than twenty years, talked about this.

'Go on,' he said.

'The reeds grew very high at the edge of the water. I remember seeing Jessye burst out of them chasing a squirrel.'

Anna paused a moment. Liebe lay on her back in the long grass, voluptuous pink-skinned belly soaking up the sun.

'She chased it across the field and towards the big main road. My mother ran after her, shouting her name but Jessye didn't stop.'

Tekkies laid the carrot he was cleaning down and was still.

'A big yellow car came around the bend, very fast. It hit Jessye first. She was sucked under the wheels. My mother was next. I can't remember seeing much after that, except . . . the white of my mother's teeth and jaw, without the soft, smiling cover of her lips.'

Tekkies shook his head.

'My father explained to me afterwards, that the impact blew the soft skin of her mouth open and back. That it was the law of physics. That's all.'

'Anna.'

'Stef howled like a wolf.'

Anna looked up to see Tekkies watching her closely.

'I was eleven.'

Tekkies sat on the ground, and looked away. It helped her to continue.

'From that day to this, whenever something important happens, the first person I want to tell is her.'

'Yes,' he said softly.

'I backed into a corner of my mind, so I wouldn't ever see her mouth again, and those teeth. And I did. I kept them at bay with the help of the books I read . . . and later the ones I wrote. I kept them at bay with my book people, for almost a lifetime.'

Both were silent while the ordinary sounds of the day continued around them – birdsong, Liebe breathing in her sleep, distant traffic. But in truth, everything had altered.

Chapter Thirty-Five

The house was already humming with Love Factory business when Anna showed up at her desk. She'd woken later than usual, and felt refreshed. It had been so long since she'd slept a whole night through that she'd forgotten how it felt.

Samar was on FaceTime with Lisbet. Anna joined their tight circle. The advance copies of her adaptation of the 'Hooked' stories had gone out, to universal acclaim. Even the review on *Jamilat that Asha'ar al Aswad* was a winner.

'We'll publish part one on the open blog as bait and part two on the pay site,' said Lisbet.

'And the Middle East will come flocking,' said Nadia.

'*Inshallah*,' muttered Samar.

'On a more prosaic note,' said Nadia, 'we still don't have anyone to translate Samar's stories into English.'

'Why not translate them yourself, Samar?' asked Anna.

'Arabic I can do, beautiful English I cannot.'

'Ask Bouchra,' Nadia told Anna. 'She's your friend! And she needs this work.'

Anna felt a sudden and irresistible urge to sleep. 'Where's Tekkies?' she asked, settling in at her own desk.

'With the architect,' said Lisbet. 'He said to tell you that they haven't taken all the linoleum off the floor yet but they discovered that the whole bloody infrastructure, pillars and beams, are *bloedhout* too.'

It still seemed unreal to Anna that she and the six partners of The Love Factory were flush enough to undertake this project. After breakfast most days she and Tekkies pored over design websites together. They selected an innovative young architect, familiar with working on a budget, and were now eagerly awaiting his plans.

'Tekkies is going to make sure we see every inch of that wood,' she said.

'*Ja*, good at whatever he does, that boy.' Lisbet was scratching through a pile of papers on her overburdened desk. 'I think he gets this design thing from his wife. She was a brilliant landscape architect.'

Anna felt the words settle. She turned away and then back again to see if she'd heard right.

'What?' she asked.

'His what?' asked Nadia.

'His wife.' Lisbet looked up. 'Has everyone gone deaf?'

'Are you sure?' said Nadia. 'He doesn't act married. He's never mentioned his wife.'

'I'm sure, dammit. He's my bloody cousin.'

Anna looked out of the window and focused on calming the unfamiliar storm in her insides. 'Married?' she said.

'Yes, he's married,' Lisbet repeated, more gently this time, and she and Nadia exchanged glances.

'Oh,' said Anna.

'Who is he married to?' asked Nadia.

'She's called Sylvia.'

'Sylvia,' repeated Anna.

'But it's not simple,' said Lisbet. 'You'll have to ask him if you want to know more.'

'Why would I want to know more?' asked Anna quietly.

Lisbet's Apple watch pinged. 'Oh, shit, I've got to conference with a writer in Rome.' She consulted her computer and said, 'Oh no, hang on. She's in fucking Quebec.'

Anna walked out of the room and up the stairs. She fell onto her bed and pulled the pillow over her head.

But bed offered her no comfort. She sat up, lay down, turned onto her side, and then gave up. She walked into the door jamb on the way to the bathroom.

You can control want, but desire controls you.

Sofia phoned late that night as Anna was trying to get to sleep.

'I think I'm in love, Mama,' she said.

Anna stopped herself just in time from saying *Please don't say that.*

'His name is Alejandro, and I'm bringing him home with me tomorrow.'

'Well that's lovely.'

Anna took a deep breath.

'I'm love-sick, Mama, literally.'

The only thing love brings is trouble and strife, thought Anna as she brushed her teeth. Then she chided herself. *What the bloody hell were you thinking, Anna?*

Nonna baked bread because Friday night production meetings had begun to feel like extended family gatherings and where there was family, there was food. The kitchen smelt like a bakery and five beautiful round loaves adorned the counter when Anna came in.

'*Grazie*, Nonna,' she said.

She so badly wanted to add, 'Save me, Nonna, I'm in love with a married man.' But the gift of those glorious loaves and the effort her grandmother had expended to make them, seemed like enough for one day.

'Good hair,' said Nonna. 'Straight, like I always said it should be, but keep an eye on those roots.' Then she headed up the stairs to put her face on, which meant a dab of foundation and some pink lipstick.

Anna was tempted to tell her grandmother that she was a month late in noticing her hair, hence the roots, but just then the motley crew of The Love Factory began to dribble into the kitchen.

They came in twos, like the animals in Noah's ark. Stokely and Farhad, Nadia and Lisbet, and Cordelia showed up with Samar on the computer screen held open in front of her.

Sofia arrived home for the weekend with her young beau, Alejandro, on her arm.

'Hello!' said Anna to the olive-skinned young man in front of her. 'I've heard so much about you.'

Alejandro shook Anna's hand and then kissed her on both cheeks. He was so *there*, for someone so young, so very complete. *He has been well loved*, she thought, and then she prayed he would love her Sofia well too.

Anna had never before welcomed one of her children's chosen into their home. The sight of Sofia and this boy, so closely bound, gave her pause.

Sofia called out, 'Everyone, this is Ale.'

There was a chorus of greeting. The newcomer made his way around the room, sprinkling, it seemed, his personal variety of gold dust.

Farhad took one look at him and whispered to Cordelia, 'He'd make a beautiful well-boy.'

'Also a good camel,' said Cordelia and she smiled.

Stokely greeted Alejandro in perfect Spanish and, once again, Anna wondered how he came to acquire his myriad skills.

The oven timer pinged, Anna put the huge casserole dish of stew on the table and said, 'Come and get it, everyone.'

★

Sixteen-year-old Luke, outgrowing his shoes every six weeks, needed constant refuelling but Anna knew he found it terrifying to walk in on their Friday meetings. He frequently sat on the stairs outside the kitchen door with his stomach rumbling.

Sofia found him there on her way to the loo. He put his finger to his lips to shush her. She sat on the step beside him.

Luke hung his head. 'If anyone at school finds out about this Love Factory business I'm a dead man,' he said.

Sofia ruffled his hair.

'I'm not joking, sis. I'll have to enter the witness protection programme.'

Sofia hooted.

'And there'll be no help for me if anyone actually reads one of Mama's stories.'

Just then Anna opened the kitchen door to find them sitting on the step. 'There you are!' she said. 'You must be starved, Lukey.'

He nodded.

'Come in. I made a stew.'

Anna dished Luke an enormous portion and handed it over. He stood with his plate in his hand.

'Go on, eat.'

He didn't move.

'Lukey?'

'Please, Mama, can I eat in my room?'

'No food in the bedroom, *caro*,' she said.

'It's just that someone might say something . . . weird . . . and I'll never be able to forget it,' he said.

Anna filled a glass of water for him and put it into his free hand.

'Come back if you need seconds.'

He was off like a bullet. Anna looked around and asked, 'Now where's Nonna?'

Sofia murmured, 'I think she's lying down.'

'What? Now?'

Anna went up the stairs muttering to herself, 'Why does everyone keep disappearing?' She pushed open Nonna's door. Her grandmother lay on the bed, her eyes fully open.

'Come and eat, Nonna.'

Nonna whispered, 'Tired, child.'

Anna sat on the bed beside her. 'Alejandro seems to be a hit. You want to meet him?'

'Tomorrow.'

'This is his first encounter with The Love Factory. He might need help to make it through.'

Nonna smiled faintly and said, 'My work is never done.'

'Never.'

Anna helped her grandmother to her feet but her heart fluttered with a mild sort of alarm. *Keep your eyes open, Anna, pay attention . . .*

Moments later, an entirely transformed Nonna walked into the kitchen. She headed straight for Alejandro, kissed him on both cheeks and wagged her finger in his face.

'I'm watching you,' she said.

He had the grace to laugh.

'Now let's all have a drop of Pinot Noir while Cordelia tells us some more about the history of sex,' Nonna continued, picking up a bottle. 'But please, *cara*, not the ones who wear the rubber masks. I don't give them the time of day.'

Alejandro looked around the table; his glowing face suggested he was going to enjoy every minute of this conversation.

'You can control want but desire controls you. Remember?' said Cordelia to Nonna.

Nonna waved away her objections and asked, 'So who is next?'

'Dante,' said Cordelia.

There was a groan from much of the room.

'Dante the Italian?' asked Nonna over the hubbub.

'He himself,' said Cordelia.

'Then carry on, of course.'

Tekkies walked into the kitchen just then. He brought the summer night with him.

'Sorry, everyone, Friday night traffic.'

Nonna said, 'Take a plate, my boy, and settle in to be educated.'

Chapter Thirty-Six

Anna weathered the ensuing hours with an almost out-of-body intensity, as if she was both seated beside Tekkies, and floating thirty feet above their heads.

When he'd first arrived, Anna had watched him dish a huge helping of stew onto his plate and then pull up a chair beside her. He'd sat down as if nothing had changed in the world.

His arrival had derailed Nonna's history-of-sex lesson and, instead, Lisbet and Nadia had led them into the usual Friday night business of story deadlines and reviews, followed by an update on the state of play at the building site.

All of which, Anna noticed, Alejandro paid deep attention to. It was as if he'd landed on a foreign planet and was figuring out what he needed to know in order to survive.

Now, they had reached the financial report part of the evening Tekkies opened his computer for up-to-the-minute data.

'Are you ready?' asked Tekkies, with the website up on the laptop in front of him.

There was a general chorus of assent and Tekkies did a roll call of all the stories posted that week and their sales figures.

'"Magnolia", Cordelia's new story, nine thousand and twenty-two hits to the pay site.'

They all clapped, spirits rising. After some hesitation, Alejandro joined in.

'"Kyle and Sammy Go West" by Farhad and Stokely, twenty-two thousand, three hundred, all to the pay site.'

Louder clapping.

'"Seven Birthdays" by Caroline of the foreverstudents,' and he hesitated, 'four hundred and two hits, seventy-one to the pay site.'

There was a low-level groan of disappointment.

'Need to do a little marketing there,' said Lisbet. Her computer pinged loudly. She glanced at the screen and then up at Tekkies. 'You should see this.'

He switched screens on his laptop.

Another ping. 'Oh, wow, oh fucking hell,' said Lisbet.

'Is it bad?' asked Samar from her perch in the corner of the table.

'"Hooked" in Arabic by Samar and Anna . . .' said Tekkies, '. . . got seventy-two thousand, three hundred and twenty-eight hits today,' and he grinned. 'Half of those were to the pay site.'

Anna exchanged a look with Cordelia. That was an awful lot of money.

She leaned across the table to Samar and murmured, 'Congratulations *compagna*!'

Samar smiled. 'We did it, Anna.'

As if that was not enough to take in, Lisbet added, 'Next week we will do our first trial run of "Hooked", "Magnolia", and "Kyle and Sammy" in China.'

Anna didn't hear anything after that apart from a blur of voices raised in excitement and some distant ululation that she assumed came from Samar. She got up to pour herself a drink of water and it occurred to her that maybe this is what you did when you worked from the back foot of doubt. Maybe you just opened the door to possibilities previously unimagined and put one foot in front of the other until you got somewhere.

The next thing she heard was Nonna's voice shouting, 'Anna! Pay attention.'

'I am,' said Anna automatically, and she sat back in her chair, straight as a die.

'Go on, *cara*,' said Nonna to Cordelia.

'OK then,' she said doubtfully, and began again, 'Dante was married . . .'

So is Tekkies. Did you know? Anna wanted to shout, but instead she took a breath and tried to bring herself into the here and now.

'. . . but he was really in love with the unattainable Beatrice,' Cordelia paused, 'who was, well, dead.'

'Oh come on now,' howled Farhad. 'What?'

Cordelia didn't skip a beat. 'She was dead. Which meant the desired and the desirer were blissfully joined as one.'

They all looked at her blankly.

'Anyone get this shit?' asked Lisbet.

'No swearing,' said Anna.

'Hey, can someone turn me around?' said Samar's voice. 'I can't see.'

Sofia arranged the computer so Samar could see the room then she took Alejandro's hand and kissed it.

'Feel free to skip a few hundred years, Cordelia,' muttered Nadia.

'To Freud then,' said Cordelia.

'If we must.'

Nonna thumped the table with her hand. '*Sì*, we must! Or do you want to sound like a *stupido* when those clever people, the ones who write about books, want to know who inspires your stories?'

'I'm not sure they're going to care about that, Nonna,' said Anna quietly.

'And why not?' said the old lady. 'If you are a cook you learn from the great chefs, if you are a doctor, you understand the teachings of the healers and scientists. And now we must learn how all the great thinkers have understood love. *Non parlo la verità?*'

'*Sì, Nonna*,' said Sofia. '*Bravo*.'

'I think you'd better tell us about Freud, Cordelia,' said Nadia.

'Right you are. Well, Freud said the great puzzle of

psychoanalysis was the question of what women *really* want.' Cordelia waited a few beats. 'And he concluded that it is a penis.'

The room exploded.

'I'm sure having one of those is not without its complications,' said Nadia.

'True,' muttered Alejandro, 'too true.' He seemed to be having the time of his life.

Anna watched as Tekkies threw his head back and laughed, a deep, booming sound.

Cordelia banged her spoon on the table. 'Order, order, now.'

Anna could feel the South African's arm resting lightly against the back of her chair.

'I told you it would be better as a musical,' Nadia muttered.

'Go on, my child, go on,' shouted Nonna above the noise.

So Cordelia took them on a lightning-stop tour through Jung with his view of female desire as inner goddess, and Lacan, who thought all desire was doomed, and Wittgenstein, who said desire and its fulfilment was only truly to be found in language.

'Really?' asked Anna.

'Yeah. You've got to know it and give it language to really understand it.'

'That's what we do here,' said Stokely, 'in a way.'

'I can live with that,' said Anna quietly.

The surreal nature of it all was made more so by the five

bottles of Pinot Noir that they consumed. This was not, Anna decided, a group who could hold their liquor.

Next came Reich with his view that the orgasm, however it is achieved, is the purpose of sex, and Kinsey, who disagreed and argued that women preferred men over a vibrator. *What?*

Their faces turned like startled geese towards Cordelia.

'Or another woman, of course,' she said. 'Or someone queer, trans, bi, you know, the whole rich spectrum of possibilities.'

'If they don't kill you first,' said Farhad.

'Jesus,' chimed Nadia, 'no one is going to kill you for having sex.'

'I don't know about that,' said Samar.

The gravity of her statement stilled the chatter for a moment, until Lisbet diffused the gloom with business as usual.

'I don't think I, for one, can take any more philosophy. What's the story schedule for next week, Nadia?'

'I can tell you already that we are one short,' said Nadia.

Stokely looked around the room. 'Come on, lovelies . . .'

Nonna the mischief maker turned to Lisbet. 'You, *cara*! I bet you have a love story.'

There was a moment of silence, then Lisbet took another sip of wine. 'You want my story?'

'*Sì*.'

'You sure?'

Nonna looked at Lisbet. 'I am sure.'

Lisbet took the computer off the table and disappeared into the living room.

★

Anna stood at the front door and saw them all off. Everyone except Lisbet stumbled into the night slightly giddy with wine and good news.

When Anna came back into the kitchen, Nonna raised two fingers and said, 'Two women. I bet you.'

'Nonna, where the hell did that come from?' said Anna. But she knew the answer. It was Nonna's witchery.

Chapter Thirty-Seven

Lisbet's Story

It is well known that the milk from my father's cows, reared on the fynbos and grasses of our Northern Cape meadow, is a seducer. It softens your taste buds with its sweetness and then leaves you needing more. Just like the redhead Elise, who is our neighbour, leaves me.

Elise and her family live on stony ground so her father leases pasture from mine for his two cows. Both fathers agree that milking should not be left to !Kai, the brown farmhand, who pulls too hard and leaves the cows bad-tempered and less willing to produce. So Elise and I milk together; in the barn each winter and in the summer in the lean-to on the side to catch the evening breeze that comes off the cold Atlantic.

Oh, that barn was the talk of the district when my pa

built it. Since when did a cow farmer have money to build a barn? And in those days before diamonds were discovered resting on the seabed where the Orange River meets the Atlantic. Well my father did, and the barn he built was warm in the winter and also on the summer nights when the Atlantic fog came in to make the air arctic.

The barn also made four walls around Elise the redhead and me. So, you could say it kept us alive too. It would not be so if anyone had seen us. Especially the skeletal Widow Westehuizen, who sat on her stoep at the bottom of the road and scanned the veld for misdeeds like the black-tailed kite hunted for prey. She would have had us strung up if she had half an idea of what we were to one another.

Like I said, the barn was always warm, so as we milked we slowly shed our shawls and then our bonnets. To go with her red hair, Elise's neck skin was as white as the cream on the milk. The first time I got close enough to smell her my heart beat in my chest like a hammer and I feared that my father, or !Kai, would surely walk in just as I plucked up the courage to run my lips over her neck.

I knew what I was feeling was downright wrong so I did my best to stop it. *Pinch me hard if I ever think on that redhead again*, I often said to myself as I watched her walk home across the veld. But my nights were always full of her and her soft hands and her cinched waist. *Pinch me and kick me in the shins. And just to be sure, I will bite my own hand when thoughts of her full breasts come into my mind.*

I did that until I had a row of teeth marks on the edge of each palm. I blocked up the back of my throat with my tongue like we learnt to do when we went swimming so I didn't smell her.

And through it all, she waited. Then came the day when !Kai and the two fathers set out for Port Nolloth to buy a pig.

I remember, it rained. It rarely rained in the Richtersveld, the veld was mostly watered by the fog. But that day it poured, and the warmth and hiss of raindrops on the veld outside the barn made us soft with wonder. Any rain in the desert meant an explosion of wild flowers would follow just for a few weeks before it all turned brown and dry and life went on.

Elise was like that rain for me, and she knew it. As we milked she looked at me, the way she often did, and I looked back, as I often did, and my body answered her in a way my mind could not. I could feel the slippery surge collect between my legs and my nipples go hard against the cotton of my bodice.

And then, thanks to all things holy, she decided not to wait any more. I saw her raise up her head and reach behind her to tug at the thin riempie leather strings that held her bodice tight to her chest. It loosened and she let the fabric fall around her waist. And the good Lord did not strike us down, neither me, nor her. The rain kept raining and the cows paid no heed. Her gaze did not leave my face, but mine took in those perfect milky white breasts and the quick short breaths she took beneath them that had them quiver a little with each gasp.

Before I knew it, my milking stool was rolling away from me across the floor and I was reaching across to brush the back of my fingers across her breasts. She smiled and her hands trembled. Then I was on my knees before her with a cherry nipple in my mouth. She closed her eyes and groaned. I ran my fingers up into that red hair and tugged at it. I sank my face into the space behind her ear and breathed in her rainbow of smells and it was my turn to groan. She arched her back and opened her legs so my body could slip between them. And all the while I wondered how it was that she knew me so well.

I felt a tugging at my skirt and the cool of her hands against my thigh. I blushed pink because my body would give me away. And then it came to me that she knew me because she and I were the same. Long had been the nights when we turned to our own hands for pleasure as we dreamed of the other. We learnt from our own bodies and here, finally, we both found the missing piece to our puzzle.

She laughed gently as if she knew that too and slipped her hand under my bloomers. Her fingers were shockingly cool against the heat of my body. I could no more stop myself from following where she led than fight off the certainty that God would take out his vengeance on both of us for this most particular sin.

She took the nub of my sex into her fingertips and

the pleasure poured out of me like the honey from my cousin Saartjie's hives. I could feel her move her own sex against my leg. I took her two nipples in my fingertips and I pinched. She gasped, and moved her fingers quick and hard over my sex until the whole of me slithered out onto her fingers in bliss.

Our eyes were owl-wide and dilated as we gazed at one another. No shame, just an understanding that we were home.

I pushed her gently backwards, so her head rested on the straw-strewn floor and her body remained on the stool. It was a low stool so the angle lifted her hips up to me. I kneeled in front of her. First, I undid the laces of her leather veldskoene – light, handmade calfskin shoes – and freed her long, narrow feet. I kissed the arches where the skin remained delicate. I ran my fingers up her calves and found what I knew I would, that her muscles were long, like that dancer I saw when we visited family in Cape Town three Christmases ago. I pushed her skirt up and along her skin and watched the hair stand on end as the fabric moved across it.

I knew that, in spite of my obedient character, if my pa or even the Widow Westehuizen happened to walk into that barn just then, I would've screamed, *Out, get out, I'm not finished here. You can have me when I have supped.* And they would have obeyed, such was my passion.

She groaned, impatient. Her undergarments were simple, thin cotton with a row of small buttons on the top. I undid them slowly, making sure I pulled the fabric against her sex as I did so. I watched her wet the white cotton until it was transparent and I could see she was a redhead here too.

Finally, there was nothing between my hands and her sex, swollen with want and luscious pink, like coral. A lick, and she opened further. I slid my fingers inside her and she contracted around them. I brought my mouth down on her and if she hadn't been made of strong human muscle she would have come asunder as she rose up.

Her own hands held her breasts and as I pushed into her and sucked I could feel her pleasure gathering.

She cried out and felt her whole being clench and release and clench again, in waves, as she gave into it.

If they had seen us then, so wild, they would have dragged us out like feral horses and stoned us. But they did not.

Afterwards, as we lay in the straw like seed pods cracked open, I could see by the way she looked at me with her lazy gaze, her wanton, satisfied look that said *I am yours*, that we would meet again in this place, and for the first time in eighteen years, I was complete.

Anna leant back in her chair, completely drained. It wasn't as if she'd expected her friend to have a conventional sex life, but the salty truth of her need for a female partner made Anna wonder if she'd paid enough attention to who Lisbet was.

It was the bare bones of a story but it rang true. And it came with the whiff of Lisbet's desert homeland and the longing that lived inside the people who inhabited it.

What shook Anna now, though, was the physical loneliness that must have attended Lisbet's long marriage. Her vivacious friend had lived almost her whole adult life without the matching piece to her puzzle.

Chapter Thirty-Eight

It was very late when Anna heard the front door open. She was still working on Lisbet's story and the sound alarmed her. She peered into the hallway and saw Luke close the door behind him with a studied attention, swaying on his feet.

'Lukey?'

He started when she spoke, and turned around. He had to lean against the wall for support.

'Where've you been?'

'Out,' he said.

'You didn't tell me you were going anywhere.'

'And you didn't notice I'd gone.'

His face was unduly pale.

'You OK?'

'Fine.'

'I don't think so, love.' She stepped forward to take his arm. He pushed her away and stumbled towards the downstairs loo but he didn't quite make it in time and some of his vomit splattered on the grey carpet.

Anna opened the lid. 'The sooner you get it out of your system, the better.'

She pulled off his jacket and then held his drooping fringe off his face as he retched into the bowl.

It went on for a long time. Finally, he sat back against the wall. Exhausted. Wretched. He looked up at Anna and said, 'I miss my dad.'

Then he closed his eyes.

Running long distance was Luke's way of taking time out from a noisy world. He had run cross country races across the green spaces of Hampstead Heath every Sunday morning for almost two years. Anna did her best to attend all his competitive events. He never directly asked her to but she knew it mattered to him, this morning more than most because of the excesses of the night before.

The nature of the trail meant that Luke would disappear into the trees on occasion and for these minutes she would read the paper, or chat with other parents.

Today it was raining so she was alone under Peter's golf umbrella which for some reason he hadn't taken with him. She sat on the bench near the finishing line and opened her paper, shrill with dark news about rising anti-immigrant sentiment in Europe.

She and Nonna talked about it often. Each time, her grandmother would shake her head and say, 'That can only mean trouble, Anna. Divisions in Europe are like poison, they spread all over the world, and are never forgotten. We know this, *cara*, we have tasted it.'

Luke rounded the corner at the bottom of the hill. He was in the lead but he was hurting. She could see from the way his left foot hit the track that he was injured. He kept on going, even when the front runners began to pass him.

If Anna's father had been watching he would have said, *See, Anna, the boy has grit.*

In the car on the way home Luke put the cold compress his coach had given him around his ankle and rested his foot on the dashboard.

No weight on your leg, Lukey, she remembers shouting as he ran onto the beach when he was three or four with a torn ligament. Instead of stopping he'd somersaulted onto his hands then flipped at double speed back onto one leg, and then again, just so he could keep up with the others on their way to the water.

Anna chatted as they drove home across London in the rain. She was aware that she was talking too much but there was something about the child's stoic silence that alarmed her.

When they got home they found Bouchra waiting for them in the kitchen.

Anna stopped in her tracks at the sight of her friend – so familiar and yet so shockingly new. She had to look away because it seemed to her, in a glance, that Bouchra had been plundered.

Someone has taken out my insides with an ice-cream scoop, she'd once said. And they had, Anna could see it.

Bouchra stood up when they came in, uncertain. Anna was equally unsure. It was left to Luke to bridge the gap. He limped into Bouchra's embrace and mumbled, 'Hello, Bouchra-auntie,' as he had so many times over the years.

His simple greeting brought their shared life back into the room. Every tender word spoken, every meal cooked and eaten together, every rite of passage – first bike ride, first tooth, first kiss, first shared holiday – settled around them like a familiar garment made comfortable with wear.

You don't give that up without a fight, thought Anna with a shudder. How petty their old rupture now seemed.

'Is it the Achilles?' Bouchra asked Luke.

'Sprained ankle, maybe,' said the boy.

'Sit, *habibi*.'

And he sat on the kitchen chair while Bouchra tended to his foot; packed it with ice, and raised it to reduce the swelling. She dug out the ibuprofen and gave him two because she knew, of course, where it lived.

Anna made them all a cup of tea and piled a plate high with Nonna's biscotti. They crunched and sipped together, exchanging light-hearted news of children and of events in Salina.

It was only when they were saying goodbye at the door that Anna said, 'We've got a new writer. She's based in Nablus.'

'You found someone in Palestine who writes this rubbish?'

'Actually, she found us. She's on an unpaid sabbatical and needs to make a living.'

'And now you need a translator?'

Anna nodded.

Bouchra considered her for a moment. 'Can I work here, with everyone else?'

'It's pretty cramped.'

'Doesn't matter.'

'Then of course.'

Bouchra nodded. 'OK.'

'Thank you.'

'No, don't thank me,' she started walking down the path, 'just forgive me for being an ass when your roof blew off.'

When Tekkies texted Anna to meet him at the new building he insisted, gently but firmly, that she come alone.

The purpose of this consultation, he said, was to discuss the design of Anna's personal workspace. He suggested that they meet at the end of the day, so they could see how the light changed from late afternoon to sunset.

On this visit, Anna found no cocky youngster at the entrance insistent on dressing her in protective gear, only Tekkies on a picnic blanket in her 'office' with his legs hanging over the edge into nothingness. The old windows were still out and the new glass not yet in, but it was *theirs*.

He got up to greet her and she, again, felt the kick of his physical power. 'He's a married man, Anna,' she said to herself again; it was becoming her mantra.

He showed her the newly exposed beams and the trusses

criss-crossing one another across the length of the roof now framed by a web of scaffolding.

'It'll never fall down.'

'*Bloedhout*,' Anna said, feeling the foreignness of his language roll over her tongue.

When the tour was over Tekkies pulled a bottle of red and two plastic cups out of his backpack.

'I've been saving this Syrah,' he said as he uncorked the bottle. 'It's from the Swartland, north of Cape Town. I don't think you'll have tasted anything like it.'

All of a sudden, it felt like a date. Was it a date?

Chapter Thirty-Nine

The sinking sun reflected in the windows of the surrounding buildings sent a slick of pink light into the room. Anna felt her body begin to warm up in spite of what her mind was telling her.

He poured the wine, handed her a glass and watched as she took a sip.

'Nice?'

She smiled at the flavour that flowed across her palate. 'Oh, lovely, dry anise. Hot country vines.'

He laughed. 'Exactly.'

She took another sip.

'Do you like quiet when you work?' he asked. 'Complete quiet?'

'Mostly,' she said. 'Sometimes the right music can be a life-saver, played so loud the walls shake. But ordinary life noise, like other people's phone calls and someone cooking popcorn makes me . . .'

'Tetchy?' he said.

'Yeah.'

He saw her. He did.

Anna lay back on the blanket to calm the involuntary quickening of just about every part of her. She watched the last of the daylight slide across the ceiling and wondered if he would understand if she told him that nobody had ever asked her that question before.

'We could install a pull-out wall and soundproof it for when you want to shut everything out.'

She sat up. 'You can do that?'

He smiled. 'We can.'

She saw small suns reflected in his eyes.

'And you'll need a shelf for your books,' he said.

'My books?'

'The novels.'

'Oh. Not a very big shelf.'

'I read them all.'

'The last one isn't finished,' said Anna.

'I know.'

'Oh.'

'Lisbet gave it to me.'

'Jesus.'

'She said I was making her betray her best friend but I made her do it anyway.'

Their eyes met. The crinkles around his eyes were deep.

'I *love* that boy,' he said softly.

'What boy?'

'Boubakar.'

'D'you want to know what happens to Boubakar?' she asked.

'Very much.'

'I don't know myself.'

'You will one day.'

'If I finish it.'

He glanced at her. 'Finish it, Anna.'

She stared at him. Married. Tekkies was *married*, she told herself again.

'My mother always said, find the gold, Tekkies, where other people see nothing.'

'And did you?' she asked.

'She thought so,' he said with a smile. 'I found my first radio in a dustbin in the Port Nolloth caravan park and I taught myself how to fix it. Then TVs, and then computers came along.'

It made sense to Anna that he should have been formed by such a world, and such a woman.

'Lisbet tells me you built a big tech company.'

'Not big. Small. But I was lucky when it came time to sell it.'

Anna looked at him and he at her.

'Tell me about your father,' he said.

'Oh, there's not much to tell. He taught music his whole life, he raised his children. But mostly, he just waited.'

'For what?'

'My mother to come through the door.'

'I believe it.'

'He sat in the chair by the window in the living room,' she said. 'One day, months after she'd died, I heard him say to himself, in German, ". . . she made herself a bed inside my ear. And slept in me".'

Both were quiet a moment.

'It wasn't until my German poetry class at university that I realised that it was from a Rilke poem,' she said.

'Beautiful,' he murmured.

Anna dared not look at Tekkies as they sat and sipped. Being with him on the picnic blanket as the sun moved across the city of London from luminous evening to velvet night was almost hallucinogenic.

'And you?' she asked.

'My dad was a farmer. With aspirations.'

'For what?'

'To rise up in the world.'

'Did he?'

'*Ja*, he just didn't take my mom and me with him.'

He scratched his chin, uncomfortable, Anna saw, at talking about himself.

'Is your mum in Port Nolloth?'

He nodded. 'With her bloodwood tree.'

'How did she come to be there?'

'You really want to know?'

Yes, you idiot, she wanted to shout. But instead, in her

wisdom, she leant back against a nearby pillar and waited for the chance to give in to his story, and the pulse she could see throbbing in his temple as he told it.

His tale began on the South African frontier, the wild, dry, sparsely populated landscape to which his great-grandfather fled to escape the pogroms sweeping Lithuania in the early nineteen-hundreds. Like many such immigrants, he arrived with nothing in his pocket.

He became a *smous*, a travelling salesman, selling ribbons, linen and cough syrup to farmers in the Northern Cape from the back of his wagon. Word came to him of fistfuls of diamonds in the sea at Port Nolloth and he found his way there. For a few years, he made a living selling stones. He married the lovely Rachel Kaplan who he met through the Hebrew congregation in the neighbouring town of Springbok. But by the time Tekkies' mother was born, the diamonds were over and the fields further out not yet discovered.

'Small fortunes made, and then lost, that was our story,' Tekkies said.

'Until you came along,' she said.

Tekkies' face was soft. 'There's gold in your stories, Anna,' he said finally.

Gold where there was nothing.

Before she could stop herself, the words, formed and waiting in the back of her mind, propelled themselves out of her mouth.

'Would your wife like them?'

'Sorry?'

'My books?'

She realised too late that what she wanted him to say was *There is no wife.*

Tekkies turned away from her. He didn't answer for a long time.

'She doesn't read much,' he said at last. Then he raised his hand to cover his face.

'Tekkies?' she said softly.

He glanced at Anna and she could see that he had said all he was capable of. He just didn't have it in him.

And neither, she realised, did she.

'I need to get back,' she said. 'I left a casserole in the oven for supper.'

And she got to her feet.

'Wait.'

'I can't,' she said.

He got up with her and his jaw was set. 'Please.'

'Thank you for the wine,' she said, 'and the sunset. And this beautiful building.'

And she walked across the big open space to the exit. As she did so, she felt his eyes on her every step of the way.

Chapter Forty

When Anna got home she found Luke and Nonna in the kitchen, laying the table for supper.

Luke glanced up and cocked his head. 'Have you been running?'

'Running?'

'You have pink in your cheeks like you do when you've been running.'

Nonna murmured, 'She's got the glow, that is for sure.'

'What?' snapped Anna.

'*Sto solo dicendo*, Anna, I'm just saying.'

'Enough!' said Anna to her grandmother. Nonna raised her hands in surrender.

Anna sniffed the air. 'What's that smell?' She turned her back on Luke and Nonna and pulled open the oven, a cloud of smoke billowed out. 'Shit, bugger. Somebody turned it up!'

'Whoa, Mama,' said Luke.

'Me,' said Nonna. 'That was me.'

Anna looked at her grandmother.

'Sorry. I thought that low it would never cook, and then I forgot I had done it. *Mi dispiaci.*'

'There's no dinner, Lukey,' said Anna and hung her head.

'It's OK, Mama, we can have scrambled eggs,' he said.

Nonna pushed up on the table. 'I will do the eggs,' she said, 'as penance.'

When Anna began to object, Nonna waved her finger at her and said, 'There are five things that turn a person into a danger in the kitchen.' She lifted her fingers one at a time as she listed them: 'Old age, as you have just seen with your own eyes, a bereavement, when a baby is born, the hot flushes, and falling in love.'

'Nonna, you really need to stop . . .' cautioned Anna. She looked at her grandmother, daggers drawn.

Nonna simply said, '*Cara*, have a glass of wine and let me make the eggs.'

The file named 'archive' to which the story of Boubakar had been consigned had hung on the upper left side of Anna's desktop for so long and been so consistently denied, that when Anna went to click on it she half expected it to shoot out like a hooded snake.

It was midnight and the house was quiet. Liebe was curled up under her feet.

She didn't think much about what she was doing, just that this was a reunion whose time had come. In the air were the simple facts that there was now a little money in the bank and that her children seemed more-or-less to have survived the rupture of their family life. Even Nonna had found something of a groove.

What she absolutely would not have been able to see but which was the real reason for her presence there was the one intimacy she most sorely wanted that was not hers to have. Once again, love and its shadow of loss sat on her shoulder as she sought less dangerous friendships on the page.

The manuscript opened and Anna scrolled through all sixty-two-thousand four hundred and twenty-two words. The size of it gave her comfort.

She knew better than to read it on the screen so she turned on the printer and stood by it to watch the pages roll out. Anna began to read.

At first, she stood rooted next to the printer and read each page as it rolled out but soon the machine outpaced her and she sat at the kitchen table.

She read about Boubakar and his search for his mother on the streets of London. She read about the churchgoers and the crooks, the charismatic traders and the hardy Londoners the boy came to know. She even recognised the people at the advice centre who had been her guides and teachers. She could hear the verity of their descriptions and feel the daily movement of their lives.

It was a compelling story.

Every so often she got up to retrieve more pages from the printer and sat down again to read. She had no sense of the passage of time but the hours of darkness were over by the time she was done. She sat back in her chair.

She did not, at that moment, know how to give language to the thing she now understood.

She sat and waited for the words to form. And when they came she could barely stop herself from sliding her fingers into her hair, bunching them into fists, and beginning to pull. She could do it until there was no hair left on her head.

For she had no business writing the story of Boubakar.

It wasn't *his* story.

It was hers.

She'd hung the weight of her one unbearable loss on to the coat-tails of his suffering. How then could she see *him* to write his life? How could she know the shape of his deprivation, the depth of his fear, his victories, his failures? How could she see how he tied his shoes? Or ate with his fingers? Even those vivacious imperfections that would have made him real, had sunk under her good intentions.

She hung her head at last and whispered, 'Forgive me.'

It was over. He was gone.

'We'll just go gently today,' said Stokely.

He still taught them yoga on Wednesdays but today Bouchra, Nadia and Farhad were all delayed by deadlines looming at The Love Factory so Anna and Stokely were alone.

As always, he could sense Anna's state of mind and typically, when he did this he could also feel the grit in her depths. Not today. Anna felt uncertain and un-held-up as she had in the worst of her crisis with Peter. More maybe. They went through the whole sequence very slowly. In every pose Anna felt the absence of Boubakar until she was as skinless as a rabbit. All she had was the self she stood up in. Lucky, then, that Stokely was able to gather up what was left and show her how to carry on.

Now there was just silence.

They were in the final stretching sequence when Stokely said, 'Oh, Tekkies left a message about a meeting with the window man.'

'When?'

'I think he said he'd see you in the morning. You need to approve the frames.'

Anna closed her eyes and said, 'He's married.'

'So I heard,' said Stokely. 'But then so was I once.'

Anna sat up. 'What?'

'Her name was Bea and we met on the first day of university.'

'How long did it last?'

'Not long.' He smiled. 'She's still a good friend.'

Anna lay back down on the mat. 'I think he's been married for a hundred years. He's that kind of man.'

'Not everything is how it seems,' said Stokely the reluctant sage.

Chapter Forty-One

The first few days of Bouchra's employment at The Love Factory went more smoothly than Anna could've hoped. She refrained from referring to the work as rubbish, or smut, and she laughed often.

There were some anomalies in her translations, and a certain straining after-effect that betrayed her rookie skills but, overall, Bouchra had an instinct for finding the voice of a story.

Towards the end of the week, Cordelia, Bouchra, Stokely and Anna were working in the living room when the doorbell rang. Bouchra, being the least engaged in other tasks at that moment, got up to answer it.

She came back into the room with an armful of roses.

'Oh, you shouldn't have,' said Stokely playfully.

'I don't think she did,' said Cordelia.

'There's no name on the envelope,' said Bouchra and she

proceeded to open it. As she pulled out the card, she pursed her lips.

A man in full black bondage gear, including a mask, stood on the rooftop of a building. The only part of his body that was unclothed was his very erect penis. Bouchra put the card upright on the table for everyone to see.

Cordelia groaned and put her head in her hands.

'Oops,' said Stokely.

'What is this about?' asked Bouchra.

Anna glanced at Cordelia and sighed. It was Stokely who came to her rescue.

'They're for Cordelia,' he said.

'What are?'

'The roses.'

'And the invitation . . .' said Cordelia.

'But what is it?'

'It's an invitation to an event at a BDSM club,' said Cordelia.

'And what is that exactly?'

'Bondage, discipline . . . you know.'

'Is this what you're into?'

Cordelia glanced at Anna and then at Bouchra. 'Sometimes.'

There was silence for a moment.

Anna knew that Cordelia's response didn't begin to be the whole answer. An empathetic word from Bouchra would've gone a long way just then but, instead, the newest associate of The Love Factory turned to its founding partner and said, 'Let me ask you something . . .'

'OK.'

'Has it not occurred to you that you could get hurt in one of these encounters and that it would be your own fault?'

'Not helpful, Bouchra,' said Anna.

'And how certain can you be that some crazy person won't get dangerous ideas from your stories?'

'What?' asked Cordelia.

'Hang on a second here,' said Anna. She could see that both Bouchra and Cordelia were losing their cool.

'I don't write abuse fantasies, Bouchra,' snapped Cordelia.

'There was some pretty rough stuff in the one I read,' said the Syrian.

'Those are called tropes, Bouchra, it's role play, and fantasy . . .' said Cordelia.

But Bouchra wasn't listening any more. She turned to Anna and said, 'And what about Samar?'

'What about her?' asked Anna, startled.

'What if some bearded wacko decides she should be "disciplined" for writing her stories?'

'We talked about the risks when she joined us,' said Anna. 'She chose to do it. And I think she's adult enough to make her own decisions.'

'I don't think you have any idea what you are dealing with, Anna,' said Bouchra.

'How's that?'

Bouchra turned on her. 'You're a white person! You've never had to fight for anything.'

Anna paused. She and her two friends had often referred,

in their banter, to their ethnic and racial differences. It almost always made them laugh.

This time the room fell quiet.

Bouchra faltered for a moment, then her features hardened and she looked away.

'Seems to me there's a whole lot of hate out there in the world,' said Cordelia, 'but I don't go looking for it.'

'Maybe *you* do, Bouchra,' said Stokely quietly. 'What d'you think about that?'

It was ten fifteen and Anna was late. The cocky little bugger at the building site was back at the counter. 'Here you go, love,' he said, and piled the usual gear on the counter.

'No thanks,' said Anna.

She was not going to wear his ridiculous plastic hat. He let her pass. As she waited for the ancient lift Anna could feel him eyeing her legs.

Tekkies was on a scaffold halfway up the large Georgian-era window on the far side of the room – he was scraping paint off the glass when Anna walked in. He looked down, smiled. He was alone.

'Where's the window man?'

'I lied.'

'The architect?'

'Sorry. I just . . .' He scrambled off the scaffold and approached her. 'How are you?'

Anna stared at him for a moment, then looked away.

'I'm . . . OK.'

He nodded but didn't speak.

'I should get back.' Anna reached for her handbag to take her leave.

'Can you give me a hand,' he said, 'while you're here?'

She looked at him.

'I've been trying to keep costs down by doing a lot of the floor and paint removal myself but I've run out of time.'

Anna looked around the room: a lot had happened since she was last here, all the linoleum was up and stacked in a neat pile. The pillars and beams were stripped. In the very far corner of the room was a sleeping bag, laid out under the window.

'Have you been sleeping here?'

'Only sometimes. They're coming to do the windows tomorrow and some of them are still covered in paint so I can't tell if they need to be replaced or not.'

She put her bag down on the floor.

'Thank you,' he said. 'Put those on.' He handed her a pair of gloves.

He led her to the scaffold and helped her up onto it. He gave her a window scraper and showed her how to push from the bottom of the window frame so that a curl of white paint lifted off the glass.

'You'll need more pressure than you think,' he said.

As she pushed, another strip of paint peeled off the glass and she saw sky beyond it, and the roofs of the neighbouring buildings.

Tekkies worked beside her so that when she lost her way he

was ready to right her. 'Try coming at it from the other side. Hold it like that. Watch out for your fingers.'

In this way, and together, they continued to remove the paint from the glass and the room slowly got lighter.

At one point, she stopped to suck on a blister forming on her finger. If he noticed, he made no comment, just kept working.

'Her name is Sylvia,' he said, after a long time.

There was a pause.

'I know.'

'We met at university.'

'Tekkies, you don't have to—'

But he went on, 'We chose to live in Port Nolloth because we liked it, but Cape Town was where the work was so I was away a lot.'

He was quiet for a moment, then he said, 'I was gone when the gangster kids from the township broke into our house. In court afterwards they said they only wanted to take my drill set and her computer, but they found her there too.'

'Oh God.'

'And she knew them. They were scared. So, they hit her until she stopped moving to warn her what would happen if she gave their names to the police.'

Anna whispered, 'Oh no.'

'She can't speak, or follow a conversation. She can't walk, or feed herself.'

'Tekkies—'

'And she can't read.'

'I'm so sorry.'

'For eleven years, I've told myself that she would get better, and for eleven years I've known that she would not.'

'So sorry . . .'

Anna turned to face him and he lifted his hand up to stop her. He had more to say.

She rested her head against the glass and she waited. She could see the people in the street below, small, and intent. She could hear his breath. She could smell his scent.

'It's been a long time.'

Anna understood that he meant it was time for him to let go of that.

She sat back, took off her glove and held out her hand to him.

After a time, he took it.

Chapter Forty-Two

The whole Love Factory crew was sat around the kitchen table, tucking into a spread of hummus and freshly baked flatbread, olives, tahini and spicy eggplant when Anna and Tekkies stumbled in together.

'Sorry we're late,' Anna said as she sat down, covered in dust, tired as a gravedigger, and pungent from her effort.

'*Ja*, sorry,' said Tekkies as he pulled up a chair.

Lisbet was less than pleased at their late arrival. Anna blew Sofia a kiss. She did not return it.

Anna tried again, '*Ciao amore*.'

Her daughter nodded but she did not smile.

Bouchra and Nadia both avoided her gaze.

'We started without you,' said Lisbet.

Cordelia smiled, 'The numbers are good, especially the Middle East and China.'

'Great,' said Anna and she stretched across the table for some bread.

She and Tekkies had worked in silence for the whole afternoon so that by the time it was growing dark, the whole expanse of glass and the lights of London beyond it, had been revealed.

Nonna looked up at her. 'Reem from over the road saved us from starvation.'

Anna said, 'Oh, Reem, yes.' She remembered the night she and Liebe had met her in the park and walked her home. 'It looks delicious.'

Lisbet muttered, 'I'm glad you approve.'

Anna glanced up. 'I'm sorry, what?'

Lisbet shrugged. 'I'm just saying.'

'Liebe ate the foot off the sofa . . .' said Nadia.

'Is Lukey around?' Anna asked.

'. . . because no one took her for a walk today.'

'Luke? You must be joking,' said Lisbet.

'Why do you say that?'

'He's out and about with his girlfriend, of course.'

'He didn't tell me he was going out.'

'I rest my case,' said Lisbet.

'*Bly stil*, Lisbet,' said Tekkies sharply. 'That's enough.'

There was a brief pause and then Nadia started up again. 'Your story editing is late too.'

'And that's holding up the translators,' added Lisbet.

Anna stopped eating and put her flatbread back onto her plate. 'You're all going to bust my chops because I'm late for a meeting? Really?'

Neither Nadia or Lisbet would answer. The room fell silent. Everyone stopped eating.

Maybe if they had been alone Lisbet could've said that what she really minded was how invisible she felt when she was with Anna and Tekkies. That even when they weren't in the same room she could tell they wanted to be. And Nadia might've confessed how much she envied them that. But neither of the friends were going to spill the beans in front of everyone even if they could've found the words.

The three women regarded one another, each daring the other to fold first.

Then, finally, Nadia smiled.

Anna said quietly, 'I love you too.'

'And I love this eggplant.' Lisbet glanced one last time at Tekkies and Anna.

'Oh, thank God,' said Farhad. 'I couldn't take another cat fight.'

And with that the tension in the room was dispelled and everyone returned to their dinner.

When the washing up was done and Tekkies had filled their glasses with sweet dessert wine, Nonna dipped her biscotti, and said, 'I'm wondering when Dr Thomas is going to begin our next lesson.'

Cordelia laughed. 'Oh, Nonna, you're alone in that desire, I think.'

'I want to hear,' said Samar from the screen on the table.

'And me,' said Sofia, 'otherwise I'll be a *stupido* when the clever book people show up.'

'I'm up for it,' said Lisbet. 'Too old for enlightenment but game to shake the tree.'

'Pass me the wine,' muttered Bouchra.

'OK,' said Cordelia. 'The good news is that we have arrived, at last, at some women theorists.'

'Yes!' said Sofia.

'Simone de Beauvoir, Gloria Steinham, Kimberlé Crenshaw—'

'A black woman. Now that's nice,' said Stokely.

'Who invented the concept of intersectionality,' said Cordelia. 'Huge!'

'Don't forget Martha Nussbaum,' said Anna.

'And Gayle Rubin,' said Cordelia

'What about Kristeva?' asked Sofia.

Anna glanced at her daughter and wondered when it was she had become so well informed.

'What did she say, this Kristeva?' asked Nonna.

'That the third phase of feminism, which is where we are now, must explore multiple sexual identities,' said Cordelia. 'She proposes that there are as many sexualities as there are individuals.'

'Well that's totally true,' said Sofia.

'Not where I come from,' muttered Samar from the small frame of the computer screen, 'Sorry to *always* be the bearer of bad news.'

'But wasn't the Middle East once very permissive?' asked Sofia.

'Yes. Long ago,' said Samar. 'In fact, we studied the Abbasid empire on my Women's Studies course.'

'And that is?' asked Lisbet.

'A civilisation that saw a great flowering of sexuality in its culture. It stretched from the shores of the Mediterranean to the borders of India and produced some great erotic stories.'

'OK, so, how did we get from there to here?' she asked.

'Decline,' said Samar. 'The slow loss of influence and power of the Arab world.'

'Not unlike the great United Kingdom,' said Stokely.

'It's been happening for longer in the Middle East. Long enough for it to have taken its toll on Arab identity in the whole region,' she said. 'It's easier for the fundamentalists to blame the whole catastrophe on the permissive West. So, we have become enemies.'

'And the wars have started,' said Nonna, 'As they do.'

'They have,' said Samar.

'That's terrifying,' said Sofia.

Samar smiled at the young girl. 'You can take heart that Cordelia and her third-phase feminists, and me and my Arab intellectuals, have a different vision for the future.'

'Me too!' said Sofia, 'And so do all my people.'

Anna wondered how her child found herself so effortlessly part of a community. It made her happy.

'A shared future.' Stokely murmured as if he had heard her thoughts.

'And peaceful,' said Nonna.

'Sexuality freely realised is liberty achieved,' said Samar quietly. 'For those who love . . .'

Bouchra sprang out of her seat like a jack-in-the-box. Anna could see that if she could've possibly stopped herself, she would've.

'I'm sorry,' she said and she looked at Anna, 'I know I'm on probation from my last . . .' she seemed suddenly to be at a loss for words.

'Outburst?' said Stokely.

'Outburst, thank you. But I just can't believe what I'm hearing.'

Anna could see Lisbet trying not to laugh.

'I mean I made it through the bloody theorists,' Bouchra continued and then she broke into Arabic, '*hatta hal jadbeh . . .*'

Samar laughed.

'Even that idiot Julia whatshername,' Bouchra continued, 'I shut my mouth through the whole bit about Arab erotica and the Abbasids, but that last comment about sex and liberty being one . . . I mean that is just . . .' she sucked in a breath and searched for a phrase that would sufficiently communicate her scorn, and then shrieked '. . . bat-*sheet* crazy!'

There was a stunned silence. Out of which Tekkies was heard to say, '*Ja*, well you lost me there too, Samar, I have to confess.'

'Oh, thank God,' said Bouchra, 'Somebody else has some sense.'

'But then again, I mean I'm a white South African and a . . .' he hesitated.

'Man?' muttered Cordelia.

'Man,' said Tekkies, 'So who cares what I think?'

The women stared at him.

'Right?'

'Right,' said Sofia and she got up to wash her hands at the sink. Anna watched her, wide-eyed with surprise.

Chapter Forty-Three

The technicalities of Anna and Peter's divorce were resolved simply enough. Everything of the not-very-much she had shared with her husband was split in half. Anna would keep the house until Luke finished school and then she would have to sell. Now that she was earning, she might decide to buy Peter out. It felt good to have that possibility in her future.

The children saw their father every second weekend at first and then every third. Both had busy lives and, increasingly, their weekends were taken up with friends and romance.

On one of Sofia and Luke's early weekend visits with Peter he introduced them to his girlfriend, Fern.

'She's an idiot,' said Sofia.

'I think she's just young,' said the more compassionate Luke.

'They look ridiculous together,' said Sofia. 'Yuk, yuk, yuk.'

Peter phoned Anna in late August. She remembered the

exact moment because she had her nose in a new story and, unusually for that stage, it was going well.

'You want to do what?' asked Anna, surprised.

'I want to come home.'

'Oh.'

'Anna?'

'Yes?'

'Nothing's working. Especially not Fern.'

'Oh,' said Anna.

'Well what do you say?'

'No.'

'What?'

'It's not possible, Peter.'

'Why not?'

'I don't think you want me to answer that question.'

Of course, that wasn't the end of it. She and Peter were bound together in myriad ways, and always would be, but the idea that they could begin again was impossible – that boat had sailed.

Anna had no idea how her two children got wind of their father's change of heart but it made for some rocky times in the Carlyle Road kitchen.

'But he's sorry, Mama!' said Luke.

'He's got nothing to be sorry for, Lukey. For him the marriage ended. It didn't make him a bad man.'

'Well he wants to come back to us now and I don't know what you are waiting for.'

'No, he doesn't, not really, he's going through a hard time. He'll be OK. The important thing is for you and your dad to see one another. He'll always be your father and he loves you.'

'Mama!'

'What?'

'You're a monster.'

'No,' she said, 'I just need to give Dad a chance, a real chance, to find the right person for him.'

'But it's YOU!' he shouted. 'You, and me, and Sofia.'

Anna shook her head. 'I love him, Lukey, but it's not me.'

The boy, in his fury, spat at her, 'You just don't know how!'

'How to what?'

The red patches high up on his cheeks were a measure of his rage and frustration.

'Love anyone!'

Sofia was no less opinionated. She waited for a moment when she and her mother were alone in the kitchen making breakfast smoothies to declare her hand.

Anna was forewarned by the furious speed with which her daughter chopped the ginger, washed the spinach, squeezed the orange juice. When Sofia speeded up there was trouble coming.

'You OK?' she asked.

'Course,' said Sofia. She threw a chopped nectarine and half a tray of ice into the blender and said, 'It's him, isn't it? That Tekkies?'

Before Anna could answer Sofia hit the button and the blender shrieked into motion.

'What?' shouted Anna over the noise.

Sofia paused the machine. 'I see the way you look at one another.'

'Hang on a minute!'

Sofia turned the blender up to maximum so Anna had to shout.

'He's my friend. That's all.'

'Oh, grow up, Mama, he's crazy about you,' she shouted back.

'He's married, Sofia!'

'Not really.'

Anna reached for the blender switch and turned it off. The quiet was shocking.

'The last time I looked there wasn't a way to be not really married,' she said.

'Well, you and Dad seemed to manage it.'

Anna couldn't refute that statement – neither could she fault her daughter's instinct for the truth.

She turned away and took two glasses out of the cupboard.

'Put us back together, Mama. If only for Lukey and me,' said Sofia.

And Anna would have, if she could have, instead, she put one foot in front of the other, as she'd learnt to do, and tried to keep the ship of their lives moving steadily forward.

*

Cordelia's graduation offered a welcome distraction. She had, just days before, defended her PhD and, after a gruelling four-hour session with her panel of supervisors, become Dr Cordelia Thomas. You would have thought that a family wedding was upon them, such was the hoo-ha associated with their preparations. Nadia had had the good sense to book tickets months ahead and everyone from The Love Factory had a seat.

Sofia and Anna went shopping. They found a beautiful dress for Sofia and a new pair of shoes to go with an old dress for Anna.

When the shopping was done, and the two were sharing a pot of strong tea and a plate of scones, Anna said, 'I'm sorry I can't give you what you want *amore*.'

'What's that?'

'Dad and me, together.'

Anna saw a shadow cross her daughter's face.

'No. I should've thanked you for holding it together for as long as you did,' said Sofia. 'I know what it cost you.'

'No, you don't . . . no, no.'

Sofia held up her hand to silence her mother and there were real tears gathering in her eyes. 'No. I do know.'

Anna looked at her hands.

'What I don't know,' said Sofia and she fought back her feeling, 'is what it means for me.'

'I see that,' said Anna softly.

'I mean we've discovered gravitational waves in black holes,' said Sofia, 'and invented surgeries to transform people into what they believe to be their authentic gender, but we are still light years away from sorting out how a simple family works.'

'Yeah, hard nut to crack, that.'

'I blame the patriarchy.'

Anna smiled at her earnestness.

'I'm serious. It suits the bastards. Look at Bouchra, and Nadia-auntie, and you,' said Sofia. 'All clever, ambitious women, and then you get married and start families and get sucked in and away from yourselves and the men just keep going. It's just not right, and fair, and equitable.'

'Sofia.'

'Yes, Mama.'

'Make your own money.'

'I plan to,' said the young woman, uncertain of where this was going.

'It will help you know your own mind.'

Sofia took a lungful of air. 'And what if you care about justice? What then?'

All Anna could say as she reached for her daughter's hand was, 'Choose carefully, my angel. Choose with every single cell in your body, your whole spirit and all the power of your mind.'

Anna would have liked to add, choose well so that he will know that the full expression of who you are is part of *his* purpose. So that he will love you for both your successes and your failures. Choose well, my child, so you can be allies. And walk away if you find it is not so. Walk away.

But it was too much life for one teatime. Anna kissed Sofia's hand and they asked for the bill.

Chapter Forty-Four

Nonna was the most lavish in her preparations for Cordelia's graduation. She dug out her diamanté sunglasses and her vintage Vuitton handbag, a gift from her husband on their fiftieth wedding anniversary and used only once before. That great event was Anna's wedding, and when Nonna received admiring comments about her bag she nodded her head and said, 'It is to hold my tissues when I weep.' She did not illuminate whether they were tears of grief, or joy.

When graduation day arrived and Nonna came into the kitchen so attired, Luke's eyes nearly popped out of his head. Sofia applauded Nonna's glamour and so saved the day.

'Close your mouth, Lukey,' said Nonna.

'OK.'

'A lady needs to dress up now and then.' She looked at her grandson. 'Come here.'

Luke got up and stood in front of his grandmother. She

retied his tie and when it was done she looked at him and said, 'My handsome boy. You are going to have to fight off the ladies.'

He blushed.

'But not nearly as much as I had to fight off the young men in my day, so don't you let it go to your head.'

The associates of The Love Factory took up an entire row at the ceremony. They were joined by Cordelia's diminutive mother and sister, both of whom had the same mousy brown hair and blue eyes – like peas in a pod spaced out in perfect generational bites.

Cordelia's mother was dressed carefully in a light green dress and matching shoes. She was tentative in the learned, urban world her daughter inhabited. When she and Anna used the bathroom together before the event, she glanced at herself in the mirror, tugged at her hair and said, 'Looks like I cut this lot with a knife and fork.'

Anna laughed and took her arm.

The brutalist nineteen-seventies concrete building that played host to the event took some warming up, but by the time all the undergraduates had been given their degrees, and the speakers had had their say, and all the families had wept and cheered, they came to the part in the proceedings when the PhDs were conferred. This time, the principal of King's College not only called out the name of the student but their supervisor too, and together mentor and mentee made their way to the stage accompanied by the roars and cheers of the whole crowd.

'Cordelia Thomas, supervised by Dr Frank Melford, I confer on you the degree of Doctor of Philosophy.'

The associates of The Love Factory swept to their feet. It was Stokely and Farhad who shouted the loudest; saintly Stokely, rendered banshee-like by joy for his friend. And Cordelia's mother, whooping with unselfconscious pride was a close second.

When Cordelia walked onto the stage, so small and yet so indefatigable, Anna, too, felt a great love for the wild iconoclast who, almost every day, liberated Anna and her associates from their assumptions.

The tiny Italian restaurant where they all gathered to celebrate was bursting at the seams. In her speech, Cordelia thanked her mum and dad, and her sister. But her deepest gratitude was reserved for someone named Ben: 'Ben who was my first and only love and who set me on this course, even though he didn't know it at the time . . .'

Anna knew she would have to wait for another moment to ask Cordelia more about that. Just then she heard her say, 'Come, let's dance,' and Cordelia led her mother and her sister onto the open space beyond the tables. You couldn't call it a dance floor but it could have been, the way it filled up with moving bodies. Cordelia was, to Anna's surprise, a fabulous dancer. And her mother and sister were quickly at home amongst the bopping bodies.

Farhad took Anna's hand and within minutes they were

Ginger Rogers and Fred Astaire, except more partial to sexy Motown than swing. Anna hadn't let loose like this in years; it shook up her natural joy. Before long the whole room was thumping.

When Anna looked up and saw Tekkies watching her she was surprised – and then pleased. She waved him over but he shook his head and gestured that he would prefer to watch her.

She strutted and jived and she swayed her hips. If there'd been an appropriate table to dance on she would have done that too.

Dancing was thirsty work, and Anna slipped out of the crowd to gulp down a glass of water. She saw Tekkies standing in the passage leading to the loos. He beckoned her over.

Time seemed to stop altogether as Anna stood with Tekkies in the dark, cramped passage. The music was loud; Anna wanted to ask him whether he was ready to dance yet, but neither of them seemed capable of speech.

Tekkies looked down on her and she could see he was trembling.

Then he kissed her . . . sweet as summer plums, and as their mouths met he groaned. It was a kiss like all kisses should be, with a kick in it, and heart, and the promise of more.

Anna heard a sharp sound behind her and tore herself away to see Cordelia barrel out of the crowd.

'Sofia and Luke are here, Anna!' she hissed. 'What the hell are you thinking?'

And to Tekkies she snapped, 'Get a bloody grip.'

The irony of being chided by this wayward philosopher

was not lost on Anna. That she was also right to do so added to the sting.

Anna, Lisbet and Nadia were silent in the car on the way back from the graduation party. The children had gone straight from the celebration to Peter's for the weekend. Nonna had tired early, and taken a cab.

After a few close shaves on the road Lisbet said, 'Pull over, I'm driving.'

And Anna obeyed.

'I haven't been drinking, if that's what you think,' said Anna as she strapped herself in on the passenger seat.

'Thank God,' said Lisbet, 'because who knows what would've happened if you had been.'

Nadia giggled. Lisbet snapped, 'It's not funny.'

'What's not funny?' asked Anna.

'She doesn't understand,' said Lisbet.

'What don't I understand?' asked Anna.

'That Tekkies is in love with you, you bloody idiot. Just wholly and completely in love, and he has been since the day he first laid eyes on you.'

'What?'

Lisbet did not answer. Anna could see her struggling. 'Lisbet?'

'I've seen that boy go through hell for love, I've seen him be true and devoted and then bereft. And I've seen you . . .' She faltered.

'You've seen me what?' asked Anna.

'Nothing.'

'No, we are in too far to stop now.'

Lisbet drove in silence.

'Please.'

'I've seen you live with a man you didn't love for half a lifetime.'

Anna saw the lights ahead of them change from red to green.

'And it makes me scared that you don't know what it is.'

'What is?'

'What it is to love.'

'Oh.'

'And if you don't know that, how will you take care of my boy Tekkies?'

Anna looked out of the window and focused on the struggle to manage the contents of her stomach. A lurch of the car over a traffic bump, and she lost the battle.

Chapter Forty-Five

When Anna was clean, and in her pyjamas, she sat in the open bay window of her bedroom, and dialled her brother's number on her mobile. Stefano's voice was as tender as she knew it would be.

'Sorry to phone so late,' she said.

'You OK?' he asked.

'I miss you, Stef,' she murmured.

'Miss you too, sis. When are you coming?' he asked.

'Christmas, I hope.'

'Good,' he said.

'I'll light a candle on your birthday,' she said.

Anna could hear Stef pause before he said, '*Sì. Grazie.*'

That's what her mother had done on each of their birthdays. She lit a candle and put it in the bay window of the living room so everyone would know it was a special day in their house.

'I planted gardenia today,' he said. 'In the window boxes.'

'Ah that smell.'

'Yes. In the summer it will be long enough to cut for the table.' Anna knew that this small, dignified life was all he could manage. He was marked, still, by the great loss of his childhood years.

A thought came winging at Anna from the darkness; maybe Lisbet was right, maybe she'd never risked real love either.

'I *will* marry him, Nonna,' Anna had shouted all those years ago, 'I will!'

'But, Anna, you know what *love* looks like!' her grandmother had said. 'You know, my *cara*.'

Anna would not meet her grandmother's gaze. Did she mean Anna's parents? Hearing their laughter float through the house when she and her brother were in bed, warm laughter, and the music they played together, each so perfectly attuned to the other?

'Anna, *è necessario conoscere l'amore*.' You must have love, Nonna had said, beseeching her.

Anna willed herself not to run for the door.

If she'd been older, Anna would perhaps have been able to scream at her grandmother: *I can't risk it, Nonna, don't you see that?*

Did the old woman not know that she loved Peter precisely because he would not reawaken those parts of her stunted by life's cruelty? It was his blinkered goodness that made it possible for her to give him her heart.

But she didn't know how to say that, or to even know it herself, so she'd just slammed her way out of the house and into her life with Peter.

Lisbet stuck her head around Anna's bedroom door and asked, 'How are you feeling?'

Anna looked up.

Her two friends had helped her into the house when they got home but she'd assumed they'd since gone home.

'My very first love,' Anna said, and she looked Lisbet straight in the eye, 'and I *did* love him . . .'

'I believe you.'

'. . . was a farmer's son, from Canada.'

'OK.'

'I tell you that only because he was an outsider, like me, and open-hearted.'

Lisbet spoke quietly. 'I didn't mean what I said in the car . . .'

'It was *because* I loved him . . . that I knew I would lose him.'

'Jesus, Anna, you're scaring me.'

'I knew I couldn't survive such a loss, so I basically kept him prisoner. He didn't realise it because I made it worth his while.'

'For which he was grateful, I'm sure.'

'Yet as I did it, I swear I thought to myself, *I am a danger to this man*.'

'Where were all the adults, Anna?'

'Oh, busy elsewhere. Eventually the proctor pounded on

my door. He found us asleep and almost out of our minds with hunger.'

'They failed you.'

Anna shook her head.

'Someone older should've been watching your back.'

'The shame of it,' she said, 'is with me, still.'

'Oh, that old friend, I know him,' said Lisbet.

Anna heard the weight in her words.

'Shame the despoiler.'

They sat in silence for a long time. The house around them eerily empty without the children there.

When Lisbet spoke again her voice had softened. 'Anna, my *bokkie*, you've got the chops to learn to love again.'

'I love him already, Lisbet,' said Anna, 'and I'm scared it will drive us both mad.'

'I've got a plan,' said Lisbet.

'OK.'

'Take a breath.'

'OK . . . and then?'

'I mean a deep breath.'

Anna did as she was told.

'And when you wake up in the morning go back to work and just . . . trust this.'

'Trust this?'

'*Ja*, just trust that if you and Tekkies are meant to be, you'll be. Neither of you come into this clean, right? You've got your mom, he's got . . .'

'Sylvia.'

'Right.'

'You've just got to gag your ghosts,' said Lisbet. 'And while you are at it, tell your meddling friends to shut up too.'

Chapter Forty-Six

After the first two blow-ups, whatever Bouchra was looking for by way of human connection and community she seemed to find at The Love Factory and she did it in her own way.

She showed up to work in heels, hair groomed, with perfect eyeliner and full coral lipstick. She was quite the sight next to Cordelia with her wilfully unkempt black-booted abandonment.

Bouchra carried her manuscripts between home and work in a sleek tote. At the beginning of every week she took it upon herself to fill the bowl in the kitchen with fresh flowers. She threw out the ageing cheese in the fridge, and every so often she baked a pecan pie for Luke.

Along with Friday-night-fess-ups with the whole tribe, Bouchra and Samar had hours-long meetings every Monday and Wednesday to work on the translation of the stories.

Anna often heard them giggling, or simply chatting in Arabic long after the work was done.

When Samar recruited a friend of hers in Ramallah to add a story or two, Bouchra enlisted Reem from over the road to add a little translation work to her cooking duties. On occasion, Anna would find a basket of lamb stew and fresh bread on her doorstop, with a love story in both Arabic and English script on top, like a garnish.

Once, when Anna came home from a visit to Sofia at university, she found the three Arab women gathered around the computer in fits of giggles as Samar read them excerpts from her latest story. Reem's eyes sparkled, her hand clasped shyly over her mouth.

When Samar didn't show up for her Monday meeting with Bouchra, nobody gave it much thought.

She didn't show up for the Wednesday session either. Bouchra tried to reach her repeatedly through that long day but there was no response.

'Shit, Anna, this is not good,' she said.

'No, it's not, but maybe she's having technical problems. Or has a cold. Or something?'

'You have no idea what could be happening to her in bloody Nablus. Do you?' snapped Bouchra.

'No,' said Anna. 'Do you?'

'No, but I didn't lure her into this project, now did I?'

Anna stared at her friend for a moment.

'Sorry,' Bouchra shook her head, 'sorry. You know me, I get vengeful when I'm scared.'

'I do know that, but the next time you're cruel to Cordelia for liking kinky sex, or me for being a stupid white person, or Nadia for eating too many biscotti, just know there's no more fucking room for vengeance in this house. Everybody is scared enough as it is, and tired, and struggling to live a good life. You hear me?'

Bouchra looked at her, eyes wide, and then she said, 'Yes, I hear you.'

Anna went back to her work but her hands were shaking. She could do with a peaceful day. Just one peaceful day.

On her way to the park with Liebe that afternoon, Anna stopped in at Reem's house to ask if Samar had been in touch with her directly.

'No,' said Reem, 'I've been waiting, but nothing.'

'Do you want to take the children to the park?' asked Anna.

The route they took led them past a newsagent; the children were drawn by the brightly coloured fruit displayed outside. The youngest stood in front of a tray of mangoes.

'You want one?' asked Anna, offering the fruit to the child but he simply stared back at her.

The two older children approached, Anna offered them the fruit too.

The oldest child nodded and gently took the mango.

Reem and Anna sat on the bench in the park, the children on the soft grass.

They each approached the eating of the mango in an entirely different way, but all were equally grave. The littlest child simply bit into the flesh, separated skin from pulp in her mouth and then spat the skin onto her small hand. The elder boy stripped the skin off with his fingers, strip by meticulous strip until the fruit was peeled. He held the skinless golden fruit in his hands and lapped at it like a cat. The middle child watched both his siblings then simply twisted the fruit back and forth in his hands until it was pulped, then he made a hole in the skin and 'drank' it.

Anna could have watched them for ever.

In truth, the hardest thing about Samar's disappearance, if that was what this was, was the unknowability of the danger facing her. They were all peering into a murky well.

'Will Samar be OK?' asked Anna finally.

'I don't know.' Reem looked at her feet. 'It depends who finds out what she's writing. It depends what else is going on. It depends.'

On Monday Bouchra once again sat herself at her computer at the assigned conference time with Samar. Everyone in the room around her continued the toing and froing of their working day but in truth the whole lot of them were listening for Samar's voice. When it didn't come, an air of anxious restlessness settled on all of them.

'I finished her new story last night,' said Bouchra, 'and I swear, Anna, it could start a feminist revolution all on its own.'

'What's the story?'

'Well there's no actual sex.'

'Oh?'

'Or revolution. Or bondage, or masks, or whips . . .'

'OK, OK, Bouchra.'

'But I tell you if anyone gets in the way of those two consummating their love, there'll be a riot.'

Chapter Forty-Seven

Anna took Samar's story and settled into the armchair by the window.

Samar's Story

The very first time I see Daleel, he is washing a car in the crowded street outside the hotel in old Jerusalem. His arms are so thin it seems he will die of hunger before he reaches the tailgate, I am sure of it – *zay ma ana shayfak amami* – just as I am sure of seeing you now. But he makes it to the end and when he is done every surface of that car shines and the wheel rims too.

The words, 'This is what my love looks like,' arriving in my mind. I am thirteen.

Daleel has light green eyes and brown skin – my mother says those pale eyes make him look like some kind of *jinn* – strange spirit creature – but I find them beautiful.

I start work at the hotel when I am fourteen and my mother's knees have become too swollen for her to polish the floors and her knuckles too bent to hold the iron. I cry on my last day of school and so does my teacher. She says it is a waste of a good mind to let me go. But she knows we are Palestinian in the time of the wall and lucky to have the work.

The sun is hot and the air dry almost every day of the year so the sheets dry quickly. I must stand on a chair to reach the washing lines in the courtyard behind the hotel. The wet sheets are heavy but when they are all hung out, row after row, they make a beautiful forest of white. I must say it satisfies me.

Daleel brings me bread and hummus on Saturdays after he's been to his mother's house. He lives far away and during the week he must sleep in the garage where they park the cars. He brings olives and peppers too because he knows we have little to spare in my house. His mother is a kind woman.

My walk to work is long and it involves hours of waiting in the dust to cross through the wall. I wash my feet and hands at the tap at the back door of the hotel every morning before I start work.

Daleel watches me slip off my street shoes, then my socks. He sees the way I hold my bare foot under the stream of water from the tap.

I smile at him when it is done and he tilts his head and grins.

Every year that passes, I give Daleel a little more of my heart, but we never, in all that time, even brush against one another's skin, hair, hands. He doesn't ask and I don't offer but we feed off one another with our eyes.

There comes a time when I no longer need to wash and iron the sheets myself, we send them out to the machine laundry. I am promoted to head cleaner and now it is my job to polish floors, vacuum carpets and clean all the hotel rooms. It is more work and I am often tired.

Every morning I stock my trolley with clean sheets and towels, with small soaps, shampoos and body lotions. I like the one that smells like magnolia best. I unscrew the top and I smell each one. One small fingertip in the lotion and then I rub it behind my ear because I know Daleel will smell it as I pass him on my way from the hotel to the street at the end of the day.

I wear the hijab, of course. Daleel and I are both devout.

In the hotel business, there is much to learn. The first lesson is that the guests who have the most money are not immune to bad behaviour. I am busy cleaning the best suite in the hotel when the guest insists that his phone has been stolen. In fact, he says I probably stole it. He points at my headscarf and he says, 'It is well known that you and your kind are thieves.'

The second lesson is that the bad-mannered guest has

the power to spoil my life. The life I plan to have with Daleel.

I beg for a chance to help the guest find the phone before he complains to the management. First I search the room. I won't describe the things I find in there as I'm cleaning up, it will make you blush. But there is no phone.

I see the paper slip, filled out in Daleel's hand, confirming that the guest has a car parked in the hotel garage. I run there.

Daleel finds the phone slipped down between the seats of the guest's car. He hands it to me and as I take it I stand in the calm of his presence and take a breath. It is more valuable than air. This faith that the people you depend on are where they are meant to be.

We are alone in the garage, alone for the first time, *habibi* and me.

'Will you come back for some tea?' he says.

I nod my head.

I return the phone to the ungrateful guest. 'Bring water and wine,' he says, and closes the door.

Daleel makes me strong tea on the burner in the corner of the garage. I see the narrow cot where he sleeps, his candle, his shoes.

He pulls a crate out from under a shelf for me to sit on as I drink tea. We do not speak.

There is a small tear in my thick woollen tights just above my knee. It is winter and the mornings are bitter.

Daleel can't take his eyes off the soft skin this hole reveals, and the promise it offers.

The following day I choose those same tights. I contrive to go to the garage again, and this time, without a word, I invite Daleel to brush his fingers over the hole in my tights.

The day after that, he pushes his little finger into the hole and the heat builds up in every part of me, even those I do not have a name for.

Each day he and I become a little bolder. Each day the shape of who we are for one another changes.

My mother asks me why it is that I am washing my hair on a week night. I usually save that for the weekend when I can use the tap in the courtyard and sit on the roof to let it dry.

Never mind, I tell her, it will dry as I sleep.

I go to the garage during my lunch break. He is waiting for me. When did he get so tall, so smooth-skinned, so firm in his arms and his back?

He leads me to the corner where we are sheltered by the storage cupboard. I untie my headscarf and let it fall.

My mother says my hair is my *ommi bitsammih tagi* – my crowning glory. I can see that he thinks so too as the dark curtain of it falls around my face.

Daleel looks at me for a long time.

I step closer to let him know that I would forgive him for touching me.

But he does not.

Instead, he says, 'Turn around.'

I feel the tail of my hair flick the top of my thighs as I twist. All the women in my family have very long hair, that's one thing we can be grateful for, though like my ma says, long hair never helped put food on the table.

I feel Daleel take a step closer and again he says, 'Turn around.'

I do as he asks and he is close enough for me to smell the cinnamon on his breath.

He takes another step. I turn around without him telling me this time. I stand as still as I can, barely breathing until I feel him reach out to touch my hair.

He runs his hand along the whole length of it and every strand rings from the touch of his fingertips. Then I feel him roll it around his hands, fold after fold, and bring it up to his face.

I turn around to face him and I see him breathe in my smell.

I undo the buttons of my jilbab and he slips his hands around my naked waist. I tell him with my eyes that I want more.

He leads me to the corner behind the storage cupboard. He lays a blanket on the floor.

I take his body into mine and he lights a fire there that will burn for as long as the sun rises in the morning and sets at the close of the day.

Chapter Forty-Eight

It was with barely concealed anxiety that Anna watched Bouchra settle in at her desk and dial Samar's number at the assigned time on Monday. And then again on Wednesday.

For the first time since her childhood, Anna closed her eyes and prayed.

Halfway through the hour, when all the associates of The Love Factory had once again lost heart, Samar's face flickered onto the screen.

Bouchra sprang to her feet. 'Holy Mary Mother of God, where the hell have you been?'

'Hello to you too, my friend.'

'Don't hello me, I've been worried sick.'

They all gathered around the computer.

'My grand-auntie Lely died last week,' said Samar by way of explanation.

'I'm sorry to hear that,' said Anna.

'She was ninety-four and more than ready.'

'Last week?' said Bouchra. 'And you didn't think it worth mentioning?'

'Sorry. I tried to text and to email but nothing works in Gaza.'

'Gaza?'

'We do it quickly so there wasn't a lot of time for planning.'

'Gaza?' exclaimed Bouchra again.

'She wanted to be buried in Gaza,' said Samar.

'Well that's considerate of her.'

'Bouchra!' said Anna.

'She was devout, so she needed to be buried in her family cemetery beside her husband. Unfortunately, the family cemetery is on the Israeli side of the wall.'

'Oh, I don't like where this is going,' said Nadia and covered her eyes with her hand.

'We asked for permission to cross the wall but it was denied.'

'So?'

'Well first we thought we could take her across on the back of a donkey, you know, where the wall is still unfinished.'

'What?'

'But all the donkeys in Gaza are busy, or dead.'

'Stop,' said Bouchra.

'So we put her body into a wheelbarrow and pushed her through one of the storm-water drains and on to the graveyard in the middle of the night. It took until dawn to dig her grave.'

Bouchra put her hand on her heart. 'Oh my sister.'

'Yeah, sorry,' mumbled Nadia.

'So sorry,' said Anna.

'Thank God they didn't find you there,' said Bouchra and she sat down.

'Yes. And now my auntie lies beside her husband where she needed to be, and I am back at my desk.'

'Thanks be to God,' said Bouchra.

Samar smiled and said in Arabic, '*Alhamdulilah*.'

Relief blew into the offices of The Love Factory on the heels of Samar's safe return. Bouchra was light-headed with joy, so much so that she stopped Cordelia in her tracks on her way to the loo and gave her an entirely unexpected hug.

Nadia's managerial instinct told her that this was the moment to enforce any unpleasant tasks. For months, she had been trying to sit Anna down with her financial planner. She had watched her friend become fiscally literate in her domestic life but it caused her pain to know Anna had not the faintest idea how to put her savings to work. Now she bundled her into an Uber and sent her off to the city.

'I think my friend Nadia wants you to teach me how to invest my money,' said Anna to the man in the wonderful suit.

'And what do *you* want me to do?' he asked her.

'To make sure I'm never a burden to my children. And, if I can, I'd like to leave them enough to get a good start.'

And as she said it, Anna realised she wanted that very much.

He got up and stood at his window overlooking the city.

'What do you see?'

'Buildings?' said Anna.

'Yes, and on the horizon?'

'Cranes?'

He nodded.

'Lots of cranes,' she said.

'When you see this many cranes, in a political climate like ours, you must assume there is trouble coming.'

'Oh,' Anna said and she thought that she should introduce this clever man to her nonna.

'It's debt. It's inflated and dangerous. And it's going to collapse.'

'Right,' said Anna. 'And so?'

'I would advise you to invest a portion of your wealth in a standard portfolio of stocks and bonds but keep the lion's share in cash until the market falls. Then you buy at the low end of the market and send me a bottle of single malt in thanks.'

'I bought a share in our offices, but I don't think I'll ever be able to buy anything else.'

He laughed. It was clear that he thought she was joking.

'Will I?'

'Ms Vallerga-Fuchs.'

'Yes?' She had not heard her maiden name spoken that formally for many years – it was a negotiated settlement of a name, and typical of her parents.

'It appears that you already can.'

On the very hot days that followed, Anna and Liebe took to having an early morning swim in the ladies' pond on Hampstead Heath.

The first time they did so, Liebe caused a fracas by chasing the ducks. She had learnt since that they were off limits and all she could do was paddle past them whining faintly.

Anna and Liebe were back and Anna stepping out of the shower when they heard Tekkies' voice in the hallway.

The last three days of every month Tekkies took the train from Paddington Station to a small village in the Cotswolds to see his wife in the care home where she had lived for close to ten years. Now he was back.

Liebe's passion for the man had grown over the months since he'd arrived in their lives. She shot out of the room and bounded down the stairs barking loudly.

Anna would've done the same if she hadn't had to pull on some clothes. She grabbed a pair of jeans, and one of Sofia's T-shirts from an anti-austerity rally that said, *It's Time To Grab The Goldmen By Their Sachs!* She wore not a spot of make-up and her hair was long and sleek down her back.

Something about all of that seemed to knock the air out of Tekkies' lungs as she came down the stairs.

'Oh, Jesus,' muttered Nadia who stood beside him in the hallway.

Anna blushed from the top of her head to the bottom of her feet – she'd dreamt of him the night before – it meant he was there, so to speak, in her body.

'Um, come in . . . coffee you had? Sorry. I mean . . .'

'I know what you mean,' he murmured.

'You can't go out into the world in that, Anna,' said Nadia. 'Go and put on some grown-up clothes.'

'What?'

The only downside of swimming in the ponds was that Anna always emerged with waterlogged ears. She'd been dogged since childhood with what her doctor had called mole tunnels instead of ear passages.

Now she hit herself on the side of the head to unblock her ears and said, 'What did you say?'

'Get dressed,' said Nadia. 'You have some furniture to buy, and remember I don't want any old desk. I want—'

'Glass, I know,' said Anna, and she headed upstairs to dress like the co-owner of a successful company – she chose a blue linen shirt-dress with a tie waist.

The furniture shop was stacked to the ceiling with used pieces of every kind. It wasn't quite junk but neither was it designer quality. Anna watched Tekkies scour through the stacks.

'Try this one,' he said as he pulled a metal-framed chair away from the wall. 'Looks like a Mies van der Rohe knock-off.'

She sat down. 'Oh, this'll do for me.' And she ran her hands over the armrests.

'Actually it's from the period, I think.'

'Oh, yes.' She paused. 'How is Sylvia?' she had to ask.

He glanced at her. 'She's OK,' he said. 'I told her about you.'

'Oh.'

Anna would have liked to have heard what he'd said about her because she wasn't sure at all what it would have been. But now was not the time.

She and Tekkies chose some rugs and light fittings, they

picked out an armchair for Farhad, and a glass desk for Nadia.

Their route back to the Tube station took them past the white-stone boutique that had once contained the blue coat.

It snagged Anna once again. This time a pair of high-heeled black shoes in the window caught her eye. Something about them made her think of black birds.

'What?'

'Black birds,' she repeated. 'Are you deaf?'

'No.'

'I am,' she said and she laughed. She turned and walked up the white stone steps. He watched her for a moment and then he followed.

Chapter Forty-Nine

The attention Anna received from the shop assistants was less ambivalent than it had been on her first visit. They seemed to flutter, weightless, towards the tall man by her side. Did they see money in him, and good looks, or simply the Darwinian strong man?

Anna looked at the shoes, felt the weight and shape of each in her hands. While she waited for the shop assistant to come back with the pairs she had chosen to try on, she saw Tekkies gravitate to the clothing rails.

She watched him consider each garment, as he had the furniture that morning, fully attentive to touch and colour and cut. He moved quickly and then he pulled a dress off the rail and held it up to the light.

'This one,' he said.

It was made of silk the colour of dried corn, overlaid with a latticework print, Islamic in feel, and as fine as those on the ancient tombs her father had shown her on a trip they made to India in her early teens.

'For me?'

'For you.'

Anna took the dress and felt the lightness of its silk.

The man who had dressed her in this shop all those months ago came to mind, only this time it was someone she hungered for.

She stepped out of her linen dress and into the silk one. Up close, she saw the unusual beauty of its artistry yet more keenly.

Tekkies had chosen well. When Anna saw her reflection in the mirror, she was, somehow, more herself.

Anna had never shared her nonna's devotion to luxury brands or their knock-offs. If she did have any sort of style, she'd learned it unconsciously from her mother – even as a young girl she could see that her mama looked different – more sly and self-aware, more herself than anyone she knew.

'Style is thinking,' her mother had said.

'Thinking?' the child had asked.

'It is what you wear because of who you are inside.'

And that was true of Anna, in the silk dress Tekkies had chosen with a slit from her knee almost to her underwear, and those legs; her father's legs, long, and slender.

Sometimes it took someone else to help you see what was there.

'*Oy, kyk nou*,' she heard Tekkies whisper to himself as he watched her walk barefoot across the carpet on her tiptoes.

It was only later that she learnt that this Yiddish/Afrikaans mash-up – *wow, just look at that* – was reserved for moments of extreme feeling.

She walked high on her toes, how long was it since she had done that?

Ballerina syndrome.

That's what they called it.

He watched her slip her fine-boned feet into the black bird shoe the assistant held out for her.

'Something softer, I think,' Anna heard Tekkies say to the shop assistant. 'She has tender feet.'

He knew that by looking, by being *seelenvoll.*

Anna's childhood had been dogged by the trials of finding shoes she could wear.

'Oh, come on, lovey!' her mother had said when, aged three, Anna wept as she tried on her first pair of black school shoes.

'Do they hurt?' she'd asked her. 'Really hurt?'

The little girl nodded, they hurt. 'Like stones rubbing on my skin.'

Anna slipped on the next pair of shoes the assistant brought her, also black birds in their shape and refinement, but made of silk – they felt like clouds. It was her natural elevation, ballerina syndrome. And he knew it.

Anna and Tekkies looked at one another.

She sat on the bench. He kneeled to test the hold of the leather sole. He slipped his fingertips into the shoe where her arch was. Anna felt her pulse begin to race.

When she tried to tell him that, he shushed her.

A groan escaped from between her teeth. The truth was she wanted him to hook one hand on the arch of her foot and trail the other up her leg, higher and higher until he slipped his fingers inside her underwear.

But he would not, she knew it, not here.

'Ask me to lunch, Tekkies,' she said.

'To lunch?'

'Yes.'

His eyes were huge, and round, and black.

'Come to lunch with me. Leave it on. All of it.'

He handed his credit card to the sales assistant. 'We'll take them, *dankie* . . . thank you,' he said and he cleared his throat. 'The dress, the shoes . . . everything.'

They stumbled out of the shop. If he hadn't been holding her hand she would have fallen.

They hailed a taxi.

'Connaught,' he said.

'Hotel?'

'Yes, or Browns, doesn't matter.'

And then Tekkies kissed her. The heat in it made her gasp.

Her phone screeched. She ignored it; it bleated. She looked at the caller ID. Luke. She answered.

'Everything all right, Luke?'

'Are you close, Mama?'

'Close?'

'I'm at the orthodontist.'

Oh no. She'd forgotten. Anna made herself calm down.

'I *am* close, as it happens,' she said. 'I'll be with you in about five minutes.'

'Because they are going to put those mean metal things at the back of my teeth,' said her son.

'Five minutes.'

She hung up and looked at Tekkies. 'I think we are going to have to slow down or my whole life is going to go up in smoke.'

Tekkies sat back against the seat and nodded. He ground his teeth together and Anna could see that he too was about to explode.

When Anna walked into the orthodontist, every last person in the waiting room looked up at her and did not look away again until she had sat down.

Most of them had no idea why she was so compelling but Anna knew it was because of the lust beating in her veins.

She sat beside Luke and said, 'Sorry I'm late. I had a very long phone meeting with a publisher in China.'

Luke looked at her and asked, 'Is that where you got the fancy dress? China?'

Later that day Anna heard Nonna whisper to Farhad, 'Anna has found her sheikh.'

Farhad whispered back, 'Hallelujah.'

'Except the sheikh is married.'

'Oh no.'

'Not happily . . . *grazie a Dio.*' She crossed her chest. 'But still married.'

That night, Anna lay on her bed in her pyjamas, and asked herself how the hell she was going to get through the night.

When she and Luke had got home from the orthodontist that afternoon she'd changed out of her dress and made dinner. She'd chatted happily as she, Nonna and Luke had eaten and then she'd cleaned up – but none of it had calmed her racing body.

Anna retrieved her computer from the kitchen. Then she lay on her bed and began to write.

Chapter Fifty

This time Anna did not call on Jessica for help although she gave thanks for her with double feeling. Jessica and her tropes had cleared the way for Anna to dare her own imaginings – and only something true to her alone could ease the pressure cooker of her lust.

She reached back to the heat of that afternoon and wrote about black birds – she wrote in honour of the paramours that make us see ourselves in a different light. And she wrote about Italy.

Black Bird

'May I order for you?' I ask the beautiful stranger with skin the colour of chestnuts.

'Yes,' he says and I wonder at the forces that have brought us to this table.

I asks for grilled shrimp, harvested fresh that morning in waters just beyond the harbour. It comes cooked, for moments only, in white wine, garlic and chilli.

He feeds me with his fingers. And I him with mine.

The flavours are bright and sharp. It's the difference between the London where I live and work, and my luminous south.

We sip red wine, dark and nutty, that grows, I tell him, on the slopes above where we sit. He tells me about the book he is reading on the Arab conquest of Palermo in the 800s as if he had been there. I feel a stirring.

He watches me lick my fingers clean. When he leans forward to kiss my cheek I smell the heathery odour of an active person in his hair. It has not been long since he swam in the sea.

I swear . . . I never do anything like this. Not ever.

I'm a clever woman. Word in London is that I have a bright turn of mind. Bollocks, and anyway I'm tired, tired *especially* of the time I spend in my mind. Weary, also, of the cold and the rain in the north.

'Have lunch with me, please,' he'd asked that morning.

I'd hesitated.

'Come, do.'

He'd held out his hand.

And I took it. Something in his eyes swept away my caution. Something that said, Trust this. Don't let go, take it, take it!

Together we walked out of the shop where, just

moments before, he had seen me try on a beautiful pair of shoes and insisted on buying them for me. I stepped – no! I *pranced* – in my new shoes that made me think of black birds onto the cobbled pedestrian street that runs from the ancient Greek amphitheatre at one end of Taormina to the sea at the other. All I could think was, Bloody hell, has there ever been a sexier moment in my very clever life?

A taxi swept us down to the medieval harbour.

As we eat and sip our wine and talk about what matters most, the sun moves with stealth across the sky.

'A hat,' he says quietly.

'What?'

'You need a hat.'

It is true that the sun now falls directly onto my face. It is also true that, though I am dark-haired, my skin is as white as milk.

He takes off his own hat and puts it on my head, and before I can stop myself I say, 'You sound like my nonna.'

He laughs and it fills the air.

When I was a child my grandmother would trail after me with a hat in her hand, saying, 'You stubborn little *cavolo*! One day you'll just go up in a hiss of pig-headed smoke. And that will be the end of you.' My nonna had a way of saying terrible things like that and making them feel like love. She also said, 'Never forget that your real power is in your brain. You will have it even when your looks have gone.'

I feel the sweet shade his hat makes on my burning cheeks and I am grateful.

He sits back in his chair and looks at me. It's a grave kind of look. And it comes to me that he does not do this kind of thing either. And that there is something unusual at play here that is bigger than both of us, if we dare it . . .

'Come,' I say, 'a swim.' And I slip the shoes off my feet, and take his hand.

I lead him down onto the sandy beach. The heat warms the soles of my feet. I am, once again, grateful for his hat, and the firm grip of his hand in mine. We skirt the water's edge and stop in a cove, bounded on three sides by high cliffs.

It is a beautiful place. I sit with my back against a flat sloping rock and close my eyes. The heat that comes off the surface of the stone sinks into my skin, my muscles, my bones.

I feel him lift my foot and brush the sand off and then he bites me on the thin skin of my arch. I gasp.

He slips his tongue into the tender gap between my toes and, honestly, he could just as well be touching my sex. And the hunger that has lain low in me for too long rises all the way to my mouth.

'May I?' he asks.

I don't at first know what he means. Then he shows me that the dress I am wearing is such that the silk in the front can be easily folded back to bare my breasts.

'Yes,' I murmur when I understand.

My nipples are as hard and dark as cherries in the sparkling day. And it comes to me that both my mind *and* my body are alive to his touch. As I say that I realise it sounds as if I've never had good sex before. Not true. Like I said, there was Billy Jones.

'And here? May I touch you here?' he asks as he lifts the hem of my dress.

I take his hand and lead him to the sweet wet between my legs.

I hear him swear.

I swear too.

If a butterfly landed on me I would be lost. That's all it would take. But he withdraws his hand.

'Please,' I say, trembling.

'Soon,' he says.

The way my muscles and ligaments fit together seems to occupy him for quite some time. I don't have the musculature of an athlete and yet, when I arch up to meet the hand he finally slips into my underwear, I know he can feel how each of my parts work together – he has those kind of fingers, cheeky and sexy and warm. I call out and then bite my lip as my body slides into a timeless, roaring bliss.

He pulls off my underwear and in the slipstream of my orgasm he enters me, edging inch by inch into my centre. It burns as the blood rushes into the tissue.

The muscles of my bottom clench and unclench as I move against his belly, cool and rhythmical as an American country and western tune.

Come on, come on . . . I seem to say. *Give in to me.*

That he can hold on this long is a source of wonder to me. He somehow finds a way to twist my dress around my waist and pull it tight, like a belt. And tighter still, until I am flush up against him, my sex and me. I call out, and I open further, he does it, he gives in to me.

Later, when we have recovered, he leads me to the water. We slip into its salty swell. He kisses the pale skin of my collarbone and says, 'Thank you, lovely lady – thank you.'

'*No, no grazie a te,*' I say, because some things have to be said in Italian. 'Thank you too. For giving me this day.'

'And the ones that will follow,' he says.

I nod, because we both know it will not be very long before we reach for one another again. Even my nonna would agree, were she here to say it, that such a concurrence of body and mind does not come along more than once in a lifetime.

There it was. She wanted a lifetime of *him*.

Anna left the house early the following morning. She had a hair appointment; they happened with alarming frequency now, as the grey grew more plentiful. She planned to meet the others at the new offices mid-morning.

Parked on the road outside her house was Peter's old car. She looked closer and saw him in it. She knocked on the window and he looked up to see her, startled. He rubbed the sleep out of his eyes and opened the window.

'Peter! Did you sleep in your car?'

'Only part of the night.'

'Are you here to see Sofia? She's going to see the new offices at nine thirty. Lukey went running.'

'You have new offices?'

'They're not ready yet but, yes, we are bursting at the seams.'

'Congratulations.'

'I'll tell the children you stopped by.'

'I'm here to see you, Anna.'

'Peter . . .'

'Just come and sit here with me. I won't keep you long.'

She looked doubtful.

He said, 'Please.'

Anna sighed; she walked around the car and sat in the passenger seat. Neither spoke for a moment, then he said, 'You're breaking my heart.'

'Peter—'

'No, just hear me out. Not because you won't have me back. I wouldn't do that straight away, if I were you.'

'Really?'

'Yes, really.' Then he looked at her. 'I would make you wait a while.'

'Stop, Peter.'

'I hurt you, Anna.'

She shook her head and said, 'I must go.'

'Wait!'

She looked at him and saw how hardship rested on his face, it made him paler.

'Are you doing OK?' she asked.

He laughed. 'No, not really.'

'I'm sorry.'

'Me too.'

She smiled at him and he brushed the hair off her forehead. 'You look lovely.'

'Please, don't,' she said.

'I'll wait for you.'

'No, don't.'

'I don't have a choice,' he said.

'Please.'

'I'm a boat without a dock, Anna,' and he rested his head on the window and closed his eyes. 'It turns out "something simpler" doesn't do it for me.'

Anna looked down at her hands. 'Peter, I think I might have met someone. It's not clear where it's going . . .'

His arm hit the side of her seat hard. It made her flinch. Almost in the same breath he brought his forehead down on the steering wheel with a terrible force – doubly shocking for its extremity and its impulsiveness.

'Oh. Please don't do that,' whispered Anna, scared now.

He raised his arms in surrender. 'OK, OK, sorry.'

'I'm going to go now,' she murmured. And she eased the handle to open the door.

He watched her minutely.

Just before she got out he took her arm. 'I will, you know.'

'What?'

'I'll wait.'

Anna ran to her car and pulled open the door. She climbed in and slammed it shut. She put her head in her hands.

Chapter Fifty-One

The new windows installed in her office took away none of the openness Anna had loved when there were none.

The great Georgian window that she and Tekkies had scraped clean, now refreshed by some new panes of glass, let in a universe of light. It mitigated the separation between Anna's office and the rest of the floor.

And those beautiful golden planks all the way from the forests of Mozambique filled the space from end to end.

As Anna walked into the room she couldn't quite manage the difference between the pall of Peter's despair and this new beginning. She paused for a moment to catch up.

The Love Factory crew were fanned out across the open space. It was a first view of the almost-finished office for most of them and their excitement was palpable.

Amazingly, Farhad and Stokely were standing on their heads in the far corner. It made Anna laugh.

Sofia attempted the same.

'You'll break your neck,' shouted Anna from the door.

Sofia waved. 'Mama!'

'Hello, *amore*,' she called back.

Anna saw Tekkies at the far end of the room. He was looking at her with such deep attention she felt the story she'd written for him burning a hole in her handbag.

'Can we do yoga here after work if Stokely wants to run a class?' asked Bouchra.

Cordelia shook her head. 'I will take Liebe for walks at lunchtime but I will not stand on my head.'

'Me neither,' said Lisbet.

Anna looked at Cordelia and said, 'Share my office with me.'

'What?'

'Come on. We started this whole debacle side by side.'

'No offence, Anna, but your old goats and me are not friends.'

'What old goats?'

'Joni Mitchell, Mozart, the blues people, that Muddy Waters . . .'

Anna grinned.

'I'm happier over here with the millennials.'

Farhad lifted his hands into the air and said, 'Is this going to be the coolest work space on the planet, or what?'

Sofia grinned and said, 'Coolest place in the whole pyjama, like my nonna would say.'

'Where is Nonna?' asked Anna, looking around.

'She said her bones hurt,' said Sofia, 'so she stayed in bed.'

'Oh,' said Anna, and she kicked herself for not checking in on her before she left the house.

Anna and Tekkies kept as far away from one another as possible during the morning. But when she stood in her office and saw how it brought her into communion with the passing of the day *and* with everyone else in this shared endeavour, she looked at him and he back at her. She would have what she needed for the first time in her life. She mouthed the words *thank you* across the space and he nodded.

Nadia spent the rest of the morning with Tekkies and the architect, marking out where the computers would go and the manuscripts and the filing.

Anna didn't want to intrude, so as she took her leave she handed Farhad an envelope.

'Can you give this to Tekkies for me?'

He reached for the letter distractedly.

'Farhad!' she said.

'What?'

'Make sure he gets it.'

He said, 'OK, OK.'

She handed it over to him and walked away.

A few minutes later Farhad put the envelope on the temporary desk Tekkies had set up for himself in the corner.

Not long after, Nadia added a plan of the bookshelves for the far wall as she hurried by on her way to the loo.

Later still, Lisbet put a catalogue on top of it all. And Anna's story slipped out of sight.

*

Anna waited until after midnight for Tekkies to respond. He did not come, neither did he text, or call.

Finally, Anna texted Farhad. Did you give him the envelope?

Yes! came the response. I put it on his desk. He could not have missed it!!!! Now go to sleep!

You go to sleep! she wrote back.

I will if you will.

And Anna finally turned off her light.

In the days that followed Anna wanted nothing more than to ask Tekkies straight out if she'd offended him. Did he find her story stupid, or crude, or just plain embarrassing? Her fear of hearing an affirmative answer to any one of those questions kept her silent and the demands of finalising the office and preparing the move gave her little time to dwell on it.

Before either of them knew what had hit them, the month came to an end, and Tekkies went off to visit Sylvia.

Thank goodness then that Sofia and Alejandro both started summer internships in London and brought a new energy into the house. Sofia's interest in women's non-fiction writing was changing the way she saw the world. She came home with *The Argonauts* by the poet Maggie Nelson under her arm. She set up a deckchair in the allotment garden and read the memoir aloud to Anna as she weeded nettle and dandelion out of the beds. The story of enduring love between two women, a pregnancy, and shared parenthood, held them both captive with its candour.

In early September Luke began his penultimate year of secondary school. He walked into the school gates with a spring in his step.

Cordelia took it upon herself to help distract Anna from the news that Tekkies had had to delay his return to London. She invited her to join her at a movie one night, and to share a drink at the pub after the dinner dishes had been cleaned away on another. Anna was grateful.

Their many months of working together had made Cordelia and Anna masterful editors of one another's work. Their criticism was unsparing. Anna insisted that Cordelia find the connection between her academic writing skills and her colloquial sexy story stream-of-consciousness writing. Cordelia declared herself 'the SWAT team of the sentimental' and she slashed the excess out of Anna's stories. It enlivened both of their work.

Cordelia invited Anna to go to her favourite gin bar in Shoreditch on Friday night. Anna contemplated going straight there from a meeting with her financial advisor but thought better of it. Apart from Lisbet, the associates of The Love Factory had taken to dressing down when they had meetings with professionals who knew the gist of their work. It helped them to signal that their sexy-story writing efforts made them no more alive to things erotic, nor more available. It saved everyone from embarrassment. In the gin bar though, it would mean that Anna would look like a prim schoolteacher amongst London's trendy Friday night revellers and life was too short for that.

Anna looked at herself in the mirror and said, 'So what do I wear?'

Cordelia opened Anna's wardrobe. 'OK, all black.'

'Black?'

'Yeah. And a hat.'

'A hat?'

'Yes, a hat, Anna. You are making me work very hard here, I don't care what you look like, but you seem to, so give me a break.'

'OK, rummage away.'

Cordelia considered the few black garments she came across, but none took her fancy, then she pulled the silk dress Tekkies had bought out of the cupboard. She held it up and whistled.

'I can't wear that,' said Anna.

'No, you can't, but it's gorgeous.'

'Tekkies bought it for me. And those shoes.'

Cordelia fell to her knees and hauled out the black bird shoes.

'You wouldn't make it home alive if you wore these,' said Cordelia.

'I don't know what the hell is going on with him and me,' said Anna.

'Tekkies and you?'

'Yes.'

'Well, he's crazy about you,' said Cordelia, 'I know that much.'

'I wrote him a story,' said Anna.

'You did what?'

'I wrote him a sexy story.'

'Oh.'

'But he never acknowledged it.'

'Maybe he needs time to recover?'

'He's had time.'

'It's probably performance anxiety.'

'What?'

'Those men in your stories are pretty hot, Anna.'

Anna wondered for one crazy moment whether Cordelia might have a point then she lay back onto the bed and said, 'Come on, Cordelia, what am I wearing?'

'Hang on a minute.'

Cordelia found a pair of skinny jeans and a black button-down shirt. Anna double knotted an old belt of Peter's around her middle and threw on a black leather jacket.

'OK, let's go.'

Cordelia had gathered the foreverstudents together in the gin bar to meet Anna. She had long wanted to lay eyes on the young women whose stories she had edited over the past months and was pleased to find that it was mutual.

'Anna!' they shrieked, and embraced her.

They were all clever young women, funny and cool. None seemed particularly hung up on where they fell on the gender spectrum. Some flirted with the men in the room, others with the women. The Love Factory had made a small difference in most of their lives. For one writer, it meant she could complete a book of poetry she was writing, another was able to help her brother who needed a spell in rehab.

'It got me a date with Penelope,' said a skinny woman with

heavy black eyeliner. 'It ups our "cool" status by degrees, so thank you, godmother of the sexy story,' and she kissed Anna's cheek.

Anna wanted to say that she could do with a godmother herself when it came to love, but it wasn't the time or place.

They danced and they sang and Anna had a little more than was good for her to drink, but, oh, it was fun.

When it came time for her to head home, she offered to share an Uber with Cordelia.

'Um, I think we're going to go on somewhere else,' said her friend.

'OK,' said Anna, and by the frisson associated with the leave-taking, Anna knew that it was going to be one of Cordelia's BDSM establishments.

'Don't get into any trouble,' she said.

'I won't. Oh, by the way, I left a new story on your desk.'

'Really?'

'Yep, let me know what you think.'

In the taxi, Anna passed Cordelia and her posse flying along the pavement arm in arm towards their next adventure.

Chapter Fifty-Two

Anna got into her pyjamas and climbed into bed with a cup of rooibos tea. She'd been introduced to the brew by Tekkies and Lisbet; it was farmed on the slopes of the Cederberg mountains in South Africa. She thought she could taste the brackish coastal mountain water as she sipped. Anna propped Cordelia's story on her knees and began to read.

Cordelia's Story

> I'd need to be a bloody magician, a conjurer of words way beyond my skill, to be able to tell you how it feels to take off the sensible shoes of my schoolteacher life and zip my feet, calves and, finally, my thighs, into the long black boots that reach almost the whole length of my leg.
>
> It's the equivalent of a long-ago kitchen maid becoming lady of the manor. And then there is the sensation

in my stomach when my dresser (yes, I do have one of those and she's a good friend to me) tightens the corset around my waist, and the lightness of the silk underwear against my sex.

So, I won't try, I'll just say the not-so-simple truth that, for yours truly, neither one of my lives would be possible without the other.

Like most everyone in my street I ride my bicycle to work. Every morning, rain or shine, like a good lemming I set out from my little dwelling and wobble to the primary school in Battersea where I teach the year one class (which I love doing, by the way). My route through Mayfair takes me past a gentleman's club with a heavy wooden door and a man in a top hat stationed at the front. And every day the man in the top hat nods a greeting as I pass.

In the late afternoon, that very same bloke (I know, a word my mum would use and not one that fits with the lady of the manor) holds the door open for me so I can pull my bicycle into the storage cupboard. He makes me a cup of tea and asks me how it went with the little ones. His name is Gerald and he is the only person in the world who knows my complete story.

He knows it because it's all his fault. He waved me over one morning as I cycled past and the rest, as they say, is history. I thank him every time we have tea, and he laughs. He also gives me a chocolate digestive biscuit.

So, because there's more than a hop, skip and a jump

between my two worlds, it's never seemed very likely that I would find a man who'd be comfy in my happy double life. I don't even look. I had a boyfriend named Sam for about five minutes a year or two ago but he said I was never home and that I had a pathological need for secrecy.

You'll understand my surprise then when, in the middle of some very sexy stuff with a client involving a whip, I look up at the viewing window (weird, I know, Gerald only allows it for special clients) and I see a man watching me whom I recognise!

Not only that, but he's one of the only men that I've fancied, in forever! He's also completely out of my league, a head governor at my school and a fancy-pants in every possible way. He's also kind, clever and very sexy. I heard he made a lot of money in global real estate and felt now that he'd quite like to give most of it away. A good bloke but a *governor* at my school, for God's sake! (By the way, I've always wondered why the word 'governor' has survived the modernisation of education lingo but there it is, a dinosaur from the class wars.) And whatever he's called, the fact is that this man is my boss, my *ultimate* boss.

Anyway, here he is, looking at me with rapt attention as I walk across my 'playroom' in my thigh-high boots. Sink or swim is all I can think, with my heart beating like the clappers. Game on, darling. I reach for a whip.

He doesn't stay to see what I do with it.

But he's back a few days later.

I lose all interest in the client lying on the bed in front of me and I dance for my governor instead. OK, I do also let my client slip his fingers into my knickers and get me going a wee bit, while sperm gathers on the head of his penis like a cloud.

But when he growls, 'Now! Let me fuck you now!' I shout, 'No!' and I whip him across his chest. I don't say it but I think 'good luck explaining that welt to your wife'. And he loves it.

I climb up on top of him and just as I'm about to slip onto his prick, I'm not thinking of him, as you well know, I look up at the governor and he's right up against the glass, hands either side of his head. His fingertips pale from the pressure of keeping himself together. But it's the fire in his gaze that gets me. As if he wants to kill the man beneath me and insert himself there instead.

The very next morning, while the children and I are singing the good morning song (honestly, the sweetest thing in this world), the governor walks into my class-room and I know he's going to have me arrested.

Little Juliet McFarlan is sitting on my lap with her head squished into my shoulder for comfort and she's jumpy at the best of times so I can't exactly clamber to my feet and beg him not to. So, on we go around the circle singing, 'Good morning, Rachel, good morning, Siddhartha . . .' and when named, every little face breaks into a smile.

And instead of arresting me the governor sits down, crosses his legs and joins in. The children make room for him as if he was just another four-year-old. They know a good one when they see it.

I have to confess, I'm feeling like I'm hanging onto my little life with my fingernails when I cycle over to world number two at the end of the school day. Gerald seems to know that something is aflutter in me because he gives me two chocolate digestives and the big cup for my tea.

I'm not altogether surprised when the door to my 'playroom' opens and it's my governor. He is wearing a suit. As always, his shoes are shiny and his tie perfectly tied. He stands on one side of the room and I'm on the other and all I can think to say is, 'Thank you for not firing me.'

'Not at all,' he says in his clipped beautiful accent. 'It is I who should thank you.'

My governor has the best manners. He steps closer and for one moment I don't have the faintest idea how to proceed. He does. He kisses me gently, respectfully, tenderly, and as he does that my body steps in where my mind cannot and I take off his jacket. Then I undo his tie.

Truth be told, I don't always feel the turn-on with my clients, sometimes it's more of a game. But now, now I'm trembling in my limbs and my fingers. He takes my hands into his and he says, 'Steady now.'

His fingers slip down the small buttons on the back of my blouse and then across my behind. And with no further ado he pinches my spot! You should know that nobody finds that spot the first time. In fact, hardly anyone ever does, it's the only place on my body over which I have absolutely no control. It comes to me just then that he'd studied me as he stood behind the glass. He knew! He moves straight from there to the nub of me swelling inside those silk knickers and when he feels my wetness he sucks in a long breath. I would follow him across the hottest desert to have more of that touch but he stops.

Oh man, it's clear as day that I'm going to have to up my game if I'm going to hold my own with this wily silver fox.

I choose the finest whip from the cabinet and with an almost invisible flick of my hand it meets his back skin. He gasps.

'Take them off,' I say. I mean his trousers because it's time, you know.

He doesn't move. The whip flicks out again and this time he cries out and undoes his trousers. I can see the distended rise of his penis through his underwear. I can see the hunger in him but he still will not yield his remaining clothing.

I take a big risk because I have an instinct and that's always your best friend in the game of love. I grab the big whip out of the cabinet. It flies through the air and scorches a welt across his back. He groans, not a pain but a pleasure sound. I read him right.

I whisper, 'Show me.'

And he stands up and takes off his underwear. Now I'm feeling ten feet tall and armed – but the sight of him so large and aroused makes me falter. What a beautiful man.

I lay the whip on the floor and walk over to him. I scoop the semen off his penis tip and put it into my mouth. He watches me and then he turns me around and begins to undo the buttons on my blouse, and when that is cast aside, the stays binding me into my corset. I will allow that, I decide, only until the breasts are free. The rest remains cinched tight around my waist.

I have been told that my breasts are a lightning rod, maybe my best feature. I don't know, I find my arse pretty effective, but I have to say when handled right my nipples are a highway to all the other erogenous zones and they can really wind me up. He knows, as he would, how to handle them, small, discreet and erect, but when he goes for both nipples at once I hiss, 'Don't,' because God only knows what will happen if he touches those together.

He obeys and I can see it costs him.

I have, as you would expect, a few playthings in my room along with the whips. A restraining frame, where I can suspend a body. Restrain a body. I sense with him that he would benefit from a little of that, maybe just the feet?

So, I lay him face down on the furry rug and strap

his ankles into the leather restraints. My favourite oil is patchouli and I warm it over a soft candle to make it slide on easy and slick. I rub it on his thighs and around his apple-bottom cheeks, and I swear I've never seen anything as sexy. And when I slip my pinky into his hole, he jerks like a colt and says, 'Just don't kill me.'

He doesn't mean kill me dead, he means kill me with pleasure, and I say, 'I won't if you won't.'

And I can see him smile and he says, 'Promise.'

He doesn't say 'deal' or anything transactional like that, he says, 'promise.' And I take his penis in my hand and he bites his teeth together and groans to stop himself coming.

'Not yet, governor,' I whisper and he laughs. As he does that I push deeper into him and the laugh becomes a lovely deep sound. I can tell he's just about to lose it and in the heat of this big highway he shouts.

'You. I need you.'

I push in close where he can reach me and his fingers move against my clit barely at all before I'm swearing like a trooper and gushing. He lets me ripple against his fingers until it is over and then he gently lays me down on the furry carpet under him.

I'm tight now. He kneels in front of me against the constraints and before I know what's what he enters me and says the words, 'Mine, mine, mine.'

I swear it feels like another go at the first time. It is downright extraordinary. He pushes in ever quickening thrusts and just before I lose it for the second time I hear him growl, 'Now you can kill me.'

Anna sat back against the bed cushions. Cordelia had found her voice. The dry wit of her prose could not have been written by anyone else. She kicked the whole *Fifty Shades of Grey* shtick into the long grass, if only because the *woman* was the one with the whip *and* she got to tell the story. Anna sent her friend a text: **Love this story Miss Kikki Hunter!**

Chapter Fifty-Three

'But what happened to the fisting?' asked Anna when she and Cordelia were alone in the office on Monday morning. 'I was looking forward to it.'

Cordelia laughed. 'To be honest, all I've done is read about it.'

Anna smiled. 'Well that's OK.'

'It better be.'

'What d'you mean?'

'I read books, that's what I do. Other people *do* things. I know all these people who are halfway from one gender to another, or experimenting with all sorts of shit . . . I mean, they are brilliant, functional people, who like the edge, you know . . . and then there's me. I read about it. It's not the same.'

'No,' said Anna, 'it's all a bit theoretical for me too since Peter.'

'You mean you and Tekkies haven't even reached first base?'

'Kissed, twice.'

Cordelia's eyes widened.

'Come to think of it, there's nothing going on in Nadia's bedroom either,' said Anna, 'and only slim pickings in Bouchra's. I don't know what Samar's story is.'

'Me neither, but she's raising her children alone which implies that not much is happening.' Cordelia hit her desk. 'This is bollocks, Anna; Farhad and Stokely are the only ones seeing any action.'

'Lucky we've got them holding up the side.'

'And we call ourselves The Love Factory! Fraudsters, that's what we are.'

They laughed.

'Well "The Governor" is a great story.'

'Ta, let's hope my mam never reads it. She'd march me down to the local job centre and say, "You wait here until you've got an honest job, Cordelia Thomas, and I don't want to hear this disgusting tosh coming out of your mouth ever again."'

'I can see that happening,' said Anna.

'Yeah,' Cordelia said. Then, very matter of factly, she said, 'I don't belong, do I? Either place.'

Out of the blue Anna recalled the speech Cordelia made on the night of her graduation about her one true love.

'Who was Ben?' she asked.

Cordelia looked up, surprised. 'Ben? Oh, he was my first love. When he was nineteen he took his new Ducati onto the M25 and was swept under the wheels of a Dutch truck full of fresh tulips.'

Anna knew not to speak.

'The truck didn't even stop.'

Truth was, it didn't surprise Anna that Cordelia had lost someone close. Those who knew such things tended to find one another.

'I'm sorry.'

'Thanks.'

Anna said, 'You belong here.'

Cordelia looked up.

'For what it's worth. You do belong here.'

Cordelia smiled at Anna, a wry, grateful, bemused grin.

'Yeah, in The Love Factory for the chaste.'

Before Anna was quite ready for it, Sofia and Alejandro's internships came to an end and they headed off to start a new term at university.

Lisbet, Nadia and the rest of the crew packed up the files and archives for The Love Factory until the front room of Anna's house was stacked floor to ceiling with boxes.

Anna wandered around the house as they worked and found herself wondering how it would be for Luke, Nonna, Sofia and her to be left here in the emptiness.

And Tekkies? What of him?

He'd sent her an enormous bunch of flowers while he was away. The enclosed card read, *Have lunch with me?*

Anna read the card over and over again – did this mean that he'd read her story and found it pleasing? Or was this a reference to their conversation in the clothing shop? He was still delayed in the Cotswolds, he said, and would be back at the end of the week.

Nadia and Lisbet oversaw the packing of the first removal van and then went with it to manage the unpacking at the new offices.

Nonna was at church and Anna was entirely alone for once. It was a weird feeling. For twenty years she had made *being there* for her family her greatest purpose, day in, day out, reliably there – it seemed to her that without much warning, she was back on the metaphorical road, not moving houses, but lives.

The doorbell rang. Anna went to open it, thinking that the team had forgotten something.

The way Nadia stood on the doorstep with the phone in her hand made Anna's heart stop beating for a moment.

'What?'

Nadia shook her head. She looked stricken.

'Is it Sofia? Luke? Nonna?'

Nadia shook her head.

'Cordelia?'

Nadia shook her head again.

'Samar?'

'Farhad,' whispered Nadia.

Anna took her friend's hand and they ran to the waiting car.

The main entrance to the hospital was bustling with people. The flower and snack shop in the foyer made the whole place smell of stale chips and air freshener. Anna, Lisbet and Nadia stood silent in the lift as it climbed up to the intensive care unit. They could hardly bear to look at one another.

'What do we know?' asked Anna.

'Nothing,' said Lisbet. 'Stokely just said to hurry.'

It had to be St Mary's. In all the intermittent visits Anna had made there over the years, the atmosphere in this hospital, and the dread that accompanied it, had never changed.

The intensive care unit was quiet. Even the nurses, familiar with the drama of life and death that hung about the place, seemed unusually subdued.

Farhad's mother sat on a blue plastic chair in the waiting room, drawn and silent. Stokely stood at the door to the ward, keeping tabs on the coming and going of the doctors.

'Is he all right?' asked Anna as she hurried to Stokely's side.

He shook his head. She could tell that he couldn't trust himself to speak. She hugged him and as she did so felt the terror thumping in his chest.

Anna sat beside Farhad's mother and took her hand. The old lady began to weep quietly.

Nonna stepped out of the lift in her church clothes. She made straight for Stokely and held his face in her hands.

A doctor appeared and called Stokely and Farhad's mother

into a consulting room. When they emerged twenty minutes later, both looked dazed.

'They think there is a fracture in his pelvis but they have to do an X-ray in the morning to confirm that,' said Stokely. 'He has a dog bite in his shoulder, lots of lesions, and a broken jaw.'

Farhad's mother added, 'They have him here for the head injuries . . .' she paused, 'and because they are fearful that there may be a rupture in his spinal cord.'

'Oh no,' said Anna, barely audible. 'No-no-no-no.'

'We don't know yet, lovey,' said Lisbet. 'Hold on.'

'Who did this to him?' asked Anna.

'It happened in the park,' said Stokely. 'He was writing at home and said he needed a break.'

Anna took his hand.

'I offered to go with him but he said I should put the beans on for supper.' Stokely paused. 'There were three of them. And a dog. He was badly bitten. Must've been when he was on the ground. They kicked him and hit him with something heavy.'

'There was a lady in the park,' said Farhad's mother, 'who heard them call my boy . . .' and she hesitated, unable to bring herself to say the words.

Stokely put his hand on her arm for comfort but she pushed it off fiercely, 'A fucking Muslim bastard,' she said. 'That's what they called him.'

'Oh, dear God,' said Nonna quietly.

Anna could see them now as they'd taken their places in the

shadows beyond Reem the night Anna found her in the park. Waiting, it seemed, for a sign from the man with his dog at his side, bouncing his way towards her on the balls of his feet, nursing his hatred.

'When he didn't come home after an hour,' said Stokely, 'I went to look for him. I found his sandal first, and then . . . him.'

'This would not have happened if he had been at home,' said Farhad's mother.

They all turned to look at her.

'What did you just say?' asked Anna.

'You heard me.'

Anna was aware that Farhad had been spending a lot of time at Stokely's house so he could avoid the trial of climbing in and out of the window, but surely none of that mattered now?

'If he had been with me I would have walked with him. I would have kept him safe.'

It was as if she had slapped Stokely's face. She turned away from them all and sat in the plastic chair with her hands in her lap.

'Oh, *caro*, poor *caro bel ragazzo*,' said Nonna and she kissed the back of Stokely's hand. 'Beautiful boy.'

'The police are looking for the ones who did it,' said Stokely. 'They have some leads.'

Nadia asked, 'Can we see him?'

Stokely shook his head. 'They say nobody can. Not until he's conscious. Sorry.'

Chapter Fifty-Four

Anna and Nadia went downstairs to the café and returned with water and fruit juice and a cup of tea for Farhad's mother.

Bouchra arrived and needed to be updated. She brought a pair of clean pyjamas in her handbag in case she had to spend the night.

Anna phoned home to tell Luke to defrost the lasagne in the freezer for his dinner.

'I'll need to stay here for a while, I think,' she said. 'Nonna is with me.'

'Tell Farhad I say hello,' said Luke.

'As soon as I can.'

Anna phoned Sofia. She told her a little more.

'Oh, Mama. How could anyone hurt that lovely man?'

'I know, *amore*, I know.'

Anna began to dial Tekkies' number and then stopped herself. She had no idea what visiting Sylvia meant to him. Would she be adding to his burdens when there was little he could do? And would it presume undue intimacy?

She settled in for the long haul with the others. A short while later Lisbet sat beside her and said, 'I phoned Tekkies. He's on his way.'

She kissed her friend on the cheek. 'Thank you.'

It would be better when he was here.

They waited. And waited. Anna watched as patients were wheeled in and out; as doctors and nurses hurried to tend to them. As administrators, caterers, security guards, cleaners, therapists, and priests, all tried to meet the needs of this vast place, occupied with the business of life and death.

But most of all she watched Stokely stand at the door to the ward that contained his true love, hour after hour, in case he woke.

The imam arrived with a small entourage. He greeted Farhad's mother and then each of them, one by one. Then he sat down and began to pray.

Stokely leaned in close and whispered in Anna's ear, 'This is not a prayer for the dying, is it?'

Anna glanced up. 'No.' At least she hoped not.

'Because he's not going to die.'

'No, he's not.'

Stokely's exhausted eyes were brimming.

Anna asked Bouchra to sit beside them and translate the prayer.

Her voice was deep and steady as she did so. 'In the Name of God, the Compassionate, the Merciful . . .'

And so it went.

When Tekkies stepped out of the lift, Anna was on her feet before she could stop herself. He took two long strides and had her in his arms. He swept on, his arm still around her, and embraced Stokely too. The two of them leant against him.

A constant chanting hum filled the waiting room.

Cordelia arrived, her face streaked with tears. She embraced Stokely and then joined the others and let the prayer wash over her.

At midnight, the night nurse on duty came into the crowded waiting room. 'I'm going to have to shut you down, I'm afraid,' she said.

They began to shuffle to their feet.

'Family can stay the night.'

Stokely glanced at Farhad's mother. She shook her head.

The rest of them said goodbye at the main entrance to the hospital. They held on to each other longer than they normally would, each bound to the other by their worry and their love for Farhad.

Anna, Tekkies, Nonna and Stokely were the last to leave. Nonna slipped her arm through Stokely's and said, 'It has been a long day.'

Anna blew Tekkies a kiss as they parted.

He smiled.

'Tomorrow?' he asked. 'Phone me when you wake up.'

'Tomorrow.'

*

It was a sleepless night for them all. Stokely stood under the shower for a good thirty minutes before falling into Sofia's empty bed.

Anna's phone rang very late.

'Hope I didn't wake you?' It was Tekkies. 'I can't sleep.'

'No, no sleep here either.'

'Anything new from Stokely?'

'Nothing.' She paused. 'How was Sylvia?'

'Sad, the same. Sweet. Absent.'

'I'm sorry.'

'I stayed longer because she's having a difficult time with her lungs.'

'How?'

'They did tests but couldn't find anything. But I think she's tired of breathing.'

'Oh, Tekkies.'

They were silent for a moment. Then she said, 'Want to seed some winter chard with me tomorrow?'

He laughed softly. '*Ja*. I do.'

'Good.'

'*Schlaf ruhig*,' he said.

'Thank you.'

'It means sleep peacefully. My mother says it to me whenever we talk on the phone. Day or night.'

Anna laughed. 'It's good advice.'

Nonna brought Anna a cup of tea in the morning.

'You never bring me tea,' said Anna, half asleep.

'Today, I think you will need it.'

'Yes. Thank you.'

She sat up to take the teacup and asked, 'Is Peter here?'

'Peter?'

'He was parked outside the other day. Just sitting in his car. I found him there.'

'Really?'

'Is he there now?'

Nonna went to the window. She scoured the cars parked on either side of the road – and then she found him, in the driver's seat, looking down at his phone.

'Is he?'

Nonna was silent for a moment. Then she kissed the cross she wore on a chain around her neck and said, 'No. He's not here, *cara*.'

'Oh good,' Anna said, and closed her eyes again.

Nonna went into the kitchen and filled a small plate with her famous biscotti. She went outside, still in her red satin dressing gown, and knocked on Peter's window.

He seemed unsurprised at seeing her and accepted the biscuits with a smile. 'Nonna, how are you?'

'No, how are you, Peter?'

'I'm OK.'

'Are you here for Lukey? Because he's gone to school already.'

'Not for Lukey, no.'

Nonna rested her elbows on the window frame and leaned down.

'You remember how it was at the beginning? When you visited Anna and I refused to serve you food.'

'I do remember.'

'And then you married her, and it was not my decision to make any more.'

'No, thankfully, it wasn't.'

'*Ecco*, enjoy those biscotti, my friend, because that is the last time anything from my kitchen will touch your lips.'

Peter looked at her with barely disguised anger. 'And it's your decision, is it?'

'Oh yes, it is now.'

He looked away and shook his head.

'It's over, Peter. And if I see you here again parked outside my granddaughter's house I will call the police. Do you hear me?'

He said nothing.

'Now give me back my plate.'

Chapter Fifty-Five

Farhad regained consciousness in the early hours of the morning.

Anna and Stokely were there for visiting hours. Farhad's mother did not greet Stokely when they arrived.

As they sat beside his bed Farhad asked them to describe what had happened to him. Stokely tried, and then Anna but Farhad couldn't seem to understand it. He'd lie there for a moment appearing to absorb it, and then he'd ask again.

'He's hurting, Anna, and he's scared,' said Stokely, 'I can see it in his eyes.'

The hospital porters came to collect him mid-morning for tests in the imaging department. It was clear he would be gone for hours.

The nurses made up a bed for Farhad's mother to nap and Stokely sat in a plastic chair in the waiting room.

'This is not right,' said Anna as she took her leave.

Stokely waved away her concern.

'I'll bring dinner.'

When Anna got home she took Liebe out to the allotment. In the days since she'd last tended the beds, the leaves of the tomato plants had become dry and yellow, leaving only the fruit to glow bright.

Farhad's peonies had long since flowered and shed their petals. She could hardly bear to think of their gardener, lying now in a metal tube, broken-boned.

Anna opened the shed and took out her tools. She attached the watering hose to the tap and laid it in the tomato bed to soak through to the roots.

When Tekkies arrived, they held one another for a long silent moment. Then they turned to the comforting task of preparing the beds for seeding. They didn't talk much but worked together, and slowly they began to restore her patch of ground.

They went inside in the early afternoon, to find Nonna making caponata.

They ate the vegetable stew together, the three of them, with a loaf of Nonna's focaccia. When they were done Anna packed some for Stokely, blended Farhad's portion to make it easier for him to eat and went back to the hospital.

By late afternoon the results of the tests had come in. In addition to his fractured jaw, they confirmed a hairline fracture of the left hip and three broken ribs. When they ruled out spinal injury, Farhad's mother wept. Then she went home to wash and change.

When Farhad was ready, Stokely fed him some of Nonna's soft vegetable stew.

Stokely held the spoon to his lips and Farhad slurped it into his mouth – spoonful by spoonful. He managed only a third of it, then Stokely wiped his mouth with a napkin. Farhad looked at him and through a jaw wired half shut he asked, 'Will you marry me?'

Stokely took a deep breath. He reached for his lover's hand and kissed it. 'You're going to have to ask me that again when you are not stuffed to the gills with Vicodin.'

And Farhad hooted despite his injuries. Then he said, slurry and sweet, 'Marry me, you fool.'

When Anna got back from the hospital she made Nonna a martini with extra olives and sat down in front of her.

'Nonna . . .'

'No, *cara*.'

'I haven't asked you anything yet!'

'You are going to ask me if that lovely man Tekkies can spend the night.'

Anna sat back her chair. 'I give up.'

'No special powers are needed to know that. But it's too soon and the children aren't ready.'

Anna looked at her grandmother. 'I could send them to Peter's?'

Her nonna lifted her finger and shook it at Anna.

'First, he must convince me of his good intentions,' she said.

'Oh, really?'

'Yes, your father's not here and I'm your oldest family member.'

'That's rich coming from you, Nonna, you of the wild night in the ferry building.'

'In peace time, we can do things right.'

'Which means?'

'No sex until I say so!'

Anna burst out laughing. 'You are joking, right?'

Nonna grinned and said, 'Give the children a little time to get over their dad and this terrible thing with Farhad. Especially Luke. Do it right and it will go better for him.'

Anna nodded. And then sighed. '*Si, Nonna. Farò come tu dici.*' I will do as you say.

Planning the wedding of Stokely and Farhad had Anna and The Love Factory crew in a flurry.

Stokely was taken up with overseeing Farhad's rehabilitation. The fracture in his left hip meant that he could put no weight on that leg. Stokely set to work on building up the muscle strength. Both were determined that he would walk down the aisle. As the day approached everyone held their breath for a sign of acceptance from Farhad's mother, but none was forthcoming.

The wedding took place, as requested by the betrothed, in the allotment gardens behind Farhad's boyhood home.

Everyone from The Love Factory, along with Sofia, Luke, Reem and relatives of both families, contributed to the decoration of the garden. It was an autumn theme, so no peonies, but an 'aisle' was created out of sweet pea frames wound with begonia and delicate autumn leaves.

Both Stokely and Farhad wore black.

Farhad wasn't able to walk unaided down the aisle after all, but his crutches were garlanded with flowers and his face radiant. When they reached the halfway mark they stopped for Farhad to catch his breath.

A murmur of surprise swept through the crowd and the two grooms turned to see Farhad's mother, adorned in a traditional wedding sari, make her way through the guests.

They watched her take her place on the podium next to Stokely's mother in her hot pink pantsuit.

She looked at her son and put her hand on her heart as if to say; I'm sorry.

There was not a dry eye in the crowd as Stokely and Farhad continued their unsteady passage down the aisle.

As the grooms had wanted, their two mothers acted as witnesses for the ceremony. And beyond them stood Anna, as maid of honour and sidekick to the celebrant. She wore the beautiful silk dress that Tekkies had picked out for her with its deep gold and fine latticework pattern. And yes, the black birds on her feet. She found his eyes in the crowd.

'Let us prepare ourselves for love and rejoicing,' said the stooped and greying celebrant. 'For Stokely and Farhad are going to be married this day, and it is their wish to share their love and their joy with you. As we celebrate with them, let us also renew our faith in the power of love, which holds us, and nurtures us, and makes us one, in spite of time, death, and the space between the stars.'

Anna had come across this special man when she contacted the office of lesbian, gay, bisexual and transgender concerns at her local council. He and the two grooms had met several times to plan their ritual.

The celebrant turned to Farhad and said, 'Do you, Farhad Latif, take this man Stokely Edwards as your wedded husband, to honour and love him until the end of your days.'

'I do.'

'And do you, Stokely Edwards, take this man Farhad Latif to be your lawfully wedded husband . . .'

'I do.'

As the two men exchanged rings, Cordelia's voice rang out over the congregation, clear as a bell.

I can hear his heart beat for a thousand miles
And the heavens open every time he smiles

She and Luke stood at the side of the crowded congregation and she sang to the accompaniment of his saxophone.

And when I come to him that's where I belong
Yet I'm running to him like a river's song

He give me love, love, love, love, crazy love
He give me love, love, love, love, crazy love

The mothers, one Jamaican, the other Pakistani, took one other's hands and pledged silently to honour their boys and their tender love. No matter what gossip, jealousy and complaint would pepper their future, these two women knew how precious was this love, one son for another.

Chapter Fifty-Six

For the reception, they had laid down a wooden dance floor in the allotment garden and hired a couple of tall gas heaters. Reem and her group of Syrian friends had prepared a simple feast of lamb kebabs, bitter green salad, olives and warm flatbread.

Tekkies and his ensemble played the first set. At Sofia and Luke's urging they had added three new songs to their repertoire in preparation. They opened with Beyoncé's 'Dance for You' with Cordelia on vocals.

Anna was unprepared for the giddy groupie she became when she watched Tekkies play his drums. He was just plain good at it, polished and instinctive. She stood on the edge of the dance floor and gazed at him.

Stokely danced and Farhad swung his body in time with the music. When they invited the guests to join them, Stokely's two sisters wowed everyone with their moves. Once it was hopping, Farhad moved to the edge of the dance floor and he and Anna watched as Stokely and his mum joined his sisters. The four of them brought the house down.

Bouchra was there with Majd, who clearly wanted to be somewhere else. She was having none of it.

'You go home, Majd, I'm not ready yet.'

'Come, Bouchra.'

'I will not.'

Anna watched him step back and consider Bouchra as she snaked her way in amongst the dancers. Did he notice, Anna wondered, how lithe she was, and joyous too?

'Well I'm going,' he called out, as petulant as a child.

'Don't wait up,' said the vivacious Syrian, and she waved. He looked astonished.

Nadia and Aalim danced by, cheek to cheek. There was a pathos about them that came from the uncertainty of how long their 'arrangement' would keep them together.

'Is there anything that boy can't do?' Farhad asked, watching Tekkies play.

She smiled. 'Want me to get you a chair?'

'No. I don't want my husband to look over and see me sitting down like an old man.'

'Then lean against me so you don't get tired.'

So he did, it felt good. They watched the dancers in silence for a moment.

'I've got it,' said Farhad.

'What?'

'The thing your boy Tekkies can't seem to do.'

'What's that?'

'Get you into bed.'

Anna flinched and the sudden movement upset their delicate balancing act. Farhad recovered.

'What I don't know is, what you're waiting for.'

'The children,' she said, jittery. 'Nonna says I need to go slowly.'

'I don't think any reasonable person would consider them children any more, Anna.'

Sofia and Luke danced in the arms of their respective partners, very much on their way to adulthood. That very afternoon, as the wedding guests were gathering, Luke had finally introduced Anna to his girlfriend.

'Mama, this is Lien Hua.'

'Hello, Lien Hua, so pleased to meet you!'

The young woman's smile lit up her face.

Now Anna looked at her feet, and a rogue sentence fell out of her mouth before she could stop it: 'Maybe he doesn't really want me. Have you considered that?'

Farhad laughed, then covered his mouth at his indelicacy. 'Sorry.'

'He hasn't responded to the sexy story I wrote for him,' she said.

'That was a sexy story you had me put on his desk?'

Anna looked away and mumbled, 'Not sexy enough. Clearly.'

'You're scared,' Farhad said quietly and he turned to look at her. 'There's no room for fear, Anna. Not now.'

She turned away.

'Some bastard could take all this away from you in an instant, in the time it takes to breathe in.'

The first set ended and the crowd shouted for more. Anna saw Farhad swing his body over to the podium and talk animatedly into Tekkies' ear. At first the South African seemed entirely bewildered by what he was saying. Then he looked over at Anna and smiled.

Tekkies and his band played three encores. He kept his eyes on Anna as he played. When the DJ finally stepped in, he made straight for her on the dance floor.

As he took her into his arms he said, 'I hear there is a story waiting for me?'

'There was once,' said Anna.

He pulled her in closer and she could feel his hand on the small of her back, insistent, strong. 'Then I will find it. I can promise you that.'

The way she looked at him suggested it would be worth his while.

In the fading hours of the celebration, before they all stumbled off to bed, Nonna walked up to Tekkies at the bar and asked him to come for dinner.

'Next Wednesday at eight,' she said. 'Don't be late.'

It was way past midnight and everyone in the Carlyle Road house was asleep except Anna. She could never sleep after a good party but tonight it was the thought of Tekkies finding and reading her story that kept her up.

She busied herself putting the wedding flowers into fresh water to share out when next the team were together.

The doorbell rang.

Anna opened it to see Tekkies holding up the envelope that contained her story.

They looked at one another.

He held out his hand to her. 'You're coming with me,' he said.

'Yes, I am,' and she took it.

He drove her to the new building. They took the stairs two at a time all the way to the sixth floor. They locked the door behind them, looked at one another for a long moment. He opened his mouth to talk and she raised her finger to his lips to shush him.

He ran his fingers across her cheek and then into her hair. He lifted her face up to his and he kissed her. It was the kind of kiss that made all others forgettable.

'No orthodontists?' he asked.

'No,' she breathed.

'No grandmother?'

'No, no, no.'

'Just me and you.'

'Yes.'

'*Yes!*'

She bit him then, on the tender skin of his left ear.

He took her lip between his teeth and caught it, not breaking skin, yet laying claim. Anna's legs began to tremble.

As he released her lip he said, 'I love you.'

She looked at his lined, beautiful face, marked by loss.

'Yes,' she whispered. 'And I you.'

And she did. She loved the decency in him, and his steadfastness, but she also loved the runaway lust beating at his body and the power it had to upend all of that. She loved his smell and his skin and the way he looked at her just then.

She stood on her tiptoes to reach his mouth, black birds on her feet.

She undid the buttons of his shirt and peeled it off his body. She'd read the twist and length of him under his clothes over these many months but now she could touch the long, tight muscles of his arms, his ribs, the spread of black hair on his chest.

And he her. She had never in her whole born days felt anything like the fire in his precise fingers. His teeth gripped the lobe of her ear just enough to send a ringing bell from breast to belly.

'Closer,' he breathed.

And she obeyed. She would have done anything at all to stay with those fingertips.

He pushed her dress up. The sound he made when he saw his fingers mixed in with her lace and skin was not anything she'd heard before.

He laid her on the sofa and spread her body out like a

starfish. The Jewish/Afrikaans mash-up that she'd heard him utter when he first saw her ballerina feet, flew out of his mouth with yet deeper wonder, '*Oy, kyk nou – oy*, just look now.'

She reached for him.

'Wait,' he said.

'I've waited long enough for you,' she said.

'Not as long as I have, for you,' he growled. 'Not nearly as long.' And she saw he was beyond negotiation.

'Just don't kill me,' she whispered.

And it came to her that those very words had been spoken by one lover to another in Cordelia's story and in Maggie Nelson's *The Argonauts* and she knew now what they meant. *Devour me, plunder my riches, do-every-last-thing short of ending it all.*

She gave herself over to him entirely.

He did take her to the edge of what her body could manage but that was no surprise. He invited the same of her.

And he entered her with a dark sound of relief, 'Jesus, oh.'

Their union felt deep enough to pin them to the turning earth, and light enough to be taking place on a rickety walkway, or a fading ferry building.

Afterwards, as she fitted into the dip in his shoulder, she smelt the green-sea smell of him and whispered, 'Thank you, *mi amore*.'

She had a love story to tell.

Chapter Fifty-Seven

Anna, Sofia and Nonna all had their hair done by Anna's diminutive hairdresser in preparation for the launch party for The Love Factory's first printed book. It was Lisbet's idea to publish a collection of their sexy stories in one beautiful volume, and their entry into this new market seemed to be causing something of a stir.

Anna was so tied up in arrangements for the launch that she had no time to shop for a new dress, so Sofia took it upon herself to act as stylist and brought home three options for her to try.

Nonna and Sofia each favoured a different dress so Luke was brought in to arbitrate.

Without hesitation and with an acuity that silenced them all he said, 'The white one because it brings out the colour in your hair and because it looks elegant and serious, but also cool.' He shrugged his shoulders and added, 'And Tekkies will like it. Not that it matters.' Then he left the room.

Anna smiled. 'So that's that.'

And she did look elegant and serious and cool and it brought out the warmth in her hair.

Of course, the entire stable of Love Factory writers showed up at the beautiful, book-lined room at the back of London's oldest bookshop. It looked more like a library in a grand house than a bookshop.

Cordelia and her foreverstudents all arrived. As did Farhad with his ever-expanding cell of erotic writers. Luke and Lien Hua were there. Sofia had Alejandro at her side and she glowed.

Lisbet climbed up onto the balcony, a Victorian passageway raised up above the shop floor that in times past had housed early maps of China and South Asia, as the bookseller proudly explained.

'Hello, friends of The Love Factory,' Lisbet called out in a smoky baritone, and everyone cheered. 'Welcome to our first ever proper book launch party!'

Lisbet wore a red cocktail dress and her trademark leopard-skin stilettoes. Her silver blonde hair was cropped neatly on the nape of her neck, around which hung a heavy amber necklace.

'Is she channelling Marilyn, or Dolly?' murmured Anna in Tekkies' ear as they gathered to listen.

'It's Marita,' he said.

'Who?'

'Tannie Marita, her mother,' he whispered. 'That's how she shows up for church every Sunday.'

'Oh, her I have to meet.'

'As many of you will know,' Lisbet continued, 'not very long ago, and in the middle of an electric rainstorm, our very own Cordelia Thomas and Anna Vallerga-Fuchs got the idea for this little company. They posted two stories on their first ever blog and hoped for the best.'

There was a scattering of laughter.

'At last count, we had over ten million visits to our site.'

Whoops and clapping filled the room. It was hard to believe those extraordinary numbers. Even Anna found it so.

'We have a partner in Palestine who we wish could be here tonight, colleagues in China, Canada, South Africa, India and Pakistan. We translate our stories into twelve languages. And we have a growing stable of native-language writers all over the world whose work we publish in English.'

In the applause that followed Anna saw Nadia shake her head in wonder. Luke put his arm proudly around Lien Hua.

Lisbet lifted the physical book up above her head. 'And now you can hold these creamy pages in your hands and you can smell the glue that binds them.' She held the book against her body. 'As many of you know, writing fine erotica demands epic imaginative power.'

There was a scattering of applause.

'And let's not forget the role it plays in celebrating love and connection over hatred and war.'

Anna could feel the people in the room pause, and then listen in a different kind of way.

'And forgive me, I don't mean to claim too much for our modest genre, but would you not prefer to read about love, in all its complicated glory, desire with all its fire, lust and yearning for what it reveals about who we are and what we care about, than the cock fight of us-versus-them isolationism?'

The applause was peppered with shouts of agreement. Anna found herself wondering why Lisbet had not sought a life in politics.

'I know a wise Sicilian grandmother who lived through the time of Mussolini and his fascists, and she reminds us that this chapter of darkness and despots will pass. It always does.'

Lisbet raised her arms aloft and said, 'To the lion-hearts of The Love Factory, my friends!'

The bookshelves that once housed the maps of the world shook from the applause.

Sofia and Luke put on their best party playlist as Anna, Cordelia, Farhad and Stokely settled in to sign books.

The line of people snaked around the shopfront and out into the street.

Sofia was third in line.

'Could you sign it to Sofia please,' she said to her mother.

'Is that with an f or a ph?' asked Anna, mimicking the question Sofia had faced all her life long.

'With an f,' she said, and smiled. 'But make it to Sofia and Alejandro.'

Anna glanced up at her daughter.

'He asked me to go with him to Argentina, to meet his mother.'

'What?'

Whoa, slow down, take a breath, everyone. Can everyone just please – slow – down.

'When?'

'After exams are over.'

'Oh Sofia,' said Anna.

'I love him, Mama,' she said quietly. 'Really love him.'

Anna signed the book and handed it back to her. But Sofia did not move on, she slipped into the space beside her mother.

Anna smiled up at the old lady who presented her with a book. 'Please sign it to my granddaughter, Summer.'

'Summer, what a lovely name.' Anna signed and handed back the book. She glanced at her daughter. 'It's awfully fast.'

Sofia sighed with impatience.

'Wouldn't the spring be better? Just to give yourself a little more time.'

'You mean if we make it that far?'

'Yes, I do mean that.'

Sofia looked at her mother and smiled. 'You know I don't have to get your permission, don't you?'

'I do know that.'

The man in front of Anna said, 'Make it to my mother, please. Penelope. She's a big fan.'

'And that a clever woman once told me that I should choose my love with my whole heart and all the power of my mind. Well, I have.'

Anna looked up at her daughter and said, 'Please.'

Sofia nodded, reluctant. 'OK then,' she said. 'I'll wait. If we are still together in the spring, which we will be, I will have Easter in Argentina.'

Anna immediately wanted to shout, *Oh, not Easter! Not that.* But she stopped herself just in time and said, 'Thank you.'

Sofia virtually skipped through the crowds to find her love.

When Anna looked up she saw Tekkies in the doorway. He smiled at her and mouthed, 'You OK?'

Anna nodded and then she tapped at her heart.

He tapped back.

Chapter Fifty-Eight

Nonna made her famous melanzane parmigiana for dinner with Tekkies. It took her two days. She served it with a fresh green salad and followed it with vanilla semifreddo with rhubarb from the garden.

Although Tekkies had eaten at their table many times, he and Anna knew that this was different. This was Nonna's ritual, her way of saying, I accept you. She did it for him but also to show her support of Anna's union to Sofia and Luke.

Tekkies sat at the head of the table and swooned at the food that appeared before him. He loved every mouthful and Nonna clearly appreciated the flattery.

In one of the several toasts of the evening Nonna held up her glass and said, 'I wish you could have known my Pietro. Here's to him.'

'I wish so too,' said Tekkies, making his own toast.

'And my girl, the mama of Anna. Here's to her.' She raised her glass again.

Anna hung her head. Tekkies waited for her to lift it again before he raised his glass and said, 'To our loved ones who have passed. To our shades.'

Later that night, when he had gone home and everyone was asleep, Anna crawled into Nonna's bed. 'Is he going to leave me too, Nonna?'

'Not if he's got any sense.'

'What do I do now?'

The old lady turned to face her, touched her cheek and said, 'Tell your story, Anna. Straight from the horse's mouth so that the people will know the whole tale of woe and wonder that is you.'

Anna began to write a new book, different from any that she'd written before. The words that came out of her no longer swung on the rickety bridge of her loss. Neither did they cut through the water like the Sheikh's sixty-five-foot yacht. They were just themselves; clear, and simple.

Anna sat up in her bed warmth and waited for her natural impatience to tip her towards the waiting day.

She slid from under the bedcovers so quietly that the *harghgggg-p-p-p-whooshnrrrr* of her husband's snoring continued without the slightest increase in pitch or rhythm. Then she ran lightly down the stairs with Liebe, her hunting dog, at her heels.

If she'd known what turmoil the day was to bring she might've slowed her pace, but unlike some in her family, Anna was not burdened with prescience.

She pulled open the kitchen door and sucked in a lungful of frosty air; she smelled the city in it and the liquid green of the underground stream at the bottom of her garden.

As she breathed in she whispered to herself, 'I am,' and, as if willing it would make it so, she said, 'at peace.'

She wrote it in her new office with a view of the great city of London. She wrote with her children, her man, and her friends around her, and with her dog at her feet.

And every day she and Tekkies enjoyed a simple, ordinary happiness she had not known was possible.

That's not to say they were magically uncoupled from the losses that had formed them. One night when Tekkies stayed over, Anna found him sitting in the hallway at three o'clock in the morning, with Luke's old cricket bat over his knees, and ink-dark terror in his eyes.

She took his hand and led him back to bed.

A few weeks later, Anna woke with the renewed certainty that an evil force would take Tekkies away from her, if not today, then soon. When she told him that, he laid his body over hers like a manta ray and filled her up with his vitality.

They bore their ghosts together.

As the end of the year approached Anna began to make plans for all five of them to go to Salina. When she proposed to the children that Tekkies join them, Luke barely raised his head from his book, and Sofia looked at her as if to say, *Why are you even asking me? Come on, Mama!*

Stefano had whitewashed the house in honour of their visit. He greeted Tekkies with a handshake, as is the way of quiet men. Before too long, the two of them went down to the harbour to 'meet' Stef's boat.

'This is Tekkies, my grandson-in-law,' Nonna said to all and sundry. This meant that each encounter was extensive, full of questions and warm laughter. Especially when they stopped in at Natalia's shop, who produced coffee for everyone and extracted as much of Tekkies' life story as she could. 'So you are Jewish?'

'Yes, and my father was Afrikaans.'

'From Africa, you say?'

'Yes,' said Tekkies, 'from a small town by the sea. But now I live in London.'

'With the heathens,' said Natalia.

Her small shop was now famous as a distributor of the entire back catalogue of The Love Factory stories. She had expanded into the shop next door and there was a large hand-painted sign above her door saying *L'ultimo della fabbrica dell'amore.*

Anna could get no sense from her as to whether the stories had affected the islanders' actual lives, whether they enlivened what went on in the bedrooms of those long married, or gave new lovers courage, but they were certainly read avidly and with special enjoyment, except, according to Natalia, by the

Malian woman who'd arrived in the spring of Anna's mourning. The original family had since been joined on the island by two Syrian families and Natalia had taken it upon herself to subsidise their food with spoils from The Love Factory as well. When Anna saw them in the square they seemed well enough.

The weather was cool and within days of their arrival a big winter storm came in from the sea. Tekkies and Anna stood on the stone beach and watched it roll in until it broke over their heads.

They fished, sailed and ate beautiful food. Tekkies had a way of being with Luke and Sofia that respected their prior claim on their mother. He timed their swimming races from the black rock beach to the harbour, a family tradition in all seasons. He kept out of the kitchen when Nonna, Anna, Luke and Sofia began making the *buccellati*, a confection of almonds, pistachios and dried fruit in preparation for Christmas.

He also understood the sea and was a creature of it. He could read the tides and feel the degree of moisture in the gathering clouds. He could forecast coming rain by the smell on the wind. Stef, Luke and Tekkies sailed most days. They began to share a whiskey in the evenings and for the first time in years Anna heard her brother laugh.

On Anna's second evening beach walk with Nonna, her grandmother paused on the edge of the black rock beach and said, 'I think I will sit here. Anna, you carry on. I will wait for you.'

Anna knelt beside her grandmother. 'Where does it hurt, Nonna?' she asked.

'Look at the light, *cara*. Just look,' she said and she pointed at the winter sun sinking below the horizon.

A flutter of anxiety grew in Anna's chest.

A visit to the local doctor, a friend of many years, confirmed that Nonna's arthritis had worsened and that she would never walk long distances again.

They bought a three-wheel jogging stroller in Palermo and it became her chariot.

Now, in the evening, Anna would push her further and further afield. It gave Nonna joy to see the sea at the far end of the harbour again, and the allotment garden up on the mountain she had tended with Sofia in the summer.

One unusually calm day, Tekkies and Anna sailed to the old harbour at Taormina. They ate at one of the three little tables under the same ragged umbrellas Anna had written about in her story. They had the shrimp and the pasta too. She made him laugh. He slipped her sandal off her foot and rested it in his lap.

As they drank and ate, he slid his finger between her toes. Anna sat straight as an arrow in her chair.

He tipped his head to one side and considered her. 'A hat,' he said.

'What?'

'You need a hat.'

He took his off and put it on her head.

'Thank you,' she said.

Anna led him to the cave and they reached for one another. It was better than the coming together in her story.

Afterwards, they swam, in spite of the chill sea. And then they sailed back to Salina slowly until the sun went down.

Chapter Fifty-Nine

Stefano retrieved the box of decorations from the small storage loft a few days before Christmas and Luke and Sofia laid out the *presepi*, the nativity, on the table in the living room.

When Tekkies asked Nonna how long the figurines of Mary, Joseph and the three wise men had been in her family she shrugged and said, 'Always.'

These were the *presepi* of her childhood, and her mother's before her . . . and on, and on, all the way back to the Middle Ages.

Then she asked him if he might carry her up the stairs to the bathroom because her leg wouldn't listen when she told it what to do any more.

This was a first. Anna and Sofia shared a glance as Tekkies scooped Nonna up in his arms and carried her to the bathroom, waited, and then brought her back down again. Anna took her back to the doctor in the village and then one in Palermo and he simply said, 'She is old, Anna, and tired.'

Nonna rested in her three-wheel stroller in the corner of the kitchen and napped off and on as Anna, Tekkies, Luke and Stefano prepared fresh pasta and the sweet cassata and cannoli for their Christmas meal. If they had a culinary question they would wake her gently and she would instruct them and then go back to sleep.

Natalia and her family joined them for the feast on Christmas Eve and brought with them a breathtaking array of food.

After dinner, they put Nonna in her stroller and, with all the other villagers, they gathered outside the church to watch the traditional re-enactment of the Nativity. The only thing that had changed since Anna's childhood was that the three wise men had grown older.

The night air was unusually warm for this time of year and afterwards Sofia and Luke took everyone for a night walk on the beach.

Anna and Nonna stayed behind to watch the lighting of the huge bonfires on the hills above the town, the *luminari* – lit to keep the baby Jesus warm.

The stacks burned higher and higher and as they watched Nonna said, 'I was a good grandmother to Sofia and Luke, no, Anna?'

It sounded as if the words were half stuck in her throat.

'You still are,' she said, wary.

'And to you and Stefano before your mama died.'

'And after. You were more than a grandmother, Nonna.'

Nonna turned to touch Anna's cheek with her hand and she said, 'No, I was not, *cara*,' she said. She lifted her hand to halt any protestations. 'Not until much later.'

'What do you mean?'

'I was filled up, from my toes to the top of my head, with grief.'

'What?'

'Oh, we got from one end of the day to the other but I didn't manage to love you in those first few years like a mother should. Not you, or your brother.'

Anna turned towards the sea and watched night creep across the water. She heard her nonna say, 'Forgive me.'

It came to her that what Nonna had said was true, and that it mattered to her that she say it. Anna also knew that, under the circumstances, the getting from one end of the day to the other was all you could hope for.

The following morning, when Anna brought Nonna tea in bed, the old lady said, 'I don't think I'll get up today, *cara*. Just let me sleep.'

That night Tekkies asked Anna if she was afraid. She nodded, and a pit of loss opened up in her; familiar, poisonous, crippling. She could not lose her nonna. Not her irascible grandmother with her Versace knock-offs and her unassailable spirit.

Over the next few nights Anna heard Tekkies get up and check on Nonna. She could feel him watching over all of them.

After New Year, when the time came for them to pack their

bags to return to London, Nonna did not fold and stack and gather like the rest of them.

'Come on, Nonna, we'll miss the ferry in the morning if we aren't packed,' said Anna.

'I'm not coming back with you, *cara*,' she said quietly and as she said it Anna could see that she could barely shape the words with her mouth.

Anna felt a chill run up her back. She asked softly, 'What do you mean?'

Her nonna reached out her hand to her. 'I'm home, Anna,' she said.

Anna looked at her grandmother and the light and clarity in her eyes silenced her dissent. She hung her head and whispered, 'I will not go without you.'

'Go, *cara*, go to your life.'

Anna did not go.

Tekkies offered to get everyone home if they would have him. Anna contacted Peter and he agreed to step in when needed.

The two children took tender leave of Nonna as she lay in her bed. Their grief was sharp. They would not see her again.

At the port, Anna held tight to Sofia and Luke. 'I don't know how long I'll need to be here,' she said.

'It's OK, Mama,' said Luke, 'we'll manage.'

Anna saw them onto the ferry and then came back to say good bye to Tekkies.

He kissed Anna on her forehead.

She whispered, 'Look after them for me.' She touched his chest. 'They are my bloodwood.'

Chapter Sixty

The days that followed their departure were quiet if only because Anna and her nonna were mostly alone. Sometimes, a neighbour would stop by to visit, and Natalia dropped in with provisions.

Stefano would sit with them briefly in the evenings but his days were busy teaching school and fishing and he went to bed early. It wasn't until the Friday evening when Anna went to sit out in the small garden in the front of the house that Stef joined her there.

They sat in silence for a while and then he said, 'You know the worst thing about this?'

'What?'

'You remember the other ones.'

'Yes,' said Anna, and she put her hand on his shoulder.

Stef looked at her and then away again. 'When Mama died, I wanted to die too.'

'I know.'

'Too hard.'

'Yes,' said Anna. She had watched her brother lie on his bed then, and it had seemed to her like cold mud was filling him up, layer by layer.

He looked at her, solemn, and he said, 'Then you made me laugh.'

Anna leaned back in her chair. 'How did I do that?'

'You were Charlie Chaplin! Remember?'

'*The Kid*!'

'Our Lord and master.'

'Oh man,' said Anna.

'You did a slapstick trip and fell down at the end of the bed like an idiot.'

Anna laughed. 'You didn't laugh the first time.'

'So you did it again.'

'And you laughed.'

'And you did it again.'

'And you howled with laughter.'

'And that's how you saved me.'

Anna took her brother's hand.

'There were times after that,' said Stef, 'when I'd say, I need to tell Mama that my stomach hurts.'

'I remember.'

'And you would say, she already knows.' He looked at her. 'I was a lucky boy.' And he smiled.

'We still had our foal legs bent under us, Stef.'

He was silent.

'That's how Virginia Woolf described herself when her mother died. She was young too.'

'It still is that way, for me,' he said. 'Always will be.'

Anna could see that her brother knew himself and that this was his way of telling her that he could not bear to watch his grandmother take her leave of them.

So, after that, it was just them, grandmother and granddaughter.

They began the day with biscotti dipped in coffee to soften it. There would be no real meals to follow. Anna read to her. She started with *Don Quixote*, the treasure of Anna's late teenhood. Oftentimes, she couldn't tell if Nonna was listening or not, but when she stopped her hand would come up, and gesture for her carry on.

Anna spoke to each of her children and to Tekkies on most nights. Luke's school term began well and Sofia's followed. She and Alejandro were busy making plans to visit his family in Argentina over Easter.

At the end of the week Nonna stopped eating altogether. She shed what was left of her bodyweight in what seemed like a matter of days – until she was bird-like. She could no longer get into the stroller herself so Anna lifted her and laid her in it. She lay on her side so that she could see the wildflowers they passed without having to lift her head.

On Sunday morning, Nonna shook her head when Anna came to rouse her for church. She was past even that. Anna let her be.

The days passed and they no longer talked very much. Anna read her the three books from Marilynne Robinson's Iowa trilogy: *Gilead, Home* and *Lila.* She hoped these stories of hardship, faith and itinerant struggle would give her nonna comfort but if they did, she didn't say.

Sometimes Anna would lean over to kiss her cheek and Nonna would smile faintly. She could barely lift her arm off the bed.

That evening, when Anna went to say goodnight, Nonna spoke, her voice faint.

'Goodbye, my girlie,' and her words had the salt of finality on them.

'Her toes are rigid,' Anna said to Natalia when she stopped by in the early morning. 'What does that mean?'

'It means it is close, my friend. That the end is close.'

That night Anna slept beside her grandmother in the bed and Stef in the chair beside it.

She felt the precise moment when her nonna took her place at the cusp between the living and the dead.

Nonna gestured for her and Stef to lean in close and she whispered, '*C'è difficoltà per il mondo.*' There's trouble coming for the world.

'*Sì, Nonna.*'

'*Prenditi cura di quelli vulnerabili.*' Take care of the vulnerable ones.

'*Faremo come ti chiedi.*' We will do as you ask, said Stefano quietly.

All Anna could manage was a nod.

Nonna closed her eyes. Anna felt her grandmother turn to her last fight, the one that would take her, finally, away.

Stef put his head in his hands and would not look up. Anna touched his shoulder in comfort. It was not long before he escaped into sleep.

There were no more dire warnings of trouble, only faint words spoken into Anna's ear as they lay together. Anna couldn't be sure, but she thought her nonna said, 'No need for you to hurry to join me, child. Your mother is waiting for me on the other side.'

'And Pietro.'

Her nonna smiled. 'And my Pietro.'

'Thank him for me,' said Anna, tears running down her cheeks, 'for The Love Factory.' She kissed her nonna on the paper-thin skin of her forehead. 'And thank you for loving me and Stef, every day, when your own heart was breaking.'

Her nonna closed her eyes and passed into the next world without noise or fanfare.

Anna lay beside her grandmother's body for the long hours of the night that followed.

Her grief was a kick in the head, a blow to the ribs, it was a rout.

Anna could barely move when the light finally came.

She made herself wash Nonna's body with scented water. She held her marble head and then kissed the crinkly skin between her eyes.

The children and Tekkies returned for the funeral and Anna could see that it had gone well with them in her absence. She held onto Luke and Sofia for a long time when they emerged off the ferry. A decade could have passed, so changed were they all.

Anna could barely look at Tekkies because he would see that she was holding on by her fingernails to the world as it now was. He would know that what she really needed was to crawl under a caper bush and weep until the new order of things had settled.

Tekkies waited until the children turned away to greet their uncle before he reached for Anna's hand. He held her by the wrist, as you would someone who was slipping off the edge of a cliff, and then he drew her into the shelter of his body.

Farhad, Stokely, Bouchra, Nadia, Lisbet and Cordelia joined them the following day to say their own goodbyes and with them came the noise and comfort of community. That night they lit a fire on the beach and they shared wine, olives and stories about Nonna. They laughed more than they cried.

Anna watched each of their faces in the firelight as they told their stories and it came to her that they were differently bound, now, by this loss

Stefano, Anna, Sofia, and Luke carried the coffin to the start of the mountain trail which led to the collection of graves that looked over the sea. It was a long walk, and, at times, Tekkies, Farhad, Stokely, Cordelia, Bouchra and Nadia switched places with them so they could rest. In this way, they wordlessly shared the privilege of returning Nonna to her rocky soil. They were, whatever their origins, her tribe.

A long line of villagers who had known and loved her followed, singing softly.

Together, and without fanfare, they lowered the coffin into the grave on the cliff above the sea. They filled it with sand.

One by one they placed a stone at the head of the grave to mark the spot. Then they stood in simple silence as the storm clouds gathered over Salina and the waves lapped high on the pier. There would be no ferry today.

Acknowledgements

Thanks to Rasha Mansouri, constant friend, who was my first and most frequent reader. To Janet Visick who gave me sanctuary in Northern California and who read and responded even in the dead of night. To Danna Elmasry who generously shared her own thinking and watched over the Arabic transliteration. Lynne Schey for knowing what mattered most. To Bob Bharij, friend and yogi, for keeping me healthy through the hard months. Hassan Elmasry for guiding the nuts and bolts of the business plan, real and imagined. To Shefali Malhoutra for her love and laughter. To my brother and sister in law Lisa and Christopher Bonbright at whose home on Kauai island the first draft of this book was completed. And Lucia Proctor-Bonbright who shared with me her reading list, her unerring ear, and her heart.

Thanks to the fabulous Wood women; Jane Wood, my editor at Quercus books, and Caroline Wood, my agent at

Felicity Bryant, for their straight talk and their patience. To researcher Alessandra Birch for curating a transformative reading list. Therese Keating for her support in challenging times. Thanks to Rachel Aviv for her Profile of Martha Nussbaum, 'The Philosopher of Feelings', *New Yorker* July 25, 2016. Maggie Nelson for 'The Argonauts' and 'Bluets'. Judith Watts and Mirren Baxter for their book *Writing Erotic Fiction*. Shereen El Feki for her seminal book *Sex and the Citadel*. Justin Bengry, lecturer in Queer History, Goldsmiths, University of London, for reading the almost final draft and sharing his thoughts. Donald Winnicott, Kimberle Crenshaw, Elaine Scarry, Julia Kristeva, and many others whose work helped me begin to grapple with the underpinnings. And the story tellers; Angela Carter, Nicholson Baker, Norman Rush, Arthur Golden, Nora Roberts, Sei Shonagon, Elena Ferrante, Marilynne Robinson, Cervantes, Elizabeth Strout, Mary Gaitskill, Anais Nin and many more for their example. Also, Hafiz, Rilke and Elizabeth Bishop for their poetry. Lines from Seamus Heaney's book 'The Human Chain' are quoted by kind permission of Faber & Faber Limited.

Deepest thanks to the many friends who bravely shared their personal stories and so enriched the reach of this book. And special thanks to David Bonbright who walks beside me always.